HOPING FOR LOVE

GANSETT ISLAND SERIES, BOOK 5

MARIE FORCE

Hoping for Love
Gansett Island Series, Book 5
By: Marie Force

Published by HTJB, Inc.
Copyright 2012. HTJB, Inc.
Cover Design by Diane Luger
Print Layout: E-book Formatting Fairies
ISBN: 978-1942295204

All characters in this book are fiction and figments of the author's imagination.

View the McCarthy Family Tree*marieforce.com/gansett/familytree/*

View the list of Who's Who on Gansett Island here *marieforce.com/whoswhogansett/*

View a map of Gansett Island *marieforce.com/mapofgansett/*

The Gansett Island Series

Book 1: Maid for Love *(Mac & Maddie)*
Book 2: Fool for Love *(Joe & Janey)*
Book 3: Ready for Love *(Luke & Sydney)*
Book 4: Falling for Love *(Grant & Stephanie)*
Book 5: Hoping for Love *(Evan & Grace)*
Book 6: Season for Love *(Owen & Laura)*
Book 7: Longing for Love *(Blaine & Tiffany)*
Book 8: Waiting for Love *(Adam & Abby)*
Book 9: Time for Love *(David & Daisy)*
Book 10: Meant for Love *(Jenny & Alex)*
Book 10.5: Chance for Love, *A Gansett Island Novella (Jared & Lizzie)*
Book 11: Gansett After Dark *(Owen & Laura)*
Book 12: Kisses After Dark *(Shane & Katie)*
Book 13: Love After Dark *(Paul & Hope)*
Book 14: Celebration After Dark *(Big Mac & Linda)*
Book 15: Desire After Dark *(Slim & Erin)*
Book 16: Light After Dark *(Mallory & Quinn)*
Book 17: Victoria & Shannon (Episode 1)
Book 18: Kevin & Chelsea (Episode 2)
A Gansett Island Christmas Novella
Book 19: Mine After Dark *(Riley & Nikki)*
Book 20: Yours After Dark *(Finn McCarthy)*
Book 21: Trouble After Dark *(Deacon & Julia)*
Book 22: Rescue After Dark *(Mason & Jordan)*
Book 23: Blackout After Dark

More new books are always in the works. For the most up-to-date list of what's available from the Gansett Island Series as well as series extras, go to *marieforce.com/gansett*

AUTHOR'S NOTE

Welcome back to Gansett Island! So far in the McCarthy series, we've seen Mac, Janey and Grant McCarthy as well as their friend Luke Harris lose their hearts to love. And now it's Evan McCarthy's turn. Oh, Evan . . . How fun you were to write in all your confused befuddlement. You've managed to slide through life with nary a thought to love or commitment or anything that smacked of forever—that is until Grace Ryan shows up on Gansett and turns everything upside down. I hope you'll enjoy reading Evan and Grace's story while catching up with some of our favorite Gansett Island residents.

Writing about this family and their life on an island so much like my beloved Block Island has been the most fun I've ever had as a writer. Thank you for embracing my fictional family and for all the lovely reviews you've posted. I appreciate your e-mails and Facebook posts more than you'll ever know. I always love to hear from readers. You can reach me at *marie@marieforce.com*. If you're not yet on my mailing list and wish to be added for occasional updates on future books, join the mailing list here *http://marieforce.com*.

While *Hoping for Love* is intended to be a stand-alone story, you will enjoy it more if you read *Maid for Love*, *Fool for Love*, *Ready for Love* and *Falling for Love* first.

A special note of thanks to my lovely reader friend, Kat Bonner, who shared her personal journey with lap-band surgery and provided details that greatly enhanced Grace's story. Thank you, Kat, for your generosity and enthusiasm.

Finally, a huge thank you to my wonderful readers who've made it possible for me to live my dream of being a full-time writer. I love you all!

xoxo
Marie

CHAPTER 1

This moment had been a long time coming. Since fourth grade, if Grace was being truthful. That was how long she'd been madly, passionately, insanely in lust—at the very least—with Trey Parsons. Of course, she couldn't have chosen to give her heart to a mere mortal. No, she'd set her sights on a god among men, a four-sport athlete she'd adored from afar all through middle and high school. While he'd been the star of field and court, she'd been known as "the Whale," and not because of her swimming skills.

Now, ten years and a hundred and thirty pounds later, she was getting busy with her own personal god—that was if she didn't wet the bed first. Her bladder was going to explode any second now, which, from what she'd heard about "the act," was not the part of her that was supposed to explode.

They were in the V-berth of his father's fancy boat, tied up at McCarthy's Gansett Island Marina for the night—the night she *would* part with her virginity if it was the last thing she ever did. And while she wished she could focus on the divine feeling of his lips and tongue on her nipple, a more pressing need had her full attention.

She pushed on his shoulder. "Trey."

He raised his head. "What?"

"I need to get up."

Taking her hand, he flashed a sexy grin and tried to press her palm against his pulsating erection. "I'm already up, babe."

Grace pulled her hand back. "Not you. *Me*. I have to pee."

Frustrated, he flopped on the bed. "Hurry up already."

She reached for his discarded T-shirt and started to put it on.

"What're you getting dressed for? Just go." He took the shirt from her. "You don't need this."

The Grace Ryan who'd never been naked in front of another living soul clung to the shirt. But the Grace who was more than ready for a whole new life let him take it from her.

He caressed her face. "Go on. It's okay."

The tender—and unexpected—gesture gave her the courage she needed to slide off the bunk and duck into the tiny head without obsessing too much about what her backside might look like to him. Wondering if he'd hear her peeing through the wall almost made it impossible for her to go.

Oh, I'm so not cut out for this, Old Grace thought. *Yes, you are,* New Grace insisted. *You have as much right to a hot night with a hot guy as any other girl. You've certainly earned it.*

That much was true. With her arms crossed over her abundant breasts—the one part of her that hadn't benefitted from the weight loss—she took care of business and stood just as the phone Trey had left on the counter chimed with a text message.

Honestly, she didn't intend to look at it, but he was Trey Parsons after all, the stud king of Mystic, Connecticut, and she didn't trust him as far as she could spit him. So she looked.

From "Quigs," also known as Tom Quigley, Trey's best friend since grade school:

Did u nail the whale yet? Remember $500 in it for ya if u bring back proof of the cherry bomb.

Grace was frozen with shock and horror. It had all been a big joke! Weeks of dates and flowers and "romance" had all been a big, *fat* joke! And to think she'd almost given him her virginity so he could use it like a trophy to impress his asshole friends! Red-hot rage the likes of which she'd never before experienced surged through her.

"What the hell are you doing in there?" Trey called, no doubt impatient to seal the deal so he could collect his prize money.

Grace wished she could storm out there and tell him off, but the fact that she was naked made it hard for her to think about anything other than the fact that she was naked—and humiliated. Again.

Staring in the small mirror, she forced back the pain, focused on the rage and opened the door.

"I thought you just had to pee." Had she ever noticed that he pouted like a petulant child when he didn't get his way? "You were in there so long I lost my boner."

Grace threw the phone at him, narrowly missing his head. Too bad. "You left it in the bathroom." She pulled on her clothes with frantic, jerky movements, desperate to cover herself and get out of there.

"What're you doing?"

"What does it look like I'm doing?"

His blond hair was mussed from her fingers, and his blue eyes shot daggers at her. What had she ever seen in him anyway? *"Why?"*

"I'm going for a walk."

"What the hell? I thought we were having sex here!"

"Were is the key word. I need more time to think about it." What she needed was to figure out a way home that wouldn't involve calling the parents who hadn't wanted her to go on this overnight in the first place.

"You gotta be freaking kidding me. We've been dating for weeks! How much more *time* do you need?"

"I don't know." She grabbed her phone and headed for the cabin door. "I'll be back."

"Don't rush on my account."

Glancing over her shoulder, she noticed him staring at his phone. Good. Let him figure out that she was on to his sick little plan. As she climbed off the boat onto the pier at McCarthy's, her hands and legs trembled from shock and anger. On her way up the dock, the pain set in. After everything she'd been through—years of obesity, the huge decision to have lap-band surgery and all her hard work to lose the weight and keep it off for more than a year—she was still "the fat girl" to people like Trey who'd never known her as anything else.

Thank goodness she'd discovered what a total asshole Trey was before things had gone any further. When she thought about being naked in bed with him and how close they'd come . . . "Ugh!" She sank her fingers into her hair, wishing she could scrub the images from her brain.

While they'd been frolicking aboard the boat, the sun had set over Gansett's Great Salt Pond. A crowd was gathered at the Tiki Bar, where two guitarists played old favorites, not that Grace paid much attention as she walked past the bar. She had far more pressing issues —such as getting as far away from Trey Parsons as possible.

"Excuse me," she said to an older man who leaned against a cab reading the newspaper.

He glanced up at her, a friendly smile on his weathered face. "How can I help ya?"

"I was wondering—what time does the last ferry leave?"

"Ya just missed it. Left at eight."

Grace sagged under the weight of the realization that she was stuck on the island until morning. "Can you recommend a place where I might be able to get a room for the evening?"

He let out a guffaw. "On Labor Day weekend? Hate to tell ya, doll, but everything's been booked for months. There's not a room to be had on the entire island. Biggest weekend of the year, 'cept fer Gansett Race Week."

Grace conjured up an image of the camper-sized sofa in the boat's salon. It was small, but it would do for one night. "Thanks for your help," she said.

"Any time."

Since she had no choice, she turned and made her way slowly and reluctantly back to the boat, taking her time to avoid Trey for that much longer. On the way, she spent a moment appreciating the two supremely handsome men who were performing at the Tiki Bar. One of them had shaggy blond hair and a smile that wouldn't quit. He

seemed in his element playing the guitar and singing for the appreciative crowd.

The other had dark hair—Patrick Dempsey hair, she decided—a
muscular build and a face that belonged in movies. He, too, seemed
right at home on stage and sang with his partner as if they'd been
performing together for years.

Leaning against the gift shop building, Grace hummed along to
"Brown Eyed Girl" and "Turn the Page" before she reluctantly
continued down the pier to deal with Trey. As she approached the
spot where the boat was supposed to be, she did a double take.

It was gone.

"Oh my God," she whispered. "That *bastard!*"

She stared at the empty spot at the dock for a long moment before
the truth sank in. He'd left her there alone, taking her purse and
clothes with him. She was stuck on Gansett Island with no boyfriend,
no place to stay and no money. In the span of an instant, she went
from hurt to angry to scared and then to sad. What was supposed to
have been one of the greatest nights of her life had turned into yet
another disaster.

THIS, EVAN MCCARTHY THOUGHT, *IS AS GOOD AS IT GETS.* STRUMMING
his guitar in perfect harmony with his best friend on a warm late-
summer evening at the docks where he'd spent an idyllic childhood.
Playing the home crowd at McCarthy's Gansett Island Marina beat
any stage in any venue, and he'd played his share of stages and venues.

He and Owen Lawry exchanged glances as they played the last
notes of "Bad Moon Rising" and launched into their anthem, "Take it
Easy." Life was good. His album would be out by Christmas, he'd had
an awesome time with his brothers, sister and extended family during
his sister's wedding the previous weekend and the tropical storm that
followed. He'd gotten a new niece out of the storm, born to his
brother Mac and sister-in-law Maddie.

After a scary accident earlier in the summer, his father seemed to be on the mend from a head injury and broken arm. "Big Mac" McCarthy wasn't quite his old self yet, but he was better than he'd been. Evan was somewhat concerned about the unusual bickering he'd witnessed between his parents since he'd been home, but he chalked that up to the strain of his father's recovery, their daughter's wedding, a houseful of extra people and the unexpected arrival of a granddaughter during a tropical storm.

A table of pretty young women had been sending flirtatious signals to him and Owen all evening. They'd have their pick of the ladies at closing time. Since he was still staying with his folks up the hill at the "White House," the name the islanders had bestowed upon the McCarthy family home, he hoped the ladies had their own rooms at whatever hotel they were calling home for the weekend.

A nice fling over the long weekend would be just what the doctor ordered after a summer of nonstop work. He'd been feeling cooped up lately, caged and unsettled. A little mindless sex would straighten him right out—the sooner the better, as far as he was concerned. When was the last time he'd blown off some steam? That he couldn't remember was worrisome.

He joined Owen for the chorus to "Take it Easy," high off the adrenaline of performing before an appreciative audience. Here he had none of the issues with the crippling stage fright that had plagued him throughout his career. That was another reason why he loved playing on Gansett so much.

Owen grinned at him, no doubt enjoying this evening as much as Evan. The gig was actually Owen's. Evan's folks had convinced O to stay on until Columbus Day, and he'd cajoled Evan into joining him tonight. It hadn't required much arm twisting, since Evan hadn't been doing anything but hanging around the house trying to dodge his mother's increasingly probing inquiries into his nonexistent love life.

The one thing Evan McCarthy avoided like the clap was commitment, which was the last thing his mother wanted to hear, especially with his siblings falling like dominoes lately. First Mac fell for Maddie, then Janey married Mac's best friend, Joe, and then Grant fell for Stephanie. To add insult to injury, even their friend Luke Harris

6

went down hard this summer after reconnecting with his first love, Sydney Donovan. Evan had no idea what was in the water lately, but whatever it was, he wasn't thirsty.

Thank God at least Owen shared Evan's commitment to bachelorhood. So did Evan's brother Adam, who'd gone back to New York once the ferries started running again after the storm. The three of them had to stick together in the midst of all this marriage mayhem.

Owen nudged him, nodded toward a woman sitting at a table by herself, and raised a questioning eyebrow.

As Evan watched her, she swiped at tears and stared off in the distance. Unlike the other women in the crowd, she wasn't paying them an ounce of attention. Evan told himself that was okay even as his ego registered the hit.

Evan shrugged as they started into "Love the One You're With." As he sang along, he kept half an eye on the unhappy woman in the corner. Thanks to the overhead lights on the pier, he could see that she had shiny, dark, shoulder-length hair, the kind of hair that would feel like silk when you ran your fingers through it. What he could see of her face struck him as exceptionally pretty—or it would've been if it hadn't been red and blotchy from crying.

When they finished the song, Owen announced they'd be taking a short break. Usually this was the point in the program when they lined up after-hours entertainment. At their table of admirers, the perky blonde he'd been making eyes with gave Evan a come-hither smile, full of invitation. All he had to do was walk over and close the deal they'd been negotiating for hours now.

"What's with the weepy chick in the corner?" Owen asked as they set their guitars into stands.

"No clue."

"Doesn't look like she's here with anyone."

Evan looked over at her again, noting that she continued to stare off into space as if she had no clue she was in the midst of a bar full of people having fun.

"We're not under any obligation here, are we?" Owen asked warily, eyeing the tableful of friendly women.

"You're not, that's for sure."

"Dude, just because your folks own the place—"

"WWBMD?"

Confused, Owen stared at him. "Huh?"

"What would Big Mac do?" Evan asked, knowing the answer to his question before he asked it.

Wincing, Owen said, "Bring a gun to a knife fight, why don'cha?" He accepted a couple of beers from a waitress and handed one to Evan.

"I could ignore it and go about my life, but his voice would be in my head, ruining whatever fun I might be trying to have," Evan said. "He'd be saying, 'How could you leave that gal crying all alone, son? Especially when she's a guest at our place? That's not the kind of man I raised you to be.'"

Owen busted up laughing. "Jesus, you sound just like him."

"Years of intensive training, my friend." Evan took another look at the young woman, confirming she was still there and still miserable. With a resigned sigh, he said, "Wish me luck."

Owen touched his bottle to Evan's. "Go get her, tiger. I'll entertain the other ladies for both of us."

"Gee, you're a pal." Like a condemned man heading to the gallows, Evan started toward the corner table. As he passed the perky blonde, he sent his regrets with a shrug and a rueful grin. Would've been fun. He approached the corner table and plopped down, startling the crying woman. "Now tell me this—what in the world could've ruined such a great night for such a pretty lady?"

CHAPTER 2

*G*race was surprised to discover that the singer with the Patrick Dempsey hair was even more handsome up close. She wiped frantically at the dampness on her face.

"What's wrong?" he asked, his brows knitting with concern.

The last thing she wanted was to unburden herself to another guy who probably had his pick of women. She was done with gods. A regular mere mortal was what she wanted now. A nice nerdy guy would do just fine.

"Nothing." Extending a hand under the table, she reached for her purse before she remembered she didn't have her purse. Trey had taken it.

"Wait," he said when she started to rise. "Whatever it is, I might be able to help."

"You think so?" She couldn't help the snarky tone.

"I know for sure I can't help if you don't tell me what has you so upset."

Since she hardly had any better options, Grace flopped back into her chair. "Fine. You want to know? Here it is. My boyfriend—no wait, that's giving him too much credit. My *date* for the evening left me here alone with no money, no clothes, nowhere to stay."

He stared at her. "What do you mean he left you?"

"I mean he took off on his fancy boat with all my stuff." She held up her cell phone. "Except for this, which is of no use to me whatsoever, since anyone who could rescue me is on the mainland."

"Wow, what an asshole."

"Ya think?"

He pushed his beer across the table. "You need that more than I do."

She gratefully reached for the bottle and took a drink. The first sip went down so well, she took a second. "Do you have a name?"

"Evan McCarthy."

"Any relation?" she asked, gesturing to the marina sign.

"My folks."

"Nice place."

"We like it. So where're you from?"

"Mystic, Connecticut."

"I like it there. Pretty town."

"You're good—at the singing and stuff."

He flashed a devastating grin, complete with sexy dimples. Life was so unfair. "Gee, thanks."

"Your friend is getting ready to start again. Shouldn't you be up there?"

Crooking a rakish eyebrow, he said, "Trying to get rid of me?"

Heat flooded Grace's face, forcing her to look away from him. "I don't want to keep you from your work."

He shrugged. "Owen can cope without me for a bit." Propping his elbows on the table, he leaned in closer to her. "So what're we going to do about this dilemma of yours?"

"It's certainly nothing you need to worry about. I didn't tell you because I wanted you to do anything about it."

"Now that I know, I can't *not* help you."

"That's a double negative," she said primly and then wanted to shoot herself for sounding like such a prude. Old habits died hard. It occurred to her that, pre-weight-loss, a man like Evan McCarthy never would've bothered to speak to her, let alone offer to help her.

His ringing laughter warmed her, even though she knew that being sucked in by yet another smooth-talking charmer wasn't in her best interest. "Are you a teacher or something?"

"Or something. Pharmacist."

He screwed his face into a serious expression. "A very smart profession."

"I guess," she said with a shrug. "I'm not feeling very smart at the moment."

"What's your name?"

"Grace."

"Nice to meet you, Grace. Here's what I think we ought to do. I have another couple of hours to go here, and then I could take you home to my folks' place up the hill. My sister's old room is empty since she's off on her honeymoon—not that she lives at home anymore. I'm sure we can find an old T-shirt of hers or something for you to sleep in. Tomorrow, I'll get you to the ferry landing so you can catch a ride home. Would that work?"

Grace stared at him, stunned. "I can't just go *home* with you."

"My parents are there," he said, flashing the dimples again. They were good dimples. Very good dimples. "We'll be fully chaperoned."

"That's not what I mean. I can't—"

He reached across the table and placed his hand over hers. "You're in a pinch. People on the island help each other out when someone finds themselves in a pinch. It's really no big deal, okay?"

With the heat of his hand demanding her full attention, Grace was powerless to resist the help he offered so freely. "Thank you," she said softly.

"No problem." He squeezed her hand and released it. "I'll meet you right here when I'm done, okay?"

Since she had absolutely nowhere else to be, she said, "Okay."

～

ON HIS WAY BACK TO JOIN OWEN ON THE STAGE, EVAN STOPPED ONE OF the waitresses. "See the woman sitting by herself in the corner? Could you keep her in food and drinks for the rest of the night?"

"Sure, Evan, no problem."

"Put it on my tab."

"You got it."

"Thanks."

Owen, who had started the next set on his own, sent Evan an arch look as he strapped on his guitar and joined in the chorus of "Sister Golden Hair."

After they played the last notes, Owen stayed at the microphone while he strummed his guitar. "Y'all may not realize it, but we have a real *star* in our presence."

While Evan made plans to shoot his friend after the gig, he stole a glance at Grace to find her watching them with interest. He was glad she'd stopped crying.

"The eminent Evan McCarthy, recording star straight from Nashville, Tennessee, is gracing our stage tonight."

"Shut up," Evan muttered to Owen as the tableful of women went wild cheering.

"I'm sure that with enough *encouragement*, Evan might be convinced to share the first single off his new album with us. Waddya say, Ev?"

As the crowd went wild, Evan said, "I say I'm gonna kill you for this," even though he appreciated the chance to show off one of his new songs.

Owen gestured for him to take center stage.

Evan rolled his eyes, bit back the surge of panic he'd grown accustomed to, then stepped up to the microphone and strummed the opening notes to "Here for You," the ballad he'd cowritten and hoped would launch his career. The song was about a couple trying to recover their friendship after a rough breakup. As he hit the refrain, he again sought out Grace in the crowd and found her watching him, her chin propped on her hands.

While she appeared to be enjoying the music, she still looked so hopelessly sad. Something about her tugged at him and made him want to make it all better, even though he knew it wasn't up to him. It was, however, within his power to make tonight a little better for her. So for the rest of their set, he sang to her, for her, and in his opinion, he'd never performed better in his life.

"You were awesome tonight, man," Owen said as they packed up their guitars and enjoyed a beer.

"So were you." Evan took a drink from his beer. "You got a date tonight?"

"Nah."

Evan stopped what he was doing to stare at his friend. "Why not?"

Owen shrugged. "Not in the mood."

Evan reached up to place a hand on Owen's forehead. "You're not feverish. Have you seen a doctor lately?"

"Shut the fuck up," Owen said, laughing. "For your information, I'm *tired*. I'm going home and going to bed. *Alone*."

"Really, I think you need a physical or something. This isn't like you."

"I'll take that under advisement. What's the plan with Weepy?"

"Don't call her that. She's had a rough night. Her asshole boyfriend dumped her here and took off—on a boat—with her purse and all her stuff. She's truly marooned."

"Whoa. That sucks. So what're you going to do?"

"Take her home to Linda. What else?"

Owen laughed. "Dude, she'll have you two married with four kids by the morning."

Evan felt like he'd been hit by an electric cattle prod. "Jesus, you're right. Maybe I can sneak her in and out without Linda ever knowing."

"You talking about Voodoo Mama? Good luck with that."

"Oh my *God*," Evan moaned. "I promised her a place to stay. I can't renege now."

"I'd offer her a room at the Surf," Owen said, referring to the Sand & Surf, an old hotel in town that his grandparents owned. "But we're not exactly prepared for guests." Owen's grandparents had recently hired Evan's cousin Laura to renovate and reopen the hotel.

"And of course everything else is sold out this weekend."

"Looks like it's either Linda or a tent on the beach."

Evan actually considered the latter alternative before dismissing it as too impractical. He was way past the point where sand in places sand didn't belong appealed to him. "Any rumors you may hear in the morning regarding my impending betrothal are not to be believed. Got me?"

Owen snorted beer through his nose and winced from the pain. "Don't say crap like that without warning me."

While they were talking, the bar had more or less cleared out, leaving Grace alone in the corner waiting for him. "Well, here goes nothing."

"Best of luck, my intrepid friend."

"Bite me." Evan shouldered his guitar, finished his beer in one big swallow and steeled himself to deal with a devastated woman he barely knew and a calculating woman he knew all too well.

By the time Evan finally made his way over to her, Grace had begun to shiver in the cool breeze blowing in from the salt pond. Along with everything else she'd brought on their trip, Trey had taken her jacket, too.

"Ready?" Evan asked when he reached her table.

Grace's stomach knotted with nerves, but since her options were limited, she nodded and stood. "Thank you for the drinks and snack."

"No problem. Are you up for a short walk up a long hill?"

"Sure, that's fine."

"So how did someone nice like you end up with a guy who'd ditch you on an island without any of your stuff?"

"That is a very long story."

"We've got nothing but time. First boat off the island isn't for about eight hours."

Sighing, she glanced up at a sky polluted with stars. "It all began in fourth grade when he moved into my neighborhood. I've basically been in love with him ever since—or I thought I was until I saw his true colors. Tonight was our tenth date, and in all the time I spent with him, I never knew . . ."

"What didn't you know?"

"That he's an *asshole*. I nursed a crush on him for *decades*, and I had no idea that he's an *asshole*. How did I miss that?"

Evan smiled at her. "I'm shocked to hear that language coming from such a sweet face," he said with mock dismay.

Damn if that didn't make her blush. "I'm sorry. Swearing is one of my character flaws."

"Is that so? What're some of the others?"

"Inappropriate laughter."

"Seriously? Give me an example."

"At my aunt's wake, my holy roller cousin gets up and acts like a priest, leading us all in prayer. My other cousin, who is truly evil, makes a face at me, and the next thing I know, I'm bent in half, sweating from the effort to contain the laughter."

"I'd like to see that," he said, seeming delighted by her confession.

"Weddings, funerals, bat mitzvahs. You name it, I've had a laughter incident. I'm sort of known for it in my family."

"Well, it's better than being known as a drunk or a drug addict or something like that."

"I suppose that's true, but drunks and addicts can go off on benders by themselves, and the whole family doesn't have to witness their misbehavior." *Nothing like being the fat girl with a laughter problem,* she thought but didn't say.

"There is that."

"What are some of your character flaws?"

He seemed taken aback by the question. "Who says I have any?"

She rolled her eyes at him. "Get real."

"Gee, let's see. It's actually a rather long list."

"The first boat doesn't leave until eight," she reminded him.

Laughing, he turned around to walk backward in front of her as they made their way up the hill. "First, there's ambition. I'm told I have too much of it."

"That's not always a *bad* thing."

"See? That's what I think, too. But I've been told, by *people*, that my ambition tends to run my life."

"Well, since you've got an album coming from an actual record company, it looks like all that ambition is finally paying off."

"Yes, it is," he said, seeming pleased by what she'd said. "I've been rather single-minded the last few years. That's why it's good to be home for a while. I've got nothing to do but wait until late November when my album drops. Since I'll be touring all next summer, I won't get back here for a while, so I'm trying to enjoy it while I can."

"Under normal circumstances, that include having clothes, money and a place to stay, I'd imagine this is a rather lovely place to be stuck for a while."

He nodded in agreement. "My brothers and I used to spend hours plotting and scheming to get the hell out of here. It became rather confining as we got older. Lost a lot of its charm. But now, when I come back after a long stretch away . . ."

"It's home."

"Yes."

"You said ambition was *one* of your vices. What're some of the others?"

"I enjoy beer. A lot. I like women. A lot. I'm not a big fan of commitment or anything that makes me feel confined, thus my issues with living on an island for eighteen years."

"That's quite a list, and I'm very impressed to discover you're so flawed. But I'm sorry to inform you that none of your stuff can top the inappropriate laughter."

"Oh, come on! Doesn't my womanizing or commitment-phobia count for anything?"

"I'm afraid that just makes you a typical man."

"Ouch. That hurt." He rested his hand on his chest. "I'm wounded."

"Sure you are," she said, amused. "So your parents really won't mind an unexpected houseguest?"

"They really won't mind. They have five kids. They're used to rolling with it."

"Wow, five kids. Where're they all now?"

"Despite our confinement issues, two of my brothers are here. Mac, the one who runs the marina, is married to Maddie. He adopted her son, Thomas, who's three, and they had a daughter, Hailey, during the tropical storm."

"I love that they named their daughter for a tropical storm. They're sort of hexing themselves for the teenage years."

Evan laughed. "I doubt they considered that. My brother Grant is a screenwriter who used to live in LA until he chased his ex-girlfriend Abby back to the island—after she got engaged to someone else. Turns out Abby really digs the other guy, and Grant is now with Stephanie, who runs the marina restaurant. My sister Janey, who dated David for thirteen years, married Mac's best friend, Joe, on the day she was supposed to marry David. The newlyweds are due back tomorrow from Aruba, where they went on their honeymoon. They'll grab their pets and head for Columbus, Ohio, where she's in vet school at Ohio State."

Grace listened to his recitation with fascination. "What happened with David? Thirteen years is a long time."

"She caught him in bed with someone else."

"*Ouch.*"

"As strange as it may sound, I think she's grateful now that it happened. She and Joe truly belong together. He'd been in love with her for years, but she never knew."

"That's very sweet."

"They seem really happy."

"So that's two brothers and a sister accounted for."

"My brother Adam lives in New York City where he's a co-owner of a tech company. He's a computer whiz. We joke that all he needs to put a man on the moon is a laptop and an Internet connection."

"Is he married?"

"Hell, no. He's got the same commitment phobia I'm afflicted with.

Owen has it, too. The three of us are united in our plan to stay single as long as possible."

"I wish you well with that."

"What about you? Tell me you aren't going to let what happened tonight sour you on men. You had the misfortune to connect with one asshole. Doesn't mean we all are."

"I know," she said with a sigh. "I'll take a week or two to lick my wounds, and then it's back on the horse."

"That's my girl."

Something about the way he said that sent a wave of yearning rolling through her. What would it be like to be his girl? *Don't be ridiculous.* He just made it perfectly clear he's not interested in anyone being his girl. Besides, he could have *all* the girls, so why would he want just one? Especially one who'd never even had a boyfriend until recently—and look at how that had turned out.

He flipped the latch on a white picket fence and ushered her into a yard fragrant with roses.

"Smells good," she said.

"My mom's prize roses. We weren't allowed within three feet of them growing up."

"I don't blame her."

"You're supposed to be on my side."

Grace snickered at his indignation as she followed him into the spacious house.

He led her into the kitchen and flipped on a light. Peeking into the fridge, he withdrew a beer and offered her one.

"No, thanks." She'd already had two, which was far more than she normally consumed since the surgery, but tonight hadn't been an average night. "Just some water, please."

"Coming right up."

When he pressed the glass to the icemaker on the door of the fridge, Grace cast a nervous glance around. "You're going to wake them up."

"Nah, they're heavy sleepers. We used to count on that when we were kids and wanted to sneak out."

"Is that so?"

They spun at the sound of a woman's voice. Grace assumed she was his mother.

"That was Mac," Evan said quickly. "I never snuck out. Not once."

"Tell your story to someone who believes you." To Grace, she said, "Hi there, I'm Linda McCarthy."

Embarrassed to have been caught, Grace shook her outstretched hand. "Grace Ryan."

"Nice to meet you."

"Grace needed a place to crash tonight, so I offered her Janey's old room. Hope that's okay."

"Of course it is. Can I get you something to eat?"

"No, thank you. I had something earlier. And thanks for letting me impose."

"No problem at all," Linda said with a warm smile.

"What're you still doing up, Mom?" Evan asked.

"Couldn't sleep."

"Everything okay?" he asked, seeming concerned all of a sudden.

Linda shrugged. "Dad wasn't doing too great earlier. By the time I got him settled, I was wide awake."

Evan put down his beer and went to his mother. "What do you mean?"

"He was agitated." To Grace, she said, "My husband suffered a head injury earlier this summer. He's much better but still has some rough spots."

"I'm sorry to hear that. I'll pray for his speedy recovery."

Linda squeezed her arm. "Thank you."

"You should've called me—or Mac or Grant. You don't have to handle him on your own when he gets like that."

"You're all busy with your own lives. Besides, I took care of it. Nothing to worry about." She went up on tiptoes to kiss the son who towered over her. Grace would put him at six two at the very least. "I'm going up to bed. I'll see you in the morning. Grace, honey, make yourself at home."

"Thank you so much, Mrs. McCarthy."

"Please call me Linda." She waved to them on her way out of the kitchen.

Evan stared after her for a long time.

"Are you okay?" Grace asked.

"Yeah," he said, making an effort to shake off whatever had upset him.

"Do you want to talk about it?" After all, he'd listened to her troubles earlier. It seemed the least she could to do to return the favor.

"It's . . . um, well, my dad." He gestured for her to follow him to the spacious deck off the kitchen. The salt pond sparkled with lights from hundreds of boats on moorings.

Evan took off his sweatshirt and handed it to her.

Grateful for the warmth, Grace zipped it on and was immediately cocooned in his appealing scent. "What's going on with your dad?" she asked when she was settled in the chair next to his.

"He's this larger-than-life presence, you know? But ever since the head injury, he's cranky and withdrawn and sometimes nasty and not at all himself."

"That happens with head injuries."

"We've heard that over and over and over. Of course, no one can tell us how long it'll be before he's himself again—if ever."

He looked and sounded so dejected that Grace felt her heart go out to him before she could remember that she'd intended to keep her distance. "It's apt to be a while. Don't give up yet, and try to be as patient as you can with him."

"We're trying, but it's not easy sometimes. I never remember my parents arguing, and now that's all they seem to do."

"They *never* argued?"

"Not that we ever heard. They've always been more lovey-dovey than anything, which was mortifying to us." He pretended to stick a finger down his throat.

"Of course it was," she said with a laugh, even as she experienced a pang of envy over his parents' happy marriage. She had good reason—especially after tonight's disaster—to wonder if she'd ever be so lucky as to find the one person meant for her.

"What're you thinking?"

"That I envy your parents. Sounds like they have the real deal." She smothered a yawn and burrowed deeper into his sweatshirt.

"I'm sorry. I'm going on and on, and you're exhausted."

"No, it's fine. I've enjoyed talking to you."

He smiled at her, flashing those adorable dimples, and her insides melted. "Me, too. Let me show you where you'll be sleeping."

CHAPTER 3

*a*gainst all odds, Grace slept like a dead woman. When Evan shook her awake just after seven, she couldn't remember where she was, but she certainly remembered him. Of course he was even more gorgeous in the morning with rumpled hair, stubble on his jaw and bloodshot blue eyes.

"We've got an hour until the first boat," he said. "Time to grab some coffee if you're interested."

"I'm interested."

"I'll let you get ready and meet you downstairs in a few."

"Thanks for getting up early."

"No problem," he said with the dimpled grin that was too cute for words.

After he left the room, closing the door behind him, Grace took a moment to study his sister's bedroom in the bright light of day. Trophies and plaques and framed photos told the story of high school life for a petite, pretty blonde. It wasn't fair, Grace told herself, to hate his sister without having met the woman.

As she dragged herself out of bed and into the bathroom, she thanked the gods for the one physical blessing bestowed upon her—hair that could be managed with fingers when she found herself marooned on an island without a hairbrush. No toothbrush, either, she remembered, bemoaning the lack of such a necessary item. Goddamned Trey Parsons. She'd kill him when she got her hands on him.

"Hey, Grace," Evan said from the hallway, giving the door a short knock. "My mom said there're extra toothbrushes in the cabinet if you want one."

"Tell her thanks," Grace said, weak with gratitude as she found a new toothbrush and broke it open.

When she was as put together as it was possible to be without her bag of tricks, Grace made her way downstairs where Evan and his mother were having coffee.

"I was going to take you to the diner," Evan said, "but Mom beat me to the punch." He gestured to the stove, where his mother stood watch over scrambled eggs and sausage.

Grace's stomach chose that moment to grumble. Loudly. Mortified, she placed a hand on her belly, as if that could stop the sounds that often emanated from that region since the surgery.

Evan chuckled. "I'd say Grace approves of the plan."

"Sorry," she muttered as she accepted a mug of coffee from him. He put cream and sugar on the table for her. "I hope you're not going to any trouble on my account."

"It's no trouble at all," Linda said cheerfully.

A tall man with gray hair came into the room, and Linda's gaze landed on him, seeming to take a quick visual inventory. "I hope we didn't wake you," she said.

He took the cup of coffee she handed to him. "I was awake."

Grace decided he was an older version of Evan, every bit as handsome in his own way, even if his brows were furrowed and his face set into a grumpy expression. His left arm was encased in a bulky plaster cast.

"Dad, this is Grace. She stayed in Janey's room last night. Grace, this is my dad. Everyone calls him Big Mac."

"Nice to meet you," Grace said. "Thanks for the lodging."

"No problem," Big Mac muttered, taking his coffee out to the deck.

Evan and his mother exchanged concerned glances as she dished up eggs and toast for all of them.

"I'm going to take mine outside to join Dad," she said to Evan. "Let me know if I can get you two anything else."

"Thanks, Mom."

"Yes, thank you, Linda—for everything. I really appreciate it."

"We're happy to have you. I hope you'll come back to see us again sometime."

"I'd like that."

Linda took two plates and headed for the deck.

Evan jumped up to help her with the door and then slid it closed behind her. As he rejoined Grace at the table, he let out a deep sigh. "Sorry about that. He's usually a lot more hospitable, especially with our friends."

"He was fine. It's early, and he didn't expect to find a stranger at his table."

"It's certainly not the first time he's been greeted with unexpected guests at the breakfast table."

"So you make a habit of bringing home strays?"

His lips formed a hint of a smile, and Grace was oddly relieved to see his expression lose some of the concern he'd directed at his father. "Not usually. My mother gets a little too *hopeful* when she sees me with a friend of the female persuasion."

That made Grace laugh. "Something tells me you don't give her many opportunities to get her hopes up."

"You got it."

"Well, I appreciate you taking one for the team by bringing me home."

"It was a huge risk, that's for sure," he said gravely, which set her off into a fit of laughter. "In light of this *huge* risk I took on your behalf, I find your laughter *highly* inappropriate."

His haughty tone only made her laugh harder. "I'm sure you do," she said, wiping the tears from her eyes.

"A guy takes a big risk for a lady, and this is the thanks he gets. I see how it is."

Grace rolled her eyes at him and laughed some more. He was just too cute, and it was fun to laugh with him—and at him. "After what happened last night, I didn't expect to laugh again for a while, so thanks for that."

"Happy to be of service." He gestured to her half-eaten breakfast. "Are the eggs okay?"

"They're great. I'm just full." Because she couldn't very well tell him about the stomach she'd had surgically reduced, she pushed the plate his way. "Why don't you finish it for me so your mother's feelings aren't hurt?"

"Don't mind if I do."

While he wolfed down the rest of her eggs and toast, she contemplated the dilemma of how she'd get home to Mystic and what she would tell her parents about why her purse and luggage were missing. It was definitely time to get her own place. She'd put that off long enough. Why the heck she was still explaining herself to her parents at twenty-eight years old was something she needed to rectify—and soon.

"What's on your mind over there?" Evan asked as he finished his coffee.

"Just thinking about getting home and how I'll get my stuff back from Trey."

"Text him with a suggestion that he return your stuff—immediately—or you'll call the police. That'll get his attention."

Grace smiled at his furious expression. "Yes, it will. And I won't have to talk to him ever again."

"Exactly. Do you have a mutual friend he could deliver it to?"

"As a matter of fact, there is someone I could ask. That's a great idea."

"I hate guys like him who give the rest of us a bad name."

"I'm glad there are still guys like you willing to help a perfect stranger."

Shrugging off her praise, he stood and cleared their plates. "It was no big deal."

"It was to me, and I won't forget it, Evan."

She watched him load the dishwasher and clean up the stove, impressed that he bothered to take the time.

When he turned back to her and caught her watching him, he seemed embarrassed. "Linda taught us well."

Smiling, she said, "I can see that." She pointed to the closed door to the deck. "Do you mind if I say thanks again?"

"Sure, go ahead."

When Grace slid open the door, his father's raised voice greeted them.

"I don't want to talk about it!" Big Mac said.

Uncertain of how to proceed, Grace glanced back at Evan.

His jaw set with tension, he joined her in the doorway. "Mom, Dad, Grace is leaving, and she wanted to say good-bye."

"Thanks again for your hospitality," Grace said, once again noting the breathtaking view of the salt pond from the McCarthy's deck.

Linda forced a smile as she said good-bye, and Big Mac gave a short wave.

"I'll be back after I walk Grace to the ferry," Evan said. He ushered her out of the house into bright sunshine a few minutes later. "Sorry about the tension."

"Please don't be. There's a perfectly good reason for it."

"Even though I know that, it's hard to see him 'off,' you know?"

"I can imagine. He's still healing, and he's no doubt frustrated to not be bouncing back as quickly as he'd like. I'm sure it's very difficult for him, too."

"Yeah, I guess. He hates everyone hovering over him, but what're we supposed to do?"

"Nothing else you can do but stand by him until he's back to normal."

"It's weird, because he was doing a lot better, and then suddenly it was two steps backward again."

"Do you think maybe something happened?"

"Could be," Evan said pensively as they walked into town. "I hadn't really thought of that. I just figured he was being stubborn."

"I'll bet something happened that scared him."

"Maybe."

They approached Gold's Pharmacy, and Grace took a long, measuring look. "You don't see that very often anymore," she said, gesturing to the clapboard house that served as the island's pharmacy.

"What's that?"

"A pharmacy that's not part of a chain."

"Are you with one of the chains?"

She shook her head. "I work at a hospital." Noting that the pharmacy was open early, she said, "Do we have time to go in?"

He checked his watch. "Thirty minutes until the ferry to New London leaves."

"I'll be quick."

Evan followed her into Gold's. The store was small but well organized with a pharmacy counter located in the back. A gray-haired woman was coming up the center aisle as they made their way to the back of the store.

"Hi there, Evan," she said, eyeing Grace with interest.

"Hi, Mrs. Gold. This is Grace Ryan. She's a pharmacist on the mainland, and she was interested in your store."

Mrs. Gold's eyes went wide with excitement. "Is she interested in *buying* my store?" she asked in a nasally New York accent.

Grace wasn't sure she'd heard her right. "Excuse me?"

Mrs. Gold let out a long-suffering sigh. "Mr. Gold and I have been trying to sell the store for some time now. Our grandchildren live in New York, and we'd like to be closer to them. If you know of anyone who might be interested, keep us in mind. We do a good business since we're the island's only pharmacy." To Evan, she added, "As you know, island life isn't for everyone. So the buyers aren't exactly crawling from the woodwork."

Grace's spine tingled with excitement at the idea of owning her own pharmacy. She'd never once considered such a thing. "What are you looking for in a buyer?" she asked.

Evan held up his arm and tapped a finger on his watch, reminding Grace that they needed to go. He was probably ready to be rid of her.

"Never mind," Grace said. "I have a ferry to catch."

"I'll give you the flyer," Mrs. Gold said, leading them to the front of the store, where she pressed a piece of paper into Grace's hands.

Their gazes met and held, and once again Grace experienced a tingle along her spine. Those tingles had led her into the pharmacy field in the first place and had helped her decide to have the surgery. She'd learned to pay attention to them.

"It was nice to meet you, Grace. I hope we'll see you again."

"Thank you, Mrs. Gold."

When she and Evan were back on the sidewalk, Grace folded the flyer, intending to put it in the purse she didn't have. Rather, she held it awkwardly in the same hand as her phone while they walked the short distance to the ferry landing.

"Take this," Evan said, handing her a hundred-dollar bill. "It should be enough to get you back to the mainland and home in a cab."

"It's too much, Evan! I don't need that much."

He closed her hand around the bill in a gesture that touched her deeply. "Take it, please. I'll feel better knowing you have enough to get home."

His kind words nearly brought tears to her eyes, but she blinked them back and worked up a smile for him. "I'll pay you back. I promise."

"No need. It was a pleasure to meet you. I hope everything works out for you."

"You, too. Good luck with your album and the tour and everything."

"Thanks."

They stood there for a moment before Grace pressed an awkward hug on him and managed to smack her forehead on his jaw. "Sorry." By the time she pulled back, her cheeks were heated with embarrassment. She couldn't even hug a guy properly. Maybe she should quit while she was ahead or join a convent—anything to avoid scenes such as this in the future.

Seeming amused, he rubbed his jaw. "You'd better get a move on." He nodded to the ferry and pointed to the window where tickets were sold.

"Oh, right. Well, see you."

"Take care, Grace."

She scurried off to buy a ticket and made it onto the ferry just as the horn blared out a departure warning. On the ferry's top deck, she went to the rail and was astounded to find Evan still standing right where she'd left him. Her gaze met his, and his dimpled grin hit her like a punch to the gut, sending a torrent of tingles down her spine. He raised a hand to her, and she returned his smile and the wave.

As the ferry steamed out of port, returning her to the place where she was known as the "fat girl" and "the Whale," Grace's spirits took a dive. By the time the ferry cleared the island's south bluffs, she was already planning a return visit to Gansett Island. She owed Evan McCarthy a hundred dollars. After all he'd done for her, the least she could do was pay him back.

CHAPTER 4

*E*van watched until Grace's ferry was out of sight. There'd been something strangely endearing about her, and he was sort of sorry to see her go. Not that she was his type or anything—far from it. She was the kind of girl who had "forever" tattooed on her forehead in permanent ink, whereas Evan had "one-night stand" stamped in temporary ink on his.

The truth of it, he thought as he walked over to the Sand & Surf Hotel to see if Owen was around, was that he'd liked talking to her. Even though she had to be reeling from what her so-called boyfriend had done, she'd still managed to laugh and spar with him and entertain him with her inappropriate-laughter stories.

She was a nice girl. Too nice for him, that was for sure.

At the Surf, he peeked in the windows but found no signs of life, so he continued on toward his parents' North Harbor home. The tooting of a horn stopped him, and he turned to find his father's best friend, Ned Saunders, pulling up to the curb.

"Give ya a ride?"

"I won't say no to that," Evan said, hopping into the passenger seat and kicking at the coffee cups littering the floor. "It's hot as hell."

"Whatcha doing out and about so early? Ya usually sleep in after a gig."

"I took a friend to catch the ferry."

"Ahhh," Ned said with a knowing smile. "I gotcha."

"Not that kind of friend." Evan filled him in on what had happened the night before with Grace.

"I think I met her. She asked about hotels, and I told her the island was all booked up for the long weekend. Nice of ya to help her out."

"Just doing what my dad would expect me to do in that situation, especially since she was stranded at our marina."

"A real pretty gal, as I recall."

"I guess." Evan knew better than to show too much interest in a woman, especially when he was home on Gansett, where the rumor mill ran on fumes. Throwing gas on the fire wasn't in his plan for the day. "Let me ask you something, Ned."

"Anything ya want."

"Are you worried about my dad?"

Ned's deep sigh answered for him. "He just ain't himself, is he?"

Evan shook his head. "He seemed to be getting better, but now it's like he's going backward or something. I don't know if it's Janey's wedding or baby Hailey arriving during the storm or what. But something set him back."

"Might be time to take him back to the doctor. Maybe David could help."

"I doubt Dad would want to see the guy who cheated on his daughter."

"Well, David did save baby Hailey," Ned reminded him. Mac and Maddie's baby arrived a month early during the recent tropical storm, and David's quick action had prevented a tragedy when Hailey emerged blue and not breathing. "Yer daddy is no doubt grateful about that."

Evan thought about it for a minute. "Would you mind dropping me at Mac's rather than my folks' place?"

"No problem."

"So how're the wedding plans coming?" Evan asked and watched in amazement as Ned's ruddy cheeks reddened.

"Fine."

Hooting with laughter, Evan jabbed at the older man's arm and started humming "Here Comes the Bride."

"Let's see how funny ya find it when it's yer turn."

Evan shuddered. "That'll never happen."

"Sure it won't. Betcha brother Mac was singing the same song five seconds before he knocked Maddie off her bike."

"He's made for fatherhood and family life. That's so not my scene."

"Yet."

"I plan to follow your path and settle down at sixty something."

"Don't be a fool," Ned said with an uncharacteristic sharpness that took Evan by surprise. "I missed out on everything. Never got to have kids of my own and had to share yer daddy's family."

"Sorry. I didn't mean to . . . you know . . ."

Ned waved off the apology. "Biggest mistake I ever made was not fighting fer my gal. I just let her go. Took more than thirty years to get her back." Ned's voice softened to a tone just above a whisper. "If ya find the right one, don't be a pigheaded fool and let her get away. Ya'll regret it the rest of yer life." He navigated the twists and turns of Sweet Meadow Farm Road and pulled up to Mac and Maddie's spacious home.

Evan started to get out of the car but stopped and turned back to Ned. "You were a damned good second dad to us, Ned. You still are. The way I see it, all you missed out on were the bills, the dents in your car and the enforcement of a staggering set of rules, most of which were broken on a regular basis."

Smiling, Ned cleared his throat and reached out to squeeze Evan's shoulder. "That's real good of ya to say, son."

"I only speak the truth, and I know the others would agree."

"Don't worry about yer daddy. We'll get him through this."

"I hope you're right."

"I'm always right," Ned said with a knowing smirk. "Ask yer brothers and Joe and Luke. They'll tell ya."

"I'll take your word for it. Thanks for the ride."

"My pleasure. Ya called before ya showed up here, didn't ya?"

"No," Evan said, taken aback. "Why do I have to call my own brother before I go to his house?"

Ned chuckled. "Ya got a lot ta learn about women, son, especially when they just had a baby."

"Great," Evan said as he closed the door to Ned's cab with a little more force than required.

With a cheerful toot of the horn, Ned drove off.

As Evan took the stairs to his brother's deck, it occurred to him that Ned was right. He probably should've called first. Before Mac had gotten married and become a dad, it wouldn't have been necessary for Evan to ask permission to see his brother. In fact, he'd once decided to spend a weekend with him in Miami and jumped on a plane to surprise Mac. They'd had a freaking blast, and it made Evan mad to think he needed to *call* before he showed up at his own brother's house. If his *wife* didn't like it, too damned bad.

"What the hell crawled up your ass and died?" Mac asked as he opened the screen door for Evan.

"Nothing."

"Hey, Evan," Maddie called from the kitchen. "Nice to see you. Want some coffee?"

"No, thanks." Evan immediately felt terrible for the nasty thoughts he'd directed at a sister-in-law who'd never done anything to deserve them. The fact she even spoke to him after what he'd done to her when they were in school was a damned miracle, and he would do well to remember that. "How's the baby?" he asked, because he knew he should.

"Sleeping *now*, of course." Mac shared a grin with his wife. "She's a night owl."

"She's got her days and nights mixed up," Maddie said as she came into the room and pressed a kiss to Evan's cheek.

"You're awfully perky considering you had a baby a couple of days ago and probably haven't slept since," Evan said.

Mac slipped an arm around Maddie. "My wife is a warrior."

"She must be to give birth to a McCarthy."

Maddie flashed them a winning grin. She kissed Mac and shooed them toward the deck. "Go have some brother time. Everything is under control here—for the moment, anyway."

"Call me if you need me," Mac said as he followed Evan outside.

The brothers took the stairs to the yard and strolled across the meadow where Mac and Maddie had exchanged vows just over a year ago.

"What's going on, Ev? You look all weird in the eyes."

"Do I?"

Mac nodded.

"Something's up with Mom and Dad. They're fighting. A lot. I'm worried that Dad's backsliding. Remember how good he was when the baby was born? All excited and *him* again?"

"Yeah. He was great when Maddie was in labor. I never could've gotten through it without him."

"He's back to being grouchy, the way he was before the wedding. Mom is doing her best to give him some room, but it's not easy when all he does is bite her head off. If he does that when I'm there, imagine what goes on when they're alone. I'm afraid it's probably even worse than I think."

Mac stopped walking and turned to face his brother. "Why do you say that?"

"I met this girl last night. She'd had a really rough night." He told Mac about Grace's boyfriend ditching her at the marina. "I took her home, put her up in Janey's old room, and Mom never said a word. She didn't grill me or give me the third degree or invite her back to the island for our wedding. She didn't do any of her usual *Linda* stuff. Well, she did cook breakfast for Grace before I took her to the ferry."

"Thank God for that much. Otherwise, I'd think she'd been abducted by aliens."

"Exactly! And it was all Dad could do to say hi to her, which isn't like him."

"That is strange. Normally, he'd be after her life story."

"That's what I thought, too. I'm worried about them, Mac. I've never seen them so at odds."

Mac scratched at the stubble on his jaw. "Maddie was saying that Mom seems distracted. I figured it was the baby's arrival and all the excitement of Janey's wedding. I guess I've been preoccupied myself. I haven't been paying attention."

"Who could blame you? You've had a lot going on." Evan glanced at the sprawling contemporary his brother called home and then back at Mac.

"What?"

"It's still kind of funny seeing you all domesticated. I never thought I'd see the day."

"Neither did I, but when the right one comes along . . ." Mac shrugged.

Evan was hearing that same refrain a lot lately. "No regrets?"

"Not a single one. When it's the real deal, it's the easiest thing in the world."

"Don't you ever miss your old life?"

"Nope."

"And you're okay with the idea that there'll only be *one* woman in your bed for the *rest of your life?*"

His brother held back a laugh. "Totally fine with it."

"Really?"

"Really." Mac gave up on trying to restrain his laughter. "What's with all the questions?"

Evan's skin felt hot, as if he had hives or something. "There's an outbreak of matrimony going on all around me. I'm trying to understand the allure. That's all."

Mac hooked an arm around Evan's shoulders. "Believe me, my friend, when the allure finds you, you'll understand."

"Um, okay. Whatever you say." Glancing up at the cloudless sky, Evan took a moment to appreciate the crystal-clear September day before he returned his gaze to his brother. "What'll we do about Mom and Dad?"

"I don't suppose there's much we can do. Whatever's going on between them, they need to work it out."

"What if they can't?"

"I doubt it's that dire. They're solid, man. They'll figure it out."

"Let's hope so."

LINDA MCCARTHY WATCHED HER LEFT-HANDED HUSBAND STRUGGLE TO shave right-handed and had to restrain herself from going into the bathroom that adjoined their bedroom to offer help. She'd learned the hard way that it was better not to offer assistance. He didn't want it, especially from her.

She sat on the bed, waiting as patiently as she could even as she churned with worry and fear. For the first time in nearly forty years of marriage, she was afraid for them—and utterly unprepared for this crisis. They'd never had one. Somehow they'd managed to navigate through life's craziness, run a business and raise five children without hitting a single speed bump.

It was ridiculous. She knew that, of course. Every marriage had its ups and downs. Except theirs was more about the ups than the downs. The one thing in her life Linda had always been certain of was the man she'd married and the bond that had sustained them for decades. And now, as she watched him awkwardly run a comb through his thick gray hair, she was certain of nothing.

They'd had more arguments in the last six weeks than in their whole life before then. Nothing she said was right. Nothing she did was right. From the minute Stephanie called from the marina to tell her about the accident, Linda's well-ordered life had been turned upside down.

Not even their daughter's beautiful wedding or the dramatic arrival of their granddaughter had managed to jar him out of the funk he'd slipped into. He'd rallied on both days, filling her with irrational hope that faded the next day when the funk returned.

The situation had progressed to the point where she'd decided outside intervention of some sort was probably needed. If only she could find a way to broach the subject without risking the wrath of a man who'd never shown an ounce of wrath before cracking his head in an accident that had nearly killed him.

It wasn't fair. He'd done nothing to deserve this. *They'd* done nothing to deserve it. A drunken boater had done this to them, and she'd be damned if she'd let that criminal steal the most important relationship in her life. And so when her husband emerged from the bathroom, she took a deep, fortifying breath and forced herself to look up and meet his stormy gaze.

"We need to talk, Mac."

"'Bout what?"

Linda wiped her sweaty palms on her pants. "About how you seem so unhappy, and if you're unhappy, so am I."

He retrieved a pair of shorts from the drawer. Watching him awkwardly work his way into them pained her. Her husband wasn't awkward. He wasn't angry. And he wasn't cold to her. Ever. Well, except lately.

"I'm not unhappy." He pulled a T-shirt over the broad chest that still rippled with muscles even as he closed in on sixty. "I'm pissed. I'm sick of this goddamned cast, and I'm sick of everyone looking at me like I'm addled, especially you."

Okay, that was totally unfair. Keeping a lid on her own anger, Linda stood to face him. "I am *not* looking at you like you're addled, but you're certainly not yourself. In fact, you're so far from yourself I don't even know who you are anymore." She went to him and rested her hands on his chest. "I miss you, Mac. I miss *us*. I can't bear the tension between us." Tears clogged her throat, which infuriated her. Linda McCarthy wasn't a crier.

His good arm curled around her, drawing her in close to him. The loving gesture shocked her. It'd been so long since he'd held her that the sheer relief of being near him overwhelmed her. As his fingers caressed the back of her neck, her eyes burned with tears. "I hate this," she said.

"I'm sorry. It's not your fault."

"It's not yours, either." She ran a hand up and down his back, breathing in the familiar scent of him. "I wish we could go through this together. There's no need for you to feel alone with whatever you're thinking or feeling. You've never felt the need to keep things from me before."

"It's not intentional." His body was riddled with unusual tension. "I don't know what I'm thinking or feeling. Everything in my head is so scrambled. Nothing makes sense."

As much as it pained her to pull back from his embrace, she had to take advantage of the first opening he'd given her in weeks. Steeling herself for his outrage, she looked up at him. "Do you think we ought to go see David?"

The roll of his eyes was more in keeping with the Mac McCarthy she knew and loved.

"You gotta be kidding me, Lin. You want me to see the guy who *cheated* on my daughter?"

"He also saved your granddaughter," she reminded him. "It's either him or we trek to the mainland." The fact that he didn't shut down the conversation and storm off was a positive sign, but then again, he hated leaving his precious island for any reason.

"That's playing dirty." It'd been so long since she'd heard that playful tone of voice or seen the hint of the devil in his eye that she wanted to jump for joy.

"Should I make an appointment with David?"

Scowling, he said, "I don't think it's come to that. I'm just in a bad mood. I'll try not to take it out on you anymore."

She rewarded him with her best smile. "That would be very nice. Thank you." If things didn't change, she *would* call David whether her husband liked it or not.

The stroke of his hand over her cheek nearly stopped her heart. "I'm sorry for putting you through this."

"It's going to be okay."

"Promise?"

She nodded and curled her arms around his neck. "Will you do one other thing for me?"

"Sure."

"Would you kiss me, Mac?" Combing her fingers through his hair, she drew him down to her. "I've really missed kissing you."

"Aww, Lin, I hate that you had to ask." He wrapped his good arm around her and did his best to make it up to her.

CHAPTER 5

*T*iffany Sturgil unbuckled her three-year-old daughter Ashleigh from the car seat and carried her up the stairs to her sister Maddie's deck.

"See Thomas, see Thomas!" Ashleigh squealed as she kicked her legs and tugged on Tiffany's hair. The cousins, born a few months apart, used to see each other every day when Maddie and Thomas lived in the apartment behind Tiffany's house.

Since Maddie married Mac, they saw each other a few times a week, which wasn't nearly enough for her daughter. Ashleigh would spend every minute of every day with Thomas if she had her way.

Lately, it took all the energy Tiffany could muster to get up, get dressed, feed her daughter and get through the day, so she was looking forward to a few relaxing hours with her sister, nephew and new baby niece.

Maddie met them at the door and slid it open. "Hey, guys, come in."

When Tiffany put Ashleigh down, the dark-haired toddler waddled over to her cousin and threw her arms around him. Thomas returned the embrace with equal enthusiasm. Watching them, Tiffany's eyes swam with tears.

"Could they be any cuter?" Maddie asked, slipping an arm around her sister.

For some reason, Maddie's usual show of affection undid Tiffany today.

"Hey," Maddie said, "what's this?"

Tiffany turned into her sister's embrace as weeks of horrible stress and upheaval and uncertainty finally became too much for her. And then there was the matter of their wayward father showing up thirty years after he took off without a single thought for the wife and daughters he'd left behind.

"Sweetie, what is it?"

"It's all just too much."

Maddie ran a soothing hand up and down Tiffany's back. "What happened?"

"Jim moved out of the house and took everything that wasn't nailed down. Luckily, he left us each a bed and Ashleigh's toys. Good of him, huh?"

Maddie's mouth fell open. "Are you *serious*?"

"He reminded me, on his way out with everything we own, that the house belongs to *his* family, and I'm *lucky* he's not kicking me out on my ass."

"He *said* that?"

"Those were his exact words." Tiffany dropped onto the sofa. "While I was here the other day, helping you with the kids, he took it all. I got home just as the truck was pulling away with my plates and towels and silverware. I never imagined he could be so rotten."

"Wow. Neither did I."

"I just wish I knew what happened to us. It used to be great, and then all of a sudden it wasn't. Something happened, but damned if I know what." Tiffany stared off into space, remembering all the good times. There'd been a lot of them before it went very bad.

"Do you think there's someone else?"

"I can't imagine who." Tiffany turned to her sister. "Who does he know that I don't know, too? *Who?*"

"I can't think of anyone."

"The best part is he's convinced—absolutely *convinced*—that I'm having an affair. You ought to hear him ranting and raving about how it's okay for me but not for him. I don't even know what he's talking about, and every time I try to talk to him, he takes off and won't listen. He won't *listen* to me, Maddie."

Maddie reached for her hand. "Maybe it's time to let him go, honey."

"I don't know how," Tiffany said, blinking back new tears. "He's my husband and Ashleigh's father. I've loved him for so long. Hell, I put him through law school working two jobs and this is the thanks I get? As soon as he starts making some real money, he manufactures a reason to toss me aside?"

"It's not fair."

"No, it isn't. I hate the idea of Ashleigh growing up the way we did with her father more or less out of the picture."

"He won't be totally out of the picture the way ours was. He loves Ashleigh."

"Yes, he does."

"You have to think of yourself, too, Tiff. If you're not happy, she won't be, either."

Tiffany glanced at her sister through watery eyes. "I don't have what you have with Mac. Even on our best day, it was never what you have. I want that."

"Aww, baby." Maddie drew Tiffany into a hug. "I want you to have that, too. There's nothing like being madly in love with the guy you get to live with and sleep with and do everything else with."

Tiffany laughed through her tears. "I'm sure." She drew back from her sister. "How do I go through with a divorce when I feel like I didn't do everything I could to save the marriage?"

"What else could you do that you haven't done?"

"I don't know. I'm thinking about that." She glanced at Maddie. "What about Dad?"

"What about him?"

"You never told me what happened when you saw him." Since

Maddie had just had the baby, Tiffany hadn't wanted to ask her sister about the upsetting encounter with their father.

"Before he knew who I was, he took a good long look at my boobs."

"He did not! Ugh, Maddie. That's so gross."

Maddie shrugged. "Par for the course. What happened when you saw him?"

"It was only for two minutes at Mom's place. The day he got here. He looked . . ."

"What?"

"Different from what I expected."

"Different how?"

"For one thing, he's old. I had this image in my head of him—young, blond, handsome. I wasn't expecting wrinkled, bloated, gray haired. Not so handsome anymore."

"Not so much."

"But . . ."

Maddie raised a questioning eyebrow.

"I don't want to be, but I'm curious. About him."

"Oh God, Tiff," Maddie said with a moan. "You can't be seriously saying what I think you're saying."

"You remember him! I don't have a single memory of him. All I have is pictures."

"But you know what he did to Mom and to us. What else do you need to know?"

"Nothing, I guess." The last thing Tiffany wanted was to upset her sister. "You're right."

The happy toddlers picked that moment to start pulling each other's hair. By the time their mothers broke up the melee, made lunch and got them down for naps, Hailey was awake and hungry. Maddie settled into the sofa to breastfeed the baby, and Tiffany flopped down next to her.

"Did you hear the news in town about Abby closing her store and moving to Texas to be with Cal?" Tiffany asked.

"No! Are you kidding? Wow. I wonder what Grant thinks about that."

"Why would he care?"

"He went out with Abby for years, and they lived together in LA until she moved back here to open the store. From what I've heard, she said she'd never leave the island again. But then Cal's mother had the stroke, and I guess he can't come back."

"Must be true love."

"Sounds like it. Oh well, I'm sure Grant wants the best for her. He's certainly happy with Stephanie. Mac heard that he talked to Janey about renting her place for the winter. Rumor has it that Stephanie is going to stick around on the island after the season ends, and they're going to write a screenplay together."

"Good for them," Tiffany said glumly. Everyone around her was so damned happy. "So I've been thinking."

"About?"

"Abby's store. I need a new challenge. With Ashleigh starting preschool, my day-care days are numbered, and I've got some money put away."

"What kind of store would you want?"

"Something totally different from anything we have now. I'm toying with ideas at the moment. What do you think about me as a store owner?"

Maddie thought about that for a minute. "Would you keep the dance studio, too?"

"That's the plan. I'd teach dance during the school year and have the store during the summer."

"Then I'm all for it. You're certainly well versed on how to run a business after having the day care and studio the last few years. I want you to find something that makes you really happy."

"That'd be nice."

"I was wondering," Maddie said with a calculating gleam in her eyes. "The night Hailey was born, I noticed you talking to Blaine Taylor. Call me crazy, but it seemed like there might've been some sparks flying between you and our sexy new police chief."

Tiffany's heart rate kicked into gear at the reminder of the man who was her brother-in-law Mac's good friend. "How do you know? You were writhing in labor pain."

"My eyes were working just fine. So tell me—sparks or no sparks?"

"Maybe. Some." Tiffany brushed a hand over the arm of the sofa. More like an inferno, not that she'd give her sister that piece of info. "He's kinda hot, isn't he?"

"Uh-huh," Maddie said with a giggle. "Kinda smoking hot."

Tiffany exhaled a long, deep breath. "Is it awful to admit that when I look at him all I can think about is how badly I want to *do* him so when Jim accuses me of having an affair, I can tell him he's one hundred percent correct?"

Maddie snorted with laughter, which jarred the baby. "Sorry, honey." Maddie smoothed a hand over her daughter's head to calm her. "So let me get this straight—the only reason you want to *do* our sexy police chief is to get back at Jim?"

"Of course it is."

"You're such a liar."

"I wish I could whack you with a pillow right now."

"Don't you dare," Maddie said. "So would *you* dare?"

"To do what?"

"To do *Blaine*."

"Come on. Be serious. I'm married. I can't even think about it."

"Tiff, honey, he moved out of your house and took all your stuff. I don't think you're married anymore."

Tiffany knew that, of course, but hearing her sister say it made it real. "I'm not ready to give up on Jim yet. It wasn't what you have, but it wasn't always like this."

"Maybe a hot night with the hot police chief is what you need right now. It'd be good for your ego *and* it would get Jim's attention."

The thought of spending time with Blaine Taylor made Tiffany tingle in places she hadn't tingled in for far too long. "What's his story anyway?" She was careful not to show too much interest.

"I don't know that much about him except he grew up with Mac here on the island, which is why we didn't really know him—they were older than us. He was gone for a long time but came back recently when the police chief's job opened up. Mac was thrilled when Blaine got the job, because they were good friends growing up."

"He's got that whole bottled-up, angry-bad-boy thing going on."

No one raised an eyebrow quite like her big sister. "Is that so?"

"It's kinda hot."

"Just kinda?"

"Have you always been this annoying, or am I only noticing it for the first time?"

"I've always wanted what's best for you."

"I know."

"You're probably going to need a lawyer at some point, sweetie."

"Who do you suggest I hire when my husband is the island's only attorney?"

"Don't say you heard this from me, but Grant's friend Dan Torrington is coming over soon to help out with Stephanie's stepfather's case."

"Dan Torrington? Like *the* Dan Torrington?"

"The one and only. Grant knows him from his Hollywood days. Apparently, Stephanie's stepdad is in prison for a crime he didn't commit. Grant asked Dan to look into it. They offered to meet him in Providence, but he was curious about the island."

"I'm sure one of the top criminal defense attorneys in the country would be all for taking on a piddling divorce case—if it even comes to that."

"All you'd need is to let Jim *think* Dan Torrington is taking your case."

"That's very devious, Madeline. I'm shocked and appalled to discover this evil side of you."

"It's been there all along." Maddie shifted the baby to her shoulder for burping. "I only save it for the most critical moments."

"Does Mac know about this unsavory side of you?"

Maddie hooted with laughter. "He's my favorite victim."

~

GRACE TOOK THE NOON FERRY TO GANSETT ISLAND ON THE SATURDAY after Labor Day weekend. The boat was all but empty except for an animated threesome at the table next to her. She'd hoped for a quiet passage to calm her churning mind. When she'd told her parents about her weekend plans, they'd been disdainful of her desire to return to the island. Not that she was surprised. They were rarely ever supportive of her.

Thinking of them made her sad. They were both extremely over-weight and unhealthy, which made them unhappy. Not that they would ever admit it. They'd been adamantly opposed to her having the surgery and unsupportive in the aftermath. She'd realized over time that they'd been threatened by her efforts to better herself. It had become increasingly clear that she needed to get away from their negativity if she had any prayer of a life of her own.

That made what she was about to do so wildly out of character. But when she thought about the proposal she planned to submit to Mr. and Mrs. Gold, a waterfall of tingles attacked her spine, filling her with excitement and anticipation. Other than the surgery, this was the most audacious thing she'd ever done, and she couldn't wait to get things moving.

"So who's running McCarthy's?" the blonde woman sitting next to her asked.

"Grant is still helping out even though Mac is back to work this week," the man said. "Evan has been helping, too. He's also been playing at the Tiki Bar with Owen."

Before she could take a minute to contemplate whether it was totally rude to butt into their conversation, she was spinning around to face them. "Sorry to interrupt, but are you guys talking about Evan McCarthy?"

A pretty woman with long red hair smiled at her. "Yes, we are. Do you know him?"

"I met him last weekend when he helped me out of a major jam."

"Come join us," the blonde woman said, waving her over.

"Are you sure you don't mind?"

"Of course not," the man said. He had dark hair and eyes. His foot was resting on a pillow, and crutches were propped next to him.

Grace slid into the booth next to the blonde, careful to avoid the injured man's foot between them. "I'm Grace Ryan."

"Sydney Donovan." The redhead extended her hand to Grace. "This is Luke Harris and Laura McCarthy, Evan's cousin."

"It's great to meet you all."

"So tell us everything." Laura, the blonde, propped her chin on her hand. "How did you meet Evan?"

Grace relayed the story about Trey abandoning her on the island—leaving out the about-to-have-sex and the nasty-wager-with-his-friend parts, both of which became a "big fight" in the retelling—and how Evan had come to her rescue.

"Wow," Luke said. "The guy just *left* you there?"

"Yep." Grace had gone from being infuriated to enjoying the reaction people had at hearing what a jerk Trey had been. Rather than being devastated over what he'd done, she'd decided she was damned glad she'd seen his true colors before their relationship progressed any further.

"Did you get your stuff back?" Sydney asked.

"Under threat of police action, which was Evan's idea. Trey delivered it all to a mutual friend's house the next day. Good riddance."

"What's with men these days?" Laura asked indignantly. "Are they all dogs or what?"

Sydney linked her arm with Luke's. "Not all of them."

Luke flashed her a sexy grin that made Sydney blush.

"I agree with Sydney," Grace said. "Evan restored my faith by coming to my rescue."

"What brings you back to the island?" Luke asked.

"I owe Evan some money, and I wanted to pay him back."

"Hmm," Laura said with a knowing grin. "And that's *all* it is?"

"Of course," Grace said, even though she suspected the rush of heat to her cheeks gave her away. Evan McCarthy had played a prominent role in her daydreams over the last week, and she was looking forward to see him again, even if she knew nothing could come of the slight crush she'd developed. What girl wouldn't be crushing on a guy who'd been so nice to her? Hoping to get the focus off her, she gestured to Luke and Sydney. "So how did you guys meet?"

"That is a very long story," Sydney said.

"We've got time," Laura said. To Grace, she said, "I've never heard it, either."

"Well," Syd said, "we dated for a few summers back in high school." With a hesitant look at Luke, she continued. "We went our separate ways in college. I was married to someone else, and after I was widowed, I came back to the island and reconnected with Luke earlier this summer."

"I'm sorry about your husband," Grace said.

"Thank you. He and our children were killed by a drunk driver a year and a half ago."

"My uncle told me about your terrible loss," Laura said, reaching across the table for Sydney's hand. "I'm so sorry."

Grace felt bad that her question had reopened an old wound. "Me, too."

"I'm doing much better these days, especially since the guy who hit them was sentenced to twenty years in prison last week."

Luke squeezed her other hand, and she sent him a grateful smile.

"Now that Luke has had surgery on his ankle, we're hoping he'll be back on his feet soon," Sydney said, clearly ready to change the subject. "He's a co-owner of McCarthy's Marina, and he's itching to get back to work."

"Fingers crossed," Luke added.

"How did you hurt your ankle?" Grace asked.

"There was an accident at the marina earlier this summer," Luke said.

"The one where Evan's dad was hurt?" Grace asked.

"That's the one," Sydney said. "Luke jumped onto the boat to get the guy's attention before he ran over Big Mac and Mac in the water. He saved their lives but did a number on his ankle. My hero."

"Stop it," Luke said, seeming embarrassed by the praise.

"At first we thought it was just a bad sprain," Sydney continued, "but when it didn't heal, we went to the mainland for an MRI. That showed a torn ligament, and he had surgery last week to fix it."

"Evan was telling me how grateful they are for what you did," Grace said.

"I hate to even think about that day," Luke said with a slight shudder. "It was horrible."

"I'm glad you're on the mend," Laura said.

"Let's hope," Luke said.

Laura leaned in closer to Luke and Sydney. "So are you guys going to tie the knot or what?"

Luke's entire demeanor changed, and his face took on a blank expression. "The question has been asked."

Sydney leaned into him. "I wasn't ready to make that decision yet."

"Oh, of course," Laura said. "I didn't mean to bring up a sore subject."

At that, Luke seemed to rally. "It's not a sore subject. The offer is on the table for whenever she's ready."

Sydney sent him a warm smile that made Grace want to sigh. They were obviously madly in love and working hard to figure things out. The burst of yearning that surged through her nearly took her breath away. That was all she wanted—someone she could love madly while they figured things out together. Was that so much to ask for? Well, considering the recent disaster with Trey, maybe so.

Sydney turned her focus on Laura. "So you must be excited for your new job." For Grace's benefit, Sydney added, "She's the new manager of the Sand & Surf Hotel in town."

"Oh, that sounds like so much fun," Grace said, thinking of her own business prospect on Gansett Island. When she hadn't been daydreaming about Evan McCarthy this week, she'd been obsessing over Mrs. Gold's desire to sell the island pharmacy.

"It needs a ton of work," Laura said of the hotel, "but I'm excited to get started and get the place open for next summer. I talked my brother Shane into coming over to help me out for the winter, so I'm excited about that. He's been through a rough time and needs a change, too."

"Didn't you get married earlier this year?" Luke asked.

Laura's smile faded. "Yep. I got one of the dogs, unfortunately. He didn't get the memo that when you get married, you're supposed to quit dating."

"Shut up!" Sydney said. "Are you *kidding* me?"

"I wish I was," Laura said with a sigh. "It's been a rough couple of months, but I'm looking forward to diving into a new life and a new challenge on Gansett. It's just what we need."

"We?" Syd said.

Laura patted her belly. "I'm three months pregnant. I was married just long enough."

"Whoa," Luke said. "Does he know?"

"Not yet. I figure I'll tell him when I have to. Until then, it's my little secret."

Listening to them, Grace yearned for friends like these women. They were gutsy and brave. They were survivors. She wanted to be like them. She was so tired of getting in her own way and letting self-doubt derail her dreams. Those days were over, she decided as the bluffs on the island's northern coast appeared in the distance.

Suddenly, she couldn't wait to get to Gansett and set the next phase of her life into motion.

CHAPTER 6

*G*race drove her car off the ferry and eyed the Beachcomber as she drove past. This time she'd left nothing to chance and had weekend reservations at the iconic South Harbor hotel. She also had a reservation for her car on the last boat back to the mainland Monday night. Hopefully, that trip would be a quick stay at home to pack up her old life before her new life on Gansett began.

The pharmacy was located on the main road, halfway between South and North Harbors. Grace had done her homework and found Gold's to be a solid business with an outstanding reputation. The island's only pharmacy had a built-in clientele that all but guaranteed a safe investment. She couldn't remember the last time she'd been so excited about anything, but she remained cautiously optimistic. A lot could change in a week. Maybe the Golds had already found a buyer. Maybe they wouldn't go for her proposal. Maybe—

"Okay, cut it out," New Grace said to Old Grace. "Stop with the self-defeatist thing. We don't do that anymore, remember?"

She pulled into the parking lot and stared at the two-story weathered shingle building for a long time before she was able to force herself out of the car. Whatever happened, she'd be fine. Because she was so determined to shake things up, she'd already given notice at her job in Mystic. No matter what happened this weekend, it was time to snap out of the rut she'd been in for years.

As she pushed open the door and heard the delicate tingle of the bell that announced her presence, Grace smiled as the sweetly scented air filled her senses. The place smelled the way a pharmacy should. She wandered toward the back of the store, hoping to run into Mrs. Gold. At the counter, Grace asked for her.

"She just left to do some errands," the pharmacist said. The older man was balding, with a warm smile and wire-framed glasses. "Is there something I might help you with?"

"Oh, um, well, do you happen to know if she's found a buyer for the pharmacy yet?" Grace held her breath as she awaited his reply.

His smile faded a bit. "Not yet. We keep hoping. One of these days, maybe." He took off his glasses and wiped them on the white coat he wore over a shirt and tie.

"Are you Mr. Gold?"

"Yes indeed."

Grace extended a hand over the counter. "I'm Grace Ryan—"

"You're the pharmacist from Mystic. My missus told me about you!" He took a long, measuring look at her. "Are you going to make my day, my month and my year, young lady?"

"Quite possibly."

"Oh, happy day! Pamela, take over here for a bit," he said to the woman who was working with him behind the counter. "I'll be right back."

"Okay, Mr. Gold," Pamela said, casting a wary glance at Grace.

"Right this way, Miss Ryan." He ushered Grace through double doors into a cramped office. When they were settled, he folded his hands on the desktop. "Now, let's talk turkey."

Grace appreciated his direct approach. "The truth of it is, I can't afford to buy your pharmacy."

His face fell with disappointment. "But I thought . . ."

Grace held up a hand to stop him. "This is what I propose. I've been out of college and working for close to seven years while living at home, but I don't have the credit history or collateral to get a loan.

However, I could make a sizeable down payment. If you and Mrs. Gold hold the mortgage on the remaining portion, you'd have a guaranteed monthly income." By the time she finished speaking, Grace had begun to sweat. All week she'd kept telling herself it was a long shot, but as she laid out her plan to Mr. Gold, she realized how badly she wanted him to say yes.

He ran a hand over his face as he pondered her plan. "It's not what we were hoping for, but it's not a *bad* idea."

Grace let out a sigh of relief that he hadn't rejected her outright.

"I'd need to talk it over with my missus, of course."

"Of course."

"How long are you here?"

"I've got my car booked on the five o'clock boat on Monday."

His brows furrowed. "Have you thought about what it'd be like to be here during the winter?"

That was the part Grace had wrestled with the most as she contemplated her life-changing plan. "I have, and while I know it will be very different from what I'm accustomed to, I'd become involved in the community and keep busy running the business."

"Did my missus tell you about the apartment upstairs?"

Grace's heart did a happy dance at that news. Finding a place to live in case the deal went through had been one of her other priorities for the weekend. "No, she didn't."

"Would you like to see it?"

"I'd love to."

He gestured for her to lead the way out of the office. "After you, my dear."

On her way through the store, she made a few mental notes of things she would change, but for the most part, the store seemed clean, orderly, well stocked and, most important, busy. The two registers at the front of the store had at least four people in each line, which made Grace smile.

Mr. Gold led her around to the back of the building, where a sturdy set of wooden stairs led to a deck that overlooked South Harbor in one direction and the town beach in the other. There were colorful pots filled with cheerful blooms, as well as tomato plants tied to stakes.

He gestured her through the sliding door into a spacious living and dining room. The kitchen was against the far wall and at first glance seemed to be in need of updating. She looked up to find a loft that served as the bedroom.

"Full bathroom upstairs and a half bath down here as well as a wood-burning fireplace," Mr. Gold said. "It's not much, but it's worked well for us."

"It would work for me, too," Grace said, her heart racing with excitement as she pondered paint colors and furniture and what she might need to buy. She could so see herself living here—close enough to her parents for an occasional visit but far enough away that they couldn't pop in and insert themselves into her life without invitation.

Mr. Gold handed her a pad stamped with the logo of a well-known drug manufacturer. "Write down your number, and I'll give you a call as soon as we've had a chance to talk it over."

Grace took the pen and wrote down her cell number. She handed it back to him and extended her hand. "Whatever you decide, I appreciate your consideration of my offer."

Mr. Gold put the pad on a table and folded her hand between both of his. "My missus and I are very eager to live near our grandbabies, so I hope we can work something out."

"I hope so, too. I'll look forward to hearing from you."

Filled with excitement and anticipation, Grace skipped down the stairs to her car. She hoped her next stop went as well as the first one. As she drove to the McCarthys' home, she was hit by a bout of nerves that nearly undid her. Why should she be so nervous about seeing a man she barely knew? What was the big deal?

She'd pay him back the money she owed him and then go check into her room at the Beachcomber. This weekend was her chance to explore the island and get to know the place she might be calling home before too much longer.

At some point, she'd have to break the news to her parents that she was moving, but that wasn't happening until everything was signed, sealed and delivered so there was no chance for them to try to talk her out of it.

She pulled up to the McCarthys' big white house and told herself it didn't matter that there were no cars in the driveway. If they weren't home, she could always come back again later. As she walked through the white-picket gate, the aroma of roses greeted her, reminding her of the previous weekend when Evan had ushered her through his mother's garden.

Grace rang the doorbell and waited a long time before she rang it again. When no one came, the staggering disappointment forced her to own up to how much she'd been looking forward to seeing Evan again. Which was ridiculous in light of his philosophies on women and relationships.

She felt like a wilted rose as she returned to her car. The marina seemed like the logical next place to check, so she drove down the hill, taking in the glorious views of North Harbor. "What a beautiful place," she said with a sigh. "Imagine living here and getting to see this every day."

Not that the views in Mystic were anything to sneeze at, but this . . . This was something else altogether. An open parking space caught her eye, and she grabbed it even though it was still a ways from the marina. Walking toward the pier, she started to regret parking so far away and worried about being all sweaty the first time she saw Evan again—if he was even there. The day was unusually warm for September, which meant the pier was bustling with people and bikes and dogs on leashes.

She ducked into the marina restaurant, relieved to be out of the sun, and wiped the dampness from her brow. As visions of sweaty pigs danced in her mind, she looked up to find Evan staring at her, and he didn't look at all pleased to see her. Great. Grace took a deep breath before she walked over to him.

"I'm sorry to interrupt." He'd been speaking with another man who sort of resembled him and a woman with short, spiky red hair. The other guy turned his blue eyes on her, and Grace nearly gasped. How was it possible for two men to have the market cornered on hotness?

Now that she'd gotten a look at his dazzling eyes, Grace had no doubt he was Evan's brother.

"Grace." She didn't miss the slight stammer in Evan's voice. "What're you doing here?"

He wore a yellow Bob Marley T-shirt with board shorts and flip-flops. His hair was mussed and his face sunburned, as if he'd spent the day at the beach. Of course, he had to be the most breathtakingly gorgeous man she'd ever laid eyes on. Apparently, it was her lot in life to have a thing for unattainable men.

"I, um, well, I owe you some money, and I wanted to pay you back."

"You didn't have to do that."

"I wanted to." She glanced at the other couple, who stared at her with unveiled interest.

"Oh, sorry," Evan said. "Grace, this is my brother Grant and his girlfriend, Stephanie."

"Oh," Stephanie said with a knowing look on her face. "I've heard about you."

Evan's mouth fell open. "What did you hear?"

Stephanie flashed him a saucy grin. "I'll never tell." She came around the counter and took Grace by the arm. "Come, sit. Have some of our famous chowder." Stephanie ushered Grace into a chair at one of the tables. "How about some clam cakes, too?"

Amused by the way Stephanie had taken over, Grace looked up at her. "I'd love some chowder, please."

Stephanie winked at Evan and gave Grant a hip check as she went behind the takeout counter to serve up the chowder. Watching her in action, Grace decided Stephanie was also the kind of fearless woman she'd love to have as a friend. Old Grace had gravitated to safe friends who didn't take risks. New Grace was interested in meeting people who didn't always bow to convention. With her spiky hair, pierced tongue and impertinent way of managing the McCarthy brothers, Stephanie intrigued her.

Grant's cell phone rang, and he excused himself to take the call.

While she waited for Stephanie to return, Grace cast a nervous glance at Evan. "I'm sorry if I took you by surprise."

"It's no problem." Though he said what he thought she wanted to hear, everything about his body language told her this visit was a big problem for him. He sat and stretched out his long, tanned legs. "I really don't expect you to pay me back. I was happy to help you out."

She forced her gaze off his muscular legs and onto his face. Her entire body was hot with embarrassment fueled by the awkward vibe he was putting out. "It's important to me that I reimburse you."

He tilted his head and scowled playfully, which made her heart race and her palms sweat. "I'd say this puts us at a significant impasse."

Grace raised an eyebrow and set her chin mulishly to let him know she had no plans to back down.

Laughing, he shook his head at her impudence.

Grace was dumbstruck by those damned dimples.

"Here we go." Stephanie returned with chowder, silverware and crackers. "What can I get you to drink?"

"Water would be great." Grace stared at the huge bowl of chowder, knowing she'd be able to eat only a fraction of it and wondering how she'd leave the rest without appearing rude or ungrateful.

Stephanie put a glass of ice water with lemon on the table and sat down to join them.

Grant ended his phone call and took the fourth seat.

Grace felt like a monkey during feeding time at the zoo with all eyes on her. She took a taste of the chowder and nearly moaned when the flavor exploded on her tongue. "Amazing."

Stephanie flushed with pleasure. "It's Linda's recipe. I just doctored it a bit."

"You'd better not let your pal Linda hear you say that, babe," Grant said as he reached for Stephanie's hand. "That's an ancient family recipe you're messing with."

Stephanie stuck her tongue out at Grant, which made his eyes heat with lust.

Grace wondered if Evan's eyes looked like that when he was aroused. *Stop it! You're being ridiculous. What business is it of yours what his eyes look like when he's turned on?* As she forced another taste of the savory soup past the growing lump in her throat, she noticed that

Evan continued to stare at her while feigning interest in what Grant and Stephanie were saying.

"How long are you here?" Stephanie asked.

Grace watched Evan perk up with interest as he awaited her reply. "Only until Monday." Did he look relieved, or was that her imagination?

"We'll have to go out or something," Grant said. "Show you around the island."

Evan sent his brother a stricken look.

As she blotted her mouth with a napkin, it became clear that Evan didn't want her around, and she could certainly take a hint. "That's really nice of you, Grant, and the chowder was delicious." Withdrawing the hundred-dollar bill she owed Evan from her purse, she placed it on the table and put the pepper shaker on top of it. "Thank you again for your kindness, Evan. It was great to meet you all."

Grace got up and walked out of the restaurant, reminding herself that she was beginning what she hoped would be a grand adventure. She didn't need Evan McCarthy's friendship to make her happy or complete. Pep talk aside, it was disappointing that he wasn't who she'd thought, which shouldn't surprise her in light of her recent experience with men. She'd nearly talked herself out of liking him in the first place when she heard him calling her name.

"Grace! Wait! Hang on a second."

She turned to find him running up behind her.

"What do you need, Evan?"

He reached for her hand, put the bill in it and curled her fingers around it. "I don't want that."

She grabbed his hand and pressed the bill into it. "Neither do I."

"Look, I was happy to help you out. I'm sure you would've done the same for me." He took her hand again, more gently this time, and pressed the bill against her palm, holding it there with his own hand.

The heat of his skin against hers made her throat close against a swell of emotion. Rather than risk letting him know how much his touch had affected her, she decided to concede defeat on the money. "Fine. Anything else?"

His face twisted into a stricken expression again. "I, uh . . ."

"Look, I know I took you by surprise today, but the only reason I came was to reimburse you. I'm not looking for anything else. I enjoyed meeting your brother and Stephanie. They're very cute together." She paused before she added, "It was nice to see you again." Turning away from him, she headed for her car.

"Wait." He took hold of her arm. "Don't go."

She released a deep sigh. "It's obvious I've made you extremely uncomfortable. Let me go, and we can all be more comfortable. Okay?"

"No. It's not okay. I don't want you to go."

"*Why?*"

He stared at her for an extremely long—and very uncomfortable—moment. "I thought about you this week." Each word seemed to cost him something critical.

Was it possible for words alone to render a person completely paralyzed? Apparently. She stood frozen in place, waiting to hear what else he would say.

He rested a hand on her shoulder. "When you came into the restaurant . . . In the very second you walked through the door, do you know what I was thinking?"

Since she'd also been rendered mute, she shook her head.

"I was thinking, gee, I wonder who Grace is mocking with her inappropriate laughter right now. And then I looked up, and there you were. That's kind of nuts, isn't it?"

She stared at him, still not sure she was hearing him correctly. He had to be making that up. He wasn't really thinking about her! When would he let her down easy and tell her she was a really nice girl, but he wasn't interested?

"Grace?" He waved a hand in front of her face. "Are you still with me?"

Forcing the fog from her brain, she nodded. "I'm sorry I surprised you."

"It was a good surprise. A very good surprise."

"Really?"

"*Yes,*" he said with that grin, that deliciously sexy, dimpled grin that made her heart race and her mouth go dry. "Really."

"You didn't look happy to see me."

"I was very happy to see you." His brows knitted with what might've been confusion. "I was surprised by just how much."

Attraction zinged between them like a live wire. She wanted to smooth his hair and touch the stubble on his cheek to see if it was coarse or soft.

He continued to look intently at her, as if he was memorizing every detail. "So you're here for the weekend?"

Forcing herself not to wilt under his scrutiny or the hot sun, she said, "Until Monday."

"Good."

"Why is that good?"

"Because that gives us plenty of time to hang out and have some fun."

"Oh. It does?"

"Sure does." He bent at the knees to look her in the eye. "If you want to, that is."

Summoning her best haughty tone, she said, "I'm not opposed to fun."

"Well, thank goodness for that. I'd hate to think you were a bore or something."

Grace gave him a playful shove.

He started to stumble backward, and she tittered with laughter as she grabbed him to stop the fall. Somehow she ended up pressed against his chest with his strong arms wrapped around her.

"You laughed when you thought I was going to fall," he whispered in her ear, sending goose bumps careening down her spine.

The aroma of sunscreen and hot man filled her senses, making her feel warm all over. "I most certainly did not."

"Did so."

Smiling, she relaxed into his embrace and decided this was going to be an awesome weekend.

CHAPTER 7

$\mathcal{F}$illed with irrational excitement, Laura McCarthy drove into the parking lot behind the Sand & Surf Hotel. After ten of the worst days of her life, the battered old hotel looked rather good to her. The idea of hauling her carload of stuff up three flights of stairs to the manager's apartment didn't hold much appeal, but she couldn't wait to be settled once and for all.

"No time like the present," she said as she shouldered two of the lighter bags and headed for the front porch. She dug the key Owen had given her out of her back pocket and inserted it into the rusty lock. When she twisted it, nothing happened.

"Great."

Dropping her bags onto the porch, she used both hands to try to turn the key, but it didn't budge. Why was it that Owen's key worked fine, but hers didn't? Was this a bad omen? How was she supposed to renovate and manage the place if she couldn't even get in?

"Come on," she whispered, starting to sweat as she gave it one more try.

"Princess! You're back!"

Laura spun around to find Owen Lawry loping up the stairs with a big goofy grin on his adorable face. "I thought you'd forgotten about us."

In the moment their eyes met, Laura realized she was in big trouble. She was far, *far* too happy to see him. And in light of her current predicament, she had absolutely no business being happy to see any man, let alone one who'd made it perfectly clear he was a vagabond and a troubadour with no interest in permanence of any kind. While his footloose and fancy-free approach to life was exactly what she *didn't* need at the moment, his lightheartedness was everything she needed.

"How bad was it?" he asked, his gray eyes taking a long, measuring look at her.

"Pretty bad."

He closed the distance between them and enveloped her in a tight hug that calmed the turbulence inside her.

"What happened?"

Overwhelmed by his nearness as well as the clean, fresh scent of him, it was all she could do to breathe, let alone speak, as she put her arms around him and returned the hug. "Well, between returning the wedding gifts, filing for divorce, moving out of my apartment and breaking the news to my dad that not only is my three-month marriage a bust but I'm pregnant, too, it was a rather uneventful ten days."

He chuckled softly. "I know it's not funny, but when you put it like that . . ."

"What else can you do but laugh?"

"You can get busy moving forward."

Laura could've spent all day wrapped up in his sweet comfort, but since it was time to stand on her own two feet, she drew back from him. "Success is the best revenge, right?"

"That's what I've heard."

"Then in that case, I'm in a world of trouble, because I can't even get the key to work."

"Let me help." He stepped around her, gave the key a wiggle and a twist, and the door swung open. "Madame, your kingdom awaits."

"Wait! How did you do that?"

"It's all in the wrist," he said with a wink.

Offering a sweeping wave of his arm, he welcomed her into the hotel his grandparents had owned and operated for fifty years, the same hotel that had beckoned to Laura since she was a grief-stricken little girl visiting Uncle Mac and Aunt Linda in the wake of her mother's death.

As she crossed the threshold, tears filled her eyes. Remembering the raw pain of that first summer without her mom reminded her of how much this island had meant to her then. It had soothed and healed her. Maybe it would again. She could only hope.

"Princess? Are you okay?"

She took a deep breath, summoning the fortitude to continue putting one foot in front of the other. What choice did she have? "Not yet, but I will be."

LATE ON SATURDAY AFTERNOON, EVAN STROLLED ON THE BEACH WITH Grant and Owen while Grace, Stephanie and Laura reclined in chairs, chattering like three long-lost best friends.

"The girls sure did hit it off," Grant said.

"Seriously," Owen said.

"I'm glad to see Stephanie relaxing a bit and making some friends," Grant said. "She's been so alone for such a long time."

Evan nudged his older brother. "You've got a bad case for her, bro."

"So it seems." Grant turned his formidable blue-eyed gaze on Evan. "I could say the same for you." To Owen, Grant said, "Do you think he realizes he's barely taken his eyes off Grace all afternoon?"

While Owen chortled with laughter, Evan huffed with indignation. "That's so not true."

"She's awfully pretty," Owen said. "I can certainly see why you'd be captivated."

"She's funny, too," Grant added. "I like her."

"I don't know why you guys are making such a big deal out of it."

Evan felt like he was fighting for his life or something, which was ridiculous. What did he have to be fighting about? So they'd had some laughs, so he found her attractive, so he wanted to get to know her better. Big whoop. Except even as he tried to talk himself out of it, the truth of the matter was that he was more interested in her than he'd been in any woman in like, well, ever. "We're just friends. I'm not *captivated*. Whatever that means."

"If you don't know," Owen said, "I'm not going to explain it to you."

Grant laughed at their banter.

"What about you?" Grant said to Owen. "Joined at the hip with Laura. What's that all about?"

Owen's smile quickly became a frown. "Nothing. We're friends. That's it."

"Uh-huh," Grant said with a knowing grin. "You're as full of it as he is."

"I don't know what the hell is going on around here lately," Evan said as desperation crept over him. His throat felt tight and constricted, as if he'd knotted his necktie too tightly. Except he wasn't wearing a tie. He wasn't even wearing a shirt, for crying out loud, so why was he having such a hard time getting air to his lungs?

There was absolutely no rational explanation for the way he felt when Grace was around—happy, calm, amused, aroused, intrigued, disturbed, unsettled, dismayed. All in one muddled package. Nothing about it made sense. She was just another woman in a long line of women who'd paraded through his life. He couldn't see any reason to make it into a bigger deal than it was.

And then her laughter rang out, drawing his attention to where she sat with Stephanie and Laura. Grace's hands danced with animation as she entertained them with a story that had the other two women laughing hysterically.

Evan wanted to know what she was saying. He wanted to hear the story and be in on the joke. He wanted *her*. Oh Jesus. What the hell was wrong with him? Though the day was seasonally warm with a hint of September chill in the air, Evan began to sweat.

She wasn't the kind of woman he could just *have* and discard. He'd known her only a short time, and he already knew that much about her. Grace Ryan wasn't a one-night-stand kind of gal, and he was hardly the kind of guy who was looking for more than that.

"Check him out," Grant said to Owen. "Staring again."

This time, Evan could hardly deny that he'd been gawking at Grace.

"There's nothing wrong with liking her, Ev," Grant said. "She's a nice girl."

"That's the problem," Evan said, filled with defeat. "She's too nice for me."

"Nah," Grant said, punching him lightly on the arm. "That's not true. Despite your many, *many* faults, at the end of the day, you're a good guy."

"No, I'm not." Evan thought of the many meaningless connections he'd made with women over the years, the promises he'd made and never kept. He wasn't a good guy. He certainly wasn't good enough for the likes of Grace Ryan, who was probably all about ethics and morals and permanence.

"Why do you say that?" Owen asked. "Look what you did for her when she was marooned at the marina."

"I just did what anyone would do in that situation."

"There were a lot of guys around that night," Owen reminded him. "No one else went over to her table to find out why she was crying. Cut yourself a break, man."

"I don't have any business starting something with her. She lives in Mystic, and I'm heading back to Nashville soon. I've got the tour coming up next summer. It's not the right time to start something."

"I said the same thing about me and Steph," Grant said, gazing at his girlfriend with love and affection that made Evan acutely aware of what he might be missing out on. "It seemed really hopeless, but when push came to shove and I had to decide between her and going back to LA without her, it was a no-brainer."

"Where do things stand between you guys now?" Owen asked.

"We're taking it a day at a time, but I'm renting Janey's house for the winter, and yesterday Steph agreed to stay with me."

Evan had never seen his brother look happier.

"That's cool," Owen said.

"I'm working on the screenplay about her and her stepfather's story. We're looking forward to her stepfather's Halloween court date and hoping for the best." Grant shrugged. "As long as we're together, I feel like we can get through anything."

"That's all well and good," Evan said, "and I'm happy for you. Don't get me wrong."

Grant raised an eyebrow. "But?"

"You can work anywhere. All you need is a laptop and you're good to go. I have to go back to Nashville. I'm going on tour. Where does a girlfriend fit into that?"

"I don't know," Grant said, "but if it's the right girl, you'll figure it out."

Evan knew his brother believed every word he said, but Evan wasn't convinced.

"Can I give you one piece of advice?" Grant said.

"Can I stop you?"

Laughing at Evan's scowl, Grant stopped walking and turned to face him. "Who knows what tomorrow will bring? Look at what happened at the marina this summer. Dad and Mac and Luke could've been killed in a matter of minutes. Beyond his worries about Dad, do you think Mac came out of the water thinking about anything other than getting to Maddie as soon as he could? Same thing for Luke with Sydney. It didn't take nearly being killed by a drunken boater to show them what really matters in life. They already knew. You don't want to miss out on that, Ev. And neither do you," he said to Owen. "Don't be so caught up in maintaining the status quo that you miss out on what could be the most awesome thing you've ever experienced. Trust me. You don't want to miss that."

"That wasn't a *piece* of advice," Evan grumbled. "It was a freaking speech."

Laughing, Grant tugged his brother into a headlock. When he fought his way free, Evan noticed Owen staring off into space and wondered if he was pondering what Grant had said.

"I think you'll be sorry if you don't try to figure out why you've had such a strong reaction to Grace," Grant added. "You'll regret letting her go home on Monday without getting to know her better."

Since the idea of never seeing her again filled him with irrational fear, Evan ventured a reluctant glance at the girls and found her watching him with a wistful expression on her face. Was it possible that she was equally attracted to him? There was only one way to find out.

"Keep walking," he said to his brother and best friend as he started back toward the women.

"And miss this?" Owen said as he turned to follow Evan. "No way."

"Right there with ya," Grant said, trotting along behind them.

Resigned to their interference, Evan walked to her, knowing that once he did whatever he was about to do, there'd be no undoing it. And what was he going to do exactly? He had no idea. All he knew was he wanted some time alone with her without the prying eyes of his brother, cousin and friends on them. As Grace watched him approach with a wide-eyed, curious stare, he could feel the anxiety, apprehension and hint of excitement emanating from her. Whatever was brewing between them, she felt it, too, which was comforting.

Aware that all eyes were on him, Evan held out a hand to Grace. "Walk with me?"

"Oh, um, sure." She took the hand he offered and let him help her up.

As the sweet scent of her surrounded him, it occurred to him that his attraction to her made no sense at all. She was nothing like the petite, perky blondes he usually preferred, and yet he was dying to find out if her dark hair was as silky as it looked.

He liked his women confident, experienced and willing to try new things—inside the bedroom and out. Grace didn't exactly exude confidence. While Stephanie and Laura had worn revealing bikinis to the beach, an oversized T-shirt covered Grace's bathing suit and kept her curves hidden from him. Evan didn't want to admit that he'd been dying to see her in a bathing suit and had been disappointed when she kept the cover-up on all afternoon.

She wasn't his type. It was that simple. Why, then, was he thrilled to be walking next to her on the beach and dodging the waves that teased the shore? His heart was beating funny, his mouth was dry as the sand under his feet, and he couldn't think of a single witty or charming thing to say to her. What the hell was wrong with him?

"Nice day," she said after a long period of silence.

"Uh-huh." Under normal circumstances, September was his favorite month of the year on Gansett. Cool, crisp sunny days perfect for surfing and sailing, and chilly nights ideal for bonfires on the beach. Today he was completely out of sorts and off his game.

"You're acting uncomfortable again," Grace said.

"Am I?" Startled, Evan snapped out of his musings and glanced over to find her watching him intently.

"Are you sorry you invited me to hang out with you this weekend?"

"No," he said, shocked to the core. That was the last thing he wanted her to think. Well, maybe not the *last* thing . . . "Of course not."

"Then what is it?"

"I don't know," he said, going with the truth. "I'm out of sorts."

"I'm sorry to hear that. It's been such a fun day. I was hoping you were enjoying it as much as I am."

"I've enjoyed it very much, Grace. That's kind of the problem."

"I don't understand," she said, looking and sounding confused.

Evan could tell he startled her when he reached for her hand and brought it to his lips. "I like you."

"I like you, too."

"No, I mean I *like* you." He watched with satisfaction as his words registered with her.

"Oh," she said, sounding breathless. "And that has you out of sorts?"

Nodding, he fought a sudden urge to lean in and kiss the pucker off her sweet lips. He couldn't do that with the others watching their every move, but he wanted to. God, he wanted to. Up ahead, the beach curved around a point and became the town beach. If he recalled correctly, that end of the town beach was usually sparsely populated.

"Come on," he said, giving her hand a tug.

"Where're we going?"

"You'll see."

Once they rounded the rocky point and were away from the prying eyes of their group, Evan tightened his hold on Grace's hand.

"What's the rush?" she asked as she half walked, half ran to keep up with him.

He stopped and turned to her, catching her when she all but crashed into him. Before he could talk himself out of seeing whether there was anything to this damned attraction, he crushed his mouth to hers. The moment their lips met, he had his answer. Heat streaked through him, burning away all his earlier ideas of what kind of woman he wanted. For whatever reason, he wanted *this* woman.

She let out a needy whimper as her arms encircled his neck.

"Open," he said in a harsh whisper. "Let me in." He dipped his head to recapture her mouth, more gently this time, stroking her lips with his tongue before easing his way in.

Even though she kissed him back with equal enthusiasm, there was something innocent and unschooled in her responses. Despite that, the instant her tongue met his, Evan was lost. His cock surged with need. God almighty, he hadn't had a reaction like this to a woman since he was a horny kid with no idea of how to control himself.

She stripped him of his self-control and his senses. Nothing else in the world mattered beyond the warmth of her eager mouth, the caress of her tongue, the sweetness of her lips and the press of her full breasts against his chest. He wanted her with an urgency that surprised and frightened him.

Stunned by his reaction, he tore his lips free and stared at her. He was breathing hard, as if he'd been running a race. As he came to his senses, he realized she was staring and breathing hard, too.

"Wow," he said. "That was . . ."

"Yeah." She raised her hand to her mouth and rested two fingers on her lips. "Wow."

"Will you go out with me tonight? Just the two of us?"

She studied him for what seemed like a long time before she said, "I'd love to."

Encouraged—and relieved—by her reply, he rested his hands on her hips and brought her in close to him again. "Afterward, can we do more of this?" he asked, touching his lips to hers.

"I might be persuaded."

"I love that haughty tone." He peppered his words with kisses. "It makes me feel so *chastised*."

"You're frequently in need of chastising."

"Do you give spankings, too?" Her entire face turned red, which made Evan feel bad for being so raunchy. "Sorry."

"It's okay. I'm getting used to your irreverence."

Evan slipped an arm around her shoulders and steered her back in the direction of the others. "You seem to be enjoying Stephanie and Laura," he said, looking for something—anything—to take his mind off the intense kiss.

"They're great. Stephanie and Grant are so cute together, aren't they?"

"Not sure I'd use the word 'cute.' They're in that newly-in-love stage when everything is viewed through rose-colored glasses."

"That sounds rather cynical. You don't think it'll last?"

"I guess we'll see."

"How long have Owen and Laura been together?"

"They're not together."

"Really? They've got sizzling chemistry."

"Do they? I haven't noticed."

"Then you're not looking. He's very protective of her. If they aren't together now, I bet it won't be long before they are."

"Very interesting. They said the same thing about us, you know. The sizzling-chemistry thing."

"Is that right?"

"Uh-huh. What do you think?"

"About?"

Evan rolled his eyes at her. "Our sizzling chemistry."

"Is it sizzling? I hadn't noticed."

He hip-checked her, making her laugh. "You're being mean to me."

"I'm very sorry."

"I don't think you are."

"Now who's being haughty?" she asked.

"That kiss was hot."

"It was okay." She bit her lip and looked up at him with big eyes full of mischief. "I'll bet you can do better."

"You are so going to pay for that." He stopped short all of a sudden. "Are you laughing at me?"

Shrieking with laughter, she took off running for the chairs and the safety of her new friends. Watching her go, Evan couldn't wait to have her all to himself for an entire evening. He'd show her chemistry.

CHAPTER 8

*A*s Grace hustled back to Laura and Stephanie, her heart raced with excitement and anticipation and a tiny bit of dread. She could feel Evan's eyes boring a hole in her back as he followed her to the row of chairs, where the other women sat watching them with interest.

"You guys," she said breathlessly. "I need your help."

"What's going on?" Stephanie asked, her brows knitted with worry. "Did Evan say something?"

"Yes! He asked me out! I have nothing to wear and hardly any time. You have to help me."

"We're on it," Laura said.

Both women jumped up and started folding their chairs and collecting their belongings.

"Hey," Grant said as he came out of the water with Owen trailing behind him. "Where're you going?"

"We have some errands to do," Stephanie told her boyfriend. "We'll catch up with you later."

Grace wouldn't have thought Grant capable of pouting, but there it was.

Laughing, Stephanie kissed the pout off his lips.

He hooked an arm around her to keep her close to him. "There," he said after a lingering kiss. "That's better. You can go now."

"Gee, thanks." She poked him in the belly and reached for the beach bag she'd dropped in the sand while he kissed her. "See if you boys can stay out of trouble while we're gone."

Owen bent to whisper something in Laura's ear.

Smiling, she looked up at him and nodded. "See you back at the ranch."

The three women started to walk toward Stephanie's car.

"Grace!"

She spun around to find Evan watching her with heated eyes that made her want to shiver. Only the prying stares of the rest of the group kept her from doing just that. "Yes?"

"Pick you up at seven thirty."

"See you then," she managed to say in a cool, unaffected tone that was a total lie. She was affected all right—on every possible level. While she couldn't wait to see him again in a few short hours, she was also dreading it. After her recent spate of bad luck, she couldn't help but wonder what might go wrong tonight.

When they were settled in Stephanie's old car and heading into town, Laura spun around in the passenger seat. "Tell us everything. You guys disappeared around the point, and we couldn't see you anymore."

"Which was clearly his intention," Stephanie added, glancing in the rearview mirror at Grace.

"Spill it," Laura said.

This whole thing was so new to her. Grace hadn't had much opportunity to dish with other women about men. Until she lost the weight, men hadn't exactly been lining up at her door. And the idea that a man who looked like Evan McCarthy could actually be interested in her was hard to believe. Of course, the moment she had that thought, she was infuriated with herself. Why *wouldn't* a man like Evan like her?

Oh, who was she kidding? Wait until Evan found out she was a formerly fat virgin with next to no experience with men. He'd run for his life, screaming for mercy. Her deep sigh had Laura reaching for her hand.

"What's wrong, Grace?"

As tears burned her eyes Grace wanted to shriek in frustration. For every step forward she managed to take, there seemed to be two steps backward, too.

"I'm sorry to drag you guys away from the beach," Grace said once she managed to get her emotions under control. "I think I'll cancel with Evan. I'm not up for going out tonight."

"What the heck are you talking about?" Stephanie asked. "Did you see the way he looks at you? Like he wants to devour you. Grant said he's never seen Evan look at a woman that way—ever."

Hearing that only made Grace more concerned about what might happen later. She was so afraid of how much she wanted him. Every minute she spent with him only made the yearning more acute. All the years she'd spent pining for Trey paled in comparison to what she already felt for Evan. Nothing good could possibly come of that.

"Tell us what has you so upset," Laura said. The compassion in her voice wrapped around Grace like a warm blanket.

"I want to tell you, but you have to promise you won't tell Evan—or Grant or Owen. Or anyone."

"Of course," Laura said. "We won't tell, will we, Steph?"

"Mum's the word."

"It's kind of a big deal." Grace took a deep breath and forced herself to meet Laura's concerned gaze. "I was obese for most of my life. I had lap-band surgery eighteen months ago, and I've since lost a hundred and thirty pounds."

"That's amazing!" Laura said. "Congratulations."

"Good for you, Grace," Stephanie added.

"Thanks." Grace had to force herself to get through this. "I have like zero experience with men, and I'm feeling way out of my league with Evan."

"You're not out of your league, honey," Laura said.

"He could have anyone he wants—"

"And yet you're the one he wants to devour," Stephanie said, smirking in the mirror.

Grace's pulse raced as images of Evan devouring her filled her imagination. What did that entail anyway? Swallowing hard, she said, "I have no idea what I'm doing with dating or flirting or sex or any of it."

"So you've never . . ."

As her face heated with mortification, Grace shook her head at Laura's gentle question.

"Well," Laura said to Stephanie, "we've got some work to do to get you ready."

"I'll do your makeup," Stephanie said.

"I don't usually wear makeup," Grace said.

"You do now," Stephanie replied as she pulled into the parking lot at Gold's. "We need some supplies. Let's go, ladies."

As they trooped into the store, Grace kept a lookout for either of the Golds but didn't see them.

Stephanie led the way to the cosmetics aisle and then turned to take a long look at Grace.

"We've got to do something magnificent with those eyes of yours," she said. "They're not so much brown as they are gold."

"I agree," Laura said, reaching for lash-enhancing mascara and tossing it into the basket Stephanie had looped over her forearm.

"I'm thinking a dark gray shadow with a hint of shimmer," Stephanie said, holding up her selection for Laura's approval.

"Perfect." Laura tossed a compact and oversized brush into the basket. "This bronzer will highlight her lovely tan."

"Good call," Stephanie said. "Now, about the lips."

Her head spinning, Grace followed them to the lipstick display. The staggering array of colors and textures made her eyes swim.

While Stephanie and Laura put their heads together to consult, Grace calmed herself by looking around at the store. It was quieter than it had been earlier in the day, but there were still several customers in line at the register and others perusing the aisles. From the raised pharmacy platform in the back of the store, she'd always be able to see everything that was going on. If it happened, that was. Just as she was wondering when she'd hear from the Golds, Mrs. Gold's nasally voice beckoned from the front of the store.

"Grace Ryan, is that you?"

Stephanie and Laura looked up at Grace with surprise.

"Hi, Mrs. Gold," Grace said as the gray-haired woman swooped down on them.

"Oh, I told my Henry that was you! We were getting ready to call you!"

Grace nearly stopped breathing, and her heart slowed to a crawl. "Is that right?"

"We've given careful consideration to your offer, consulted with our children, and we all agree that you should be the new owner of Gold's Pharmacy! Congratulations, honey!"

As she accepted Mrs. Gold's hug, Grace noticed Stephanie and Laura staring at her in stunned silence. Grace didn't think this would be the best time to tell Mrs. Gold that the name of her store would be changing to Ryan's Pharmacy. "Thank you so much," Grace said to Mrs. Gold. "I'm so excited."

"We'll have to sit down about all the details and apply to the town to transfer the license, but we're looking to do this as quickly as possible. We've already been to see Jim Sturgil, the island lawyer, and he's going to draw up the papers for us." Mrs. Gold seemed to realize all of a sudden that Grace wasn't alone and lowered her voice. "Might you come by tomorrow morning to talk particulars?"

"I'd love to. I'll be here."

"Wonderful." Mrs. Gold gave Grace another hug. "We can't thank you enough. I'll see you tomorrow."

She skipped off toward the back of the store.

"Oh my God!" Laura said. "*You're buying Gold's?*"

"Looks that way," Grace said with a satisfied smile. All her plans were falling into place, and she couldn't be more excited.

"Congratulations, Grace," Stephanie said. "That's awesome. I'm so glad you'll be staying on the island."

"I am, too. I already know I love it here. But do me a favor—please don't mention the news about the store to anyone yet. I don't want Evan to think that buying the store had anything to do with him, because it didn't. It was something I wanted for myself."

Until Mrs. Gold had shared the good news, Grace hadn't been aware of just how badly she'd wanted it to work out. Everything about this move felt right to her, and she couldn't wait to get settled in the cozy apartment upstairs.

"I certainly get that," Laura said. "I felt the same way about the opportunity with the hotel. It was all about doing something that I wanted for once. Don't worry, we'll keep it between us until you're ready to tell people."

Stephanie nodded in agreement. "Absolutely. That's your news to share."

"Thanks." Grace was relieved they seemed to understand. "I appreciate that. I feel much better about the idea of spending the winter here knowing you guys will be here, too."

"We'll have tons of fun," Stephanie promised.

Laura tossed the lipstick they'd chosen into the basket and steered Grace toward the checkout. "Let's get out of here. We've got to get you ready for a hot date!"

"I'M *NOT* HAVING SEX WITH HIM," GRACE PROTESTED AN HOUR LATER AS the three women crowded into the small bathroom in her room at the Beachcomber to experiment with hairstyles. Stephanie had produced a box of condoms that she'd bought for Grace on the sly when they were at Gold's.

"Just in case," Stephanie said with a knowing grin as she put them on the counter next to the sink.

Grace had dropped a hundred dollars on a black silk cocktail dress that her friends assured her was sizzling hot, and another fifty on sky-high heels that they said made her legs look a mile long. Since she had absolutely no experience with this stuff, Grace was taking their word for it.

"Read my lips: I am *not* having sex with him."

"You say that now," Stephanie said, smirking, "but don't you want to be ready, just in case?"

"Define 'ready.'"

"How to say this . . ." Stephanie looked to Laura for guidance. "You know how when you have an important event, you'd shave your legs?"

"Of course."

Laura's eyes danced with mirth as she apparently got where Stephanie was going.

Grace wished one of them would clue her in.

"If there's any chance you might have sex, you also want to shave . . ." Stephanie pointed down.

Grace finally got what she meant and gasped. "Ew, really? *All* of it?"

"I wouldn't say *all*," Laura said diplomatically. "Most would be good. Guys dig that."

Grace wondered how she'd managed to live nearly thirty years without knowing this kind of stuff. "They do?"

"Yep," Stephanie said, holding up Grace's razor and pointing at the shower. "Time to tame the beast."

Laura busted up laughing, which spurred giggles all around.

"I don't think the beast needs taming," Grace said. "I'm not going to sleep with him." Maybe if she said it often enough, she'd begin to believe it herself.

"I sleep with his brother, and I'm friends with his other brother's wife," Stephanie said. "Trust me when I tell you the McCarthy powers of sexual persuasion are not to be taken lightly."

"La-la-la, too much information." Laura stuck her fingers in her ears. "I don't want to know this stuff about my cousins."

Stephanie rolled her eyes at Laura. "As if it's news to you." Giving Grace a nudge toward the shower, she said, "Better to be ready, just in case."

The idea of sleeping with Evan filled Grace with excitement and anticipation and anxiety. "Fine, but I'm not having sex with him."

"You keep telling yourself that," Stephanie said, "but I'll bet you'll be thanking me tomorrow."

Grace eyed the other woman shrewdly. "I'll take that bet." She held out her hand. "Twenty bucks?"

Stephanie shook her hand. "Make it fifty. Laura, you're our witness."

"Duly noted. Take your shower, Grace, and then I'll do your hair."

"You guys must have better stuff to do than babysit me."

"Are you kidding?" Stephanie said. "This is fun! I can't wait to see you all dolled up in that black dress Laura found for you, and the heels. Evan will wet his pants when he gets a load of you."

Grace chuckled at that visual as they left the room and shut the door. She eyed the razor warily as she considered their instructions. "Well, they certainly know better than I do, so here goes nothing."

CHAPTER 9

*R*eady to get home to his family, Mac McCarthy locked up the marina office and restaurant. He couldn't wait to see Maddie and hear about everything the kids had been up to that day. He'd been spoiled by the weeks at home during Maddie's high-risk pregnancy, and now that he was back to work, he was far too aware of what he was missing with his family.

The sun was setting over the salt pond in a vivid display of reds, pinks, blues and purples. Knowing how Maddie loved a pretty sunset, he sent her a text telling her to take a look outside and letting her know he'd be home soon.

As was his habit at the end of the day, he took a walk down the main pier to make sure the boats were securely tied for the night. Halfway down, he stopped short at the sight of his father's familiar thatch of gray hair. Shoulders stooped, Big Mac stared down at the spot where his life had nearly come to a tragic end earlier in the summer.

Mac approached his father and rested a hand on his shoulder. "Dad? Are you okay?"

"Oh, hi, son. I didn't realize you were still here."

Mac didn't mention that his father would've had to go past Mac's truck to get to the pier. "I was just closing up for the night."

"Did we have a good day?"

Mac smiled at his father's daily question. "A very good day. A thousand more than the same day last year."

"I love that you know that."

"It's called record keeping."

"Never heard of it."

Mac laughed as he remembered how long it had taken him to wrangle the business records into shape. "Believe me, I know. So what're you doing here?"

Big Mac looked down at the water again. "Trying to remember. I keep going over and over it, and I can't recall a damned thing about what happened."

"That's probably just as well. I've heard that's the brain's way of protecting itself after a traumatic injury."

"It's damned frustrating. How am I supposed to get past it if I can't even remember it?"

The despair Mac heard in his father's voice was wildly out of character. Big Mac was never despondent. Ebullient, yes, but never despondent. Seeing him like this struck a note of fear in Mac. "What can I do for you, Dad?"

"No one will tell me what happened. I know you're all trying to protect me, but I want to know." He grasped his son's arm. "Tell me, Mac. Please, tell me."

Mac released a deep breath. The last thing he wanted was to relive one of the worst days of his life, but there was nothing he wouldn't do for his dad. "Let me buy you a beer."

"Is that your way of blowing me off?"

"Not at all." He took his father by the arm and led him to the Tiki Bar, where the bartender greeted them warmly. "Two light beers, please."

"Coming right up."

With their beers in hand and the bartender working the other end of the bar, Mac took a long look at his dad. "You're sure you want to hear this?"

Big Mac nodded. "I *need* to hear it."

Mac stared off at the boats bobbing in the salt pond, trying to find the words he needed. "We were sitting with the guys at the picnic table outside the restaurant when we saw the boat coming. He was steaming across the pond, leaving a big wake. You got pissed and got up to go meet him."

"Why me and not you or Luke?"

"Because you said you had it, and even though you put us in charge, you're still the boss."

That drew a grin from Big Mac. "Damned straight."

"So the guy was totally out of control. You know the type, all power and no skill. His crew of drunken women had managed to get the stern line to you, and you had it wrapped around the piling. Luke and I had wandered over to help when he gunned it and dragged you right off the pier."

A shudder rippled through Mac as he thought of his father disappearing from the dock. Rubbing at the stubble on his jaw, Mac took a minute to regain his composure. His father would never know that he'd had nightmares for weeks about that moment.

"I, ah . . . I looked into the water, saw you floating facedown, and I jumped."

Seeming to sense this was difficult for Mac to talk about, his father rested a comforting hand on his shoulder.

"I turned you over and . . . You weren't breathing, so I did rescue breathing until you started breathing on your own again. There was, um, blood in the water from where you smacked your head on the swim platform. The boat . . . It came close to us. Really close."

"Was that when Luke jumped?"

"Yeah. I didn't see him jump, but I heard him land. So did the captain, and he finally killed the power."

"Close call."

"Very. Luke saved both our lives by getting the guy's attention before he could run over us in the water."

"He's paid a big price for that."

"Hopefully, the surgery fixed up his ankle once and for all."

"Let's hope so." Big Mac squeezed Mac's shoulder. "I knew you'd come in after me, but not all that about the breathing and such. I needed to know so I could say thank you."

"Come on, Dad. Like you wouldn't have done the same for me or anyone."

"Were you scared?"

"Senseless. My hands shook for hours afterward. I kept trying to picture what could've happened, what it would be like if . . ." Mac shook his head. "Unimaginable."

"It's gonna happen someday," his father reminded him.

"Not like that. I'd prefer it to happen when you're about ninety-nine or so and have driven us all mad for years being a grumpy old pain in the ass. Maybe by then I might be able to conceive of life without you."

"You're a good boy, son," Big Mac said, his voice gruff. "Always were."

Though his father's words touched him deeply, Mac went for levity lest he end up bawling his head off. "Even when you were bailing me and Joe out of jail for flattening mailboxes in your truck?"

"Even then."

It wasn't like his father to miss a chance to jab at him about the mailbox incident. Mac had heard about it daily for years afterward. "You're going to be okay, Dad. I know it."

"I hope you're right."

"How's Mom doing?"

"Why do you ask?" Big Mac asked, instantly on alert. "Did she say something to you?"

"I don't know what you mean."

Big Mac tipped his head to study his son. "Don't give me that bull crap. You know something. Spill it."

Why he ever thought he could get away with being less than truthful with his father was beyond Mac. "Evan said you guys have been fighting a lot."

"Evan's got a big mouth."

"He's worried, Dad. We both are. It's not like you two to fight."

"I've been hard on her. I know that, but I can't stand the way she hovers, waiting for me to need her help with something. Drives me batty."

"She only wants to do whatever she can to help you get better."

"I know that, but the hovering is too damned much."

"What if I talk to her and ask her to back off a bit and let you fend for yourself?"

"Then she'll know I was griping to you about her, and that won't do me any good. Trust me on that."

Mac thought about that for a minute. "Then how about some romance?"

"Come again?"

"Take her out on a nice date. Wine her, dine her, and somewhere over the course of the evening let her know that you're going to be fine and it's time for both of you to get back to normal."

"Huh," Big Mac said. "You think that'll work?"

"I'm sure it will. Having done the dating thing more recently than you, I might even share a few pointers—for a price."

"What price?"

"Stop snapping at her every time she does exactly what you'd do if the roles were reversed."

"When did you get so wise about these things?"

"Right around the time I knocked a gorgeous woman off her bike."

"Best thing you ever did."

"Couldn't agree more. Now, are you going to fix this thing with Mom or what?"

"I'm gonna fix it."

"Good. Now here's what I think you ought to do."

~

TIFFANY FOLLOWED ABBY FROM THE FRONT OF THE STORE TO THE storage room in the back of Abby's Attic, the Main Street store Abby had run for the last few years.

"I've managed to sell most of what I had in stock during the going-out-of-business sale, but there's still quite a bit more back here." She gestured to the shelves that held T-shirts stacked in neat piles, toys sorted by age group and an array of Gansett Island merchandise. "Get what you can for it at this point."

"I'll send you a check for whatever I manage to sell."

"That'd be great." Abby turned to Tiffany. "You're sure you don't mind doing this?"

"Of course not. I can finish up your sale, since I don't plan to open my store until next season anyway."

"You're saving my life. I'm anxious to join Cal in Texas. His mom has been struggling after the stroke, and he sounds so down."

"Are you guys still planning to get married?"

"Eventually," Abby said with a sigh. "We had it all planned for next month here on the island, but we had to cancel when his mom got sick."

"That's a bummer."

"Big-time, but I suppose this is a glimpse at what married life will be like. You do what you have to for the other person."

"Let's hope your married life is better than mine, because mine was all about me doing what was best for *him*," Tiffany said, even though she immediately regretted her bitter-sounding tone. "Sorry. I shouldn't have said that. I'm sure it'll be much different for you."

Abby's brown eyes went soft with compassion. "I heard that you and Jim had split. I'm really sorry."

Tiffany shrugged off the sympathy. "It's for the best." If she kept telling herself that, maybe one day she'd believe it. She was bothered mostly by the fact that she'd failed to hold their family together for her daughter.

"Will you open another store in Texas?"

"I'd like to. I enjoyed this so much." She looked around the store with barely concealed sadness. "I guess we'll see how things work out with Cal's mom and figure out our next step. All that matters now is that we're together."

"I'm sure you'll figure it out."

The bells over the door rang to signify a customer, and Tiffany followed Abby to the front, stopping short at the sight of Police Chief Blaine Taylor in his oh-so-sexy uniform. His crisp white shirt offset his dark tan. Her eyes were drawn to the gun belt slung around lean hips. When her gaze dipped below his belt, she quickly recovered, forcing herself to meet golden-brown eyes that were staring directly at her.

"Hi, Blaine." Abby broke the tension that arced between Tiffany and the sexy officer. "How're you?"

"Um, good," he said, tearing his gaze off Tiffany to address Abby. "I heard you were closing down to go be with Cal."

"That's right. Tiffany is taking over my lease and opening her own store next season. We were just going over some of the particulars."

"Is that right?" Blaine said, casting another intrigued glance at Tiffany.

She still hadn't recovered from the first time he'd sent his hungry stare her way. Since her tongue was tied in knots, she nodded in response to his inquiry.

"What kind of store will it be?"

No way could she tell this particular man what she had in mind. Not when he looked at her like he wanted to chain her to his bed and have his wicked way with her. Not that she'd mind, per se, but she was still married. "It's, um, going to be a gift shop. Of sorts."

He didn't need to know that the gifts would be lacy and see-through and the toys would appeal more to adults than children. In fact, she planned to keep a tight lid on her plans for the store until it was ready to open, so no one could talk her out of it.

"Good luck with it," he said.

"Thanks."

"Is there something I can help you find?" Abby asked him.

"I need a gift for my niece's birthday. She's going to be three."

"I have a few things left she might enjoy," Abby said, leading him to the toy display.

As he followed her, he cast another heated look Tiffany's way.

She forced herself to remain calm even as she imploded from within. *Whoa*, she thought. No guy had ever inspired that kind of reaction from her with merely a look. She wondered if Abby stocked any of those foldout fans that the tourists loved. It was getting hot in here.

While Abby completed the transaction with Blaine, Tiffany hid out in the storeroom. Only when she heard the bells jingle over the door did she release the deep breath she'd been holding.

Wearing a knowing smirk, Abby came to the door. "Well, well, *well*, Ms. Tiffany. Looks like you know right where to go when you're ready to start dating again."

She couldn't even think about Blaine without her heart beating fast and her palms getting sweaty. "I have no idea what you're talking about."

"Oh *right*! That guy is h-o-t for you!"

"He is not," Tiffany said, her words ringing hollow even to her.

"Whatever you say, tiger. I need a cigarette after being in the same room with you two, and I don't even smoke!"

That drew a reluctant laugh from Tiffany. "He is rather gorgeous, isn't he?"

"Rather." Abby came into the storage room and plopped down next to Tiffany on the floor. Handing her the keys to the store, she said, "I think things are about to get very interesting for you."

Taking the keys, Tiffany curled her fingers around them. "After the hell of the last few years, I'm ready for interesting."

CHAPTER 10

*A*s he took the stairs to the Beachcomber, Evan realized he was nervous, which was ridiculous. He'd been on hundreds of dates. No, not hundreds. A hundred. Maybe . . . Suffice to say, there'd been a lot of dates. He was what some people might call a serial dater. That wasn't to say he was a jerk or anything. As Big Mac McCarthy's son, he'd been taught to treat women with the utmost respect.

Other than the unfortunate incident in high school in which he'd allowed a rumor to run wild about Maddie Chester, who was now his sister-in-law, Evan's track record was fairly clean. He'd suffered a guilty conscience over the untruths his friends had spread about Maddie, and he'd learned from it. By the time Mac confronted him on the matter and forced him to denounce the rumors in a letter to the *Gansett Gazette*, Evan had been relieved to have the chance to right a terrible wrong.

Thinking about ancient history didn't do much to dispel his nerves. As much as he enjoyed being around women, the woman he was seeing tonight was different. For one thing, she seemed far more innocent than the women he normally dated. He couldn't put his finger on why he was picking up that vibe, but it was there loud and clear. However, since she'd been on an overnight date gone bad when he met her, he assumed she wasn't *completely* innocent.

"God," he muttered under his breath. "What if she is completely innocent?"

"Talking to yourself, Cousin?"

Startled out of his musings, Evan looked up to find Laura and Stephanie coming down the stairs to the lobby.

"Hey," Evan said. "You guys are still here?"

"We had fun hanging out with Grace this afternoon," Laura said. "She's all ready."

"Oh," Evan said, his stomach twisting. He'd heard of having butterflies in the belly, but all of a sudden his butterflies felt more like seagulls. "Okay."

"Evan," Stephanie said, her hand resting on his arm and her expression grave. "Be good to her. She's a really nice girl."

"I know that. Why do you think I asked her out?"

"We know you know," Laura added, "but she's *special*. No smooth moves, you got me?"

Evan wanted to be insulted, but sadly he knew exactly what his cousin meant. "I got you."

Laura straightened the collar on the button-down shirt he'd ironed for the occasion. "You look nice, but she looks better," Laura said. "Room 320." She left him with a pat on his freshly shaven cheek and took off with her arm linked through Stephanie's.

Their laughter filled the Beachcomber's lobby as they headed for the door.

Although he didn't appreciate his cousin's attempt at humor, he was glad to see her and Stephanie laughing, since both women had been through a lot lately and deserved to have some fun—even at his expense. Climbing the stairs to Grace's third-floor room, Evan tried to calm his nerves by reminding himself that this was just another date. No big deal. Except he'd thought of little else since the sizzling kiss on the beach . . .

Outside room 320, Evan took a moment to collect himself. He

credited the odd beat of his heart to the trek up three flights of stairs. It certainly wasn't because he couldn't wait to see her. That was not at all like him. Raising his hand, he knocked on the door.

She made him wait a long, breathless moment before she opened the door. Taking in the sight of creamy curves and a sexy black dress, his mind went totally blank except for one niggling thought—this was definitely not going to be just another date.

EVAN WOULD NEVER KNOW THAT HIS REACTION TO SEEING HER DRESSED up for their date was the first time in Grace's life that she felt truly beautiful. He stared at her with such blatant desire etched into his handsome face that her legs began to quiver, which was rather dangerous when wearing three-inch heels.

He looked amazing in khaki pants and a blue dress shirt that did amazing things to his eyes. She couldn't decide what she wanted to do more—run her fingers through the thick, dark hair he'd combed into submission for the occasion or caress his smooth cheek. As she breathed in the sexy, musky scent of him, it was all she could do to keep her hands to herself.

"Let me get my purse," she said, leaving him at the doorway. As she crossed the room to the bed, where she'd left her bag, she was acutely aware of him watching her every move.

When she turned to face him again, she found him standing right in front of her. The door was closed. How had that happened without her hearing it? Grace swallowed hard as she gauged his intense expression.

"You look gorgeous," he said, his voice huskier than she'd heard it before. His hands landed on her hips to bring her in close to him.

Her purse fell to the floor with a thunk, and her hands landed on his muscular chest. She knew she should acknowledge the compliment, but her tongue was tied in knots.

"I keep thinking about that kiss on the beach," he said, his lips a mere fraction of an inch from hers. "I want to kiss you again, but you're too pretty and perfect. I don't want to mess you up."

Who cared about lipstick at a moment like this? She reached up to pull him down to her. When she thought of all the years she'd spent lusting after Trey, she almost laughed. That wasn't lust. *This* was lust. Despite her vows to Stephanie and Laura, the minute his mouth claimed hers, Grace began to wonder if she would lose the bet.

He was gentle but insistent as he seduced his way past her lips and into her mouth to flirt with her tongue.

Grace's arms encircled his neck to keep him exactly where she wanted him.

He tightened his hold on her and brought her into intimate contact with his erection.

She rubbed against him wantonly, drawing a deep groan from him that thrilled her. Encouraged by his response, she sucked on his tongue, which earned her another groan.

He cupped her ass and pushed hard against her.

Consumed by curiosity and feeling rather reckless, she ran her hand over his muscular chest to his belly and below. The instant her hand met his steely length, he broke the kiss and drew in a sharp, deep breath. She stroked him from root to tip, stunned by the length and width of him. Trey had nothing on Evan, and even though she desperately wanted to see and feel him without his pants in the way, she experienced a moment of fear as she tried to imagine *that* fitting inside of *her*.

"Feels good," he said in a strained tone.

She ventured a look up at him and found his head thrown back, his jaw clenched and his Adam's apple bobbing in his throat. Pressing her lips against his neck, she continued to move her fingers over his throbbing length. She'd gone a little wild with the razor earlier, and the feel of her silky panties on bare, sensitive skin ratcheted up her desire to combustible levels.

"Grace, God, you make me crazy." He framed her face with his hands and took her mouth again, devouring her in a series of kisses, each more heated and intense than the last.

By the time he finally drew back from her, Grace was stunned and confused and dying for more.

"I promised myself I'd go slow with you, but you're so damned sexy."

To a woman who'd spent most of her life feeling anything but sexy, Evan's words went straight to her already over-committed heart.

"I can't resist you," he said as he turned his attention to her neck, sending shivers of desire straight to her core. "I made reservations for dinner. We should go."

"Or," she said, tipping her head to give him better access to her neck, "we could get room service and stay in."

He raised his head and met her gaze, his eyes heated with desire. "You got all dressed up. I want to take you out and show you off."

"I don't care about that."

"Are you sure, Grace? I need you to know I'm not looking for anything serious—"

She rested her fingers on his lips. "I get it. Don't worry." Although her heart sank at the thought of never seeing him again, he'd been clear from the outset that he wasn't a relationship kind of guy.

He tucked a strand of hair behind her ear and studied her for a long moment.

It was all Grace could do to get air to her lungs as she waited to see what he would do. If he didn't do something—*anything*—soon, she was going to die on the spot.

And then he tipped his head and touched his lips lightly to hers, starting all over again with kisses that stripped her defenses. Since he was giving off the "slow things down" signal, she reluctantly shifted her hand from his erection and wound her arms around his neck.

She almost stopped breathing altogether when she felt the tug of her zipper and the singe of his fingers skimming over her back on the way down. Her heart beat wildly, and she hoped she could remain standing on increasingly unsteady legs. His lips were relentless on her neck, sending sensation coursing down her spine.

Her nipples strained against the tight confines of her bra, and the throb between her legs demanded her full attention.

He pulled back and rested his hands on her shoulders, edging the dress off in tiny increments that made her heart beat fast.

A million thoughts cycled through her mind: Would she measure up to other women he'd been with? Would he wonder about the scar on her abdomen? Would he be able to tell she was a virgin? Should she tell him?

"Why are you suddenly all tense?" he asked.

"Am I?"

He nodded and stopped her dress from falling the rest of the way off her shoulders. "What's wrong?"

Grace knew she'd hate herself in the morning. "I don't think I'm ready for this after all."

To his credit, he didn't exhibit an ounce of disappointment. "That's okay." He arranged her dress so it was back where it belonged. "We're not in any rush."

Relieved that he didn't seem mad with her for letting things get so far and then pulling the plug, Grace leaned her forehead against his chest. "It's not that I don't want to. I hope you know that."

His arms came around her, and his fingers combed through her hair in a gesture almost as seductive as his kisses. "It's okay, Grace. If you're not ready, you're not ready."

"We hardly know each other."

"And yet there's an undeniable sizzle."

"Yes."

"You might not believe this, but I've never experienced a sizzle quite like ours."

"Really?"

He kissed the top of her head and used a finger on her chin to compel her to look up at him. "Really," he said, punctuating the word with a soft kiss. "Let's go get some dinner. What do you say?"

He was so sweet and considerate that she wanted to take it all back and tell him she was ready to get naked with him. Instead, she turned her back to him and pointed to her zipper. With his lips teasing her neck from behind, he raised the zipper and had her about to beg by the time he was done.

"That's not fair," she said.

"Sorry." His chuckle gave him away as anything but sorry.

"Give me a minute to repair the damage." She ducked into the bathroom, closed the door and was shocked by what she saw in the mirror—swollen lips, smeared lipstick and glassy eyes.

"So this is what passion looks like," she whispered as she wiped off the lipstick and reapplied it the way Stephanie had taught her. Studying her reflection, she took cleansing breaths to calm her racing heart and out-of-control hormones.

Maybe by the time they had dinner and got to know each other a little better, she'd be more comfortable getting naked with him. He seemed to want her as much as she wanted him. He'd made it clear he wasn't interested in a relationship, and with the huge challenge she was about to undertake with the pharmacy, it wasn't a good time for her to get involved, either.

So who would be harmed by a weekend fling? No one, she decided as she blotted her lips and ran a brush through her hair. "After dinner," she whispered. "We'll try this again."

AFTER PARTING WITH STEPHANIE, WHO WAS EAGER TO GET BACK TO Grant, Laura took a leisurely walk through town, window-shopping and enjoying the salt air. As soon as the sun began to dip toward the horizon, the warmth of the day was replaced by a September chill that had Laura wishing for a sweater.

On the far end of the town, the Sand & Surf Hotel beckoned her home. A riot of gables and craggy corners illuminated by the setting sun, the hotel's shingled exterior was in need of a good pressure washing, which was just one of many items on her extensive to-do list. Thinking about the renovation and redecoration project had helped to preserve her sanity as she'd gone through the torture of ripping apart the life she'd planned to lead with her philandering husband.

For the first time since her bridesmaids had broken the news about finding her new husband's dating profile alive and well online, Laura felt like she could breathe again. Thank God she didn't have to go back to the mainland any time soon to face well-meaning friends and family members who looked at her with such pity. Instead, she could throw herself into creating a whole new life here on the island in a place where she and her unborn child could put down roots and make some friends.

The afternoon she'd spent with Stephanie and Grace had gone a long way toward restoring her spirits. Her new friends hadn't been witnesses to her epic disaster, and while they knew she was nursing deep wounds, they didn't look at her with pity or sympathy or hover around her as if she might shatter at any moment the way her friends at home did.

Laura took a deep breath of the fragrant sea air and watched a pair of gulls dive into the surf in search of dinner. She'd done the right thing moving here. No matter how things worked out at the hotel, being on the island had always felt right to her. Being anywhere other than Providence would be an improvement, but being here in the home of her heart went a long way toward soothing the still-festering wound on her soul.

Taking the stairs to the hotel, she wondered if Owen was around. As she had the thought, her heart did a funny thudding thing that she attributed to the exercise. What else could it be? Her key gave her fits again, but when she wiggled it the way Owen had shown her, it finally gave way.

Once inside, she was drawn to the music coming from the sitting room Owen used whenever he was on the island. His grandparents, who owned the hotel, made sure a suite was always clean and ready for him even as the rest of the hotel fell into disrepair.

Laura followed the music and found him sitting on a rail-back chair he'd dragged in from the dining room, facing the breathtaking view of the ocean at sunset. His broad shoulders were bent over the guitar, and his mop of dirty-blond hair was in the usual disarray. One of these days, she would probably indulge the ever-present desire to reach up and straighten it with her fingers. That thought led to another of those mysterious thuds from her heart. Resting her hand over the misbehaving organ, she knew she really ought to take it easy. She had the baby to consider.

Hesitant to disturb Owen, she stood in the doorway, mesmerized by his deep voice. She recognized the song, "Please Come to Boston," about a musician hoping to convince his love to join him on the road as she tried to lure him home to her.

Caught up in the melody and the lyrics about the man from Tennessee, she almost didn't hear her cell phone ring. Before it could bother Owen, she withdrew it from her pocket and stepped into the lobby to take the call without checking the caller ID.

"Hello?"

"What the *hell* have you done, Laura?" Her husband Justin's angry voice startled her. She hadn't heard from him since the ugly night several weeks earlier when she'd confronted him about their divergent definitions of marriage and thrown him out of their apartment. "You filed for *divorce? Are you out of your freaking mind?*"

Laura forced herself to remain calm. "What would you expect me to do?"

"Have you given any thought to how this will look to people? We haven't even been married for four months!"

"And whose fault is that? Were you thinking of how it would look to people when you made a date with one of my friends—*after* we were married?"

"I told you that was a mistake. Nothing happened. I haven't been unfaithful to you. I don't know how many ways I can say that."

"You were unfaithful the minute you made that date and showed up to keep it."

"You're being ridiculous. Meet me at the apartment tonight, and we'll talk it through."

"That's going to be impossible for two reasons—one, I'm not in Providence, and two, we no longer live in the apartment."

"What're you talking about? This is just a bump in the road. Of course we live there."

Laura hated the way her hands shook and her heart raced. Not trusting her legs, she lowered herself to the stairs that led to the second-floor guestrooms. "No, we don't. I cleaned out the apartment and returned the keys to the landlord two days ago."

"You did *what?* Where's all our stuff?"

"*Our* stuff, the wedding gifts we hadn't even opened before you started dating again, were returned. *Your* stuff will be delivered to your mother's house on Tuesday, and my stuff is with me."

"You sent it to my mother," he said, his voice flat and cold. "Fabulous. That's just great, Laura. And what am I supposed to tell her when everything I own lands on her doorstep?"

"You can tell her the same thing I was forced to tell my father when I informed him that my marriage is already over."

"*You told your father?*" Justin asked, his voice shrill and nearly hysterical. He'd spent years sucking up to her father, the judge, and was no doubt sorry to see all that hard work be for naught.

"He's extremely disappointed in you, but shockingly, he wasn't as surprised as I'd expected him to be. I guess he saw your true colors before I did."

"You're making a huge mistake, Laura." Now he sounded seriously pissed, and Laura was relieved to have a good chunk of ocean between them.

"I made a far bigger mistake in May."

"If you think I'm going to support you—"

"I want nothing from you."

"This isn't over. I won't sign these papers. Not now or ever. I'm not interested in being divorced."

"You weren't all that interested in being married, either."

"That's not true. You're being hysterical, but once you come to your senses—"

Laura had heard enough. She pressed End and clutched the phone in her trembling hand.

"Everything okay, Princess?"

Owen's soft voice cut through her shock and dismay. She looked up at him and shook her head, mortified to realize tears were rolling down her cheeks.

He sat next to her on the step and put his arm around her.

It was most natural thing in the world to rest her head on his shoulder.

"I take it the divorce news didn't go over very well."

She wiped the tears from her face. "He said he won't sign the papers. Not now or ever." The phone rang again, and Justin's name appeared on the screen.

"Once it sinks in that you're not coming back, he'll sign."

Ignoring that call and the one that followed, Laura said, "I don't think he will. He's an up-and-coming lawyer, and I'm starting to realize he valued his association with my father more than he ever valued me. He liked telling people that Judge Frank McCarthy is his father-in-law."

"Surely your father won't have anything further to do with him."

"Oh, he won't, but that won't stop Justin from taking full advantage of the family connection for as long as he can." She released a deep sigh. "I can't believe I was such a fool. He was always so smooth and full of ambition. I saw what I wanted to see and ignored the rest."

"Don't beat yourself up because you loved the guy, Laura. None of this is your fault. You know that."

She shrugged. "I guess."

"Hey, what do you say we leave this here," he said, prying the phone from her hand, "and go get some dinner? Anything you want. My treat."

"Don't you have to play at the Tiki Bar tonight?"

"Not until nine. I've got plenty of time."

"That would be nice. Thank you."

"Sure thing."

"I'm sorry to inflict my problems on you. I hope you don't feel like you have to babysit me."

"You haven't inflicted anything on me, and babysitting you is fun." He flashed an irrepressible grin that drew a reluctant smile from her. That grin was hard to resist. "You've got enough on your mind right now. Don't worry about me." He tucked a strand of hair behind her ear and looked at her wistfully, as if he had feelings for her that he was trying hard to keep hidden. Was that possible? Before she could process the discovery, his usual lighthearted expression was back in place. "Shall we?"

She took the hand he offered and let him help her up. "By all means."

CHAPTER 11

Tiffany poured herself a glass of merlot and settled into the single old armchair that remained in her living room. She'd found a flimsy card table in the garage that now held the tiny black-and-white television she'd bought with babysitting money in high school. Apparently, the castoffs hadn't appealed to Jim in his rampage. When she walked through the cavernous house, her footsteps echoed like gunshots. Poor Ashleigh thought someone had stolen all their stuff.

What was she supposed to say? *Daddy is the thief?*

Jim had certainly made his point. This was what she got for refusing to move out of the house that had been in his family for two generations. But what was she supposed to do? Her daughter needed a home, not to mention her mother, who still technically lived above Tiffany's dance studio out back, even though Francine spent most nights lately with her fiancé, Ned.

Since she'd lose her home *and* the place where she ran her dance and day-care businesses, Tiffany had refused to give up the house to Jim.

So he'd gotten even. The worst part, Tiffany decided, was she didn't even know how they'd reached this point. When had it all gone to shit? If she was being truthful, it had started to happen right around the time he graduated from law school and they returned to the island to set up his practice.

He hadn't needed her anymore. Sure, he'd needed her when he was in school in Boston and she was paying all the bills by working two jobs. But once he had that degree in hand and opened his practice, she'd gone from being his partner to being his problem.

Even though she worked and ran two successful businesses, he made sure to let her know this was *his* house and they were living off *his* money. After the first time he'd had the nerve to say that, she'd started socking away money from her day-care and dance businesses. It was almost as if she'd known, deep down inside, that she'd need it someday. Well, someday was here now, and it was time to make a new plan.

Despite her bravado, however, all she could think about was growing up without her own father, and now the same thing would happen to Ashleigh unless Tiffany could think of some way to save her marriage. Tiffany had seen her father for the first time in more than thirty years a few weeks ago, and the encounter had left her deeply shaken. While she knew Jim would be far more present in his daughter's life than Tiffany's father had been in hers, it still pained her to see her family broken.

If only she could think of some way to get Jim to talk to her. Maybe if he would listen, they could fix this thing before it went any further off course. He'd shocked her when he cleaned out the house. She hadn't seen that coming, and frankly, she wouldn't have guessed he had that level of nastiness in him. A big part of her was done with him, but then her thoughts returned, as always, to Ashleigh.

There had to be some way to fix this. While she didn't bear any illusions about herself, she knew she was generally considered attractive and maybe even sexy when she put her mind to it. Blaine Taylor sure made her feel sexy when he set his smoldering gaze on her.

"You can't think about him," she said out loud. "Focus on Jim and fixing your marriage, or you're going to end up a divorced single mother."

The whole thing was so unfair. She'd worked her ass off to get him through school, and now, just when his practice was taking off, so was he. Her emotions were all over the place. Mad one minute, then sad, then right back to furious. It would be one thing if she'd done anything to deserve the way he was treating her. But all she'd ever been was a devoted wife and mother. She deserved better.

A knock on the back door startled her. She put down the wineglass and walked over to peek through the blinds, groaning to herself when she saw Mac on the porch. What did he want? As much as she'd tried to dislike her overbearing brother-in-law, he'd grown on her since he'd married Maddie. He'd been a wonderful husband to Maddie and father to Thomas.

Hoping there was nothing wrong with Maddie or the kids, Tiffany cracked open the door. "Hey, Mac."

"Hi, Tiff. Sorry to bother you. I was on my way home and had an idea I wanted to run by you. Mind if I come in for a minute?"

Panic-stricken by the thought of him seeing her empty house, she stepped onto the porch, pulling the door closed behind her. "Ashleigh was fussy tonight, so I don't want to disturb her. What's your big idea?"

"Maddie's been stuck in the house since she had the baby, and I thought it would do her good to have a night with the girls. I wondered if you might be willing to help me out with that."

He's too good to be true. "Sure. What do you want me to do?"

"I doubt she'd be up for going *out* out, so maybe you could have it here?"

"Ahh, I don't think I can do that. I could check with Sydney about doing it there." Syd and Maddie had been friends since high school.

"Is everything okay?" Mac asked, eyeing her shrewdly. "Why do you seem so nervous?"

"I'm not nervous."

"If something's wrong, you know you can tell me. Right?"

"Sure."

"Tiff . . ."

Goddamn him and his sweetness. He was going to make her cry.

What the hell? Maddie would probably tell him anyway. She threw open the door and flipped on a light.

He followed her inside.

Tiffany watched him take in the barren emptiness that was her home before he turned to her with murder in his eyes.

"Are you kidding me?"

"I refused to move out." Tiffany shrugged. "This is what I get."

"This is bullshit! He can't get away with this."

"Looks to me like he already did."

"You need a lawyer, honey."

"Don't be nice to me, Mac. I can't take that right now."

As if she hadn't spoken, he walked over to her and wrapped his arms around her.

Tiffany tried to fight him off, but he wouldn't be deterred. Her eyes burned with unshed tears. If she started crying, she might never stop.

"Why don't you and Ashleigh come stay with us for a while? We've got plenty of room, and Maddie and Thomas would love it. So would I."

"No," she said, pulling free of him. "You guys just had a baby. That's the last thing you need."

"Tiffany—"

"No, Mac." Making an effort to soften her tone, she added, "Thank you. I appreciate that you want to help, but this isn't your problem."

"Of course it is. You and Ashleigh are family to me. Family helps family."

She wanted to remind him that her family was nothing like his, but he was only trying to help and didn't deserve her bitterness. "I'll be okay. Jim and I have a few things to work out, but it'll be fine." Tiffany wished she believed her own words.

"You're not alone in this. Maddie and I are here for you—and for Ashleigh. Whatever you need, whenever you need it."

The softly spoken words went straight to her broken heart. "Stop it."

His brows furrowed with confusion. "Stop what?"

"Stop being so nice to me. It's much easier to think you're a pain in the butt than to admit you're a rather nice guy."

Mac tossed his head back and laughed. "I'm sorry to disappoint you."

"You haven't disappointed me. You've impressed me with the way you care for my sister and her children. I was hard on you when we first met, and I've regretted that."

"Aww, jeez, keep it up and I might start to think you like me or something."

"I never said I like you, so don't get all full of yourself," Tiffany said with her trademark smirk. He was so damned sweet, and her sister was awfully lucky to have him. If she didn't love Maddie so much, Tiffany would be eaten up with jealousy. "About the thing for Maddie . . ."

"Don't worry about that. You've got too much going on."

"No, I'll take care of it. Let me talk to Syd and see if we can use her place. I'll call to invite Maddie when we have it figured out."

"Why don't you let me tell her so I can present her with a done deal. I'll tell her I'm taking care of the kids, including Ashleigh, if need be."

"That's nice of you. Thanks."

He shrugged off the praise. "Any time. I mean that."

She went up on tiptoes to kiss his cheek. "Thank you."

He gave her a quick hug. "We'll get you through this. Don't worry."

Since she couldn't speak over the lump in her throat, she just nodded as she saw him out.

MAC GOT INTO HIS CAR AND WITHDREW HIS CELL PHONE FROM HIS pocket. "Hey, baby," he said when Maddie answered. "I've got one more thing I need to take care of before I come home. Are you okay for a little while longer?"

"My mom and Ned are here, and they're giving Thomas a bath," she said with a chuckle. "From the sound of things, Thomas is winning the war."

"He usually does," Mac said, smiling as he imagined the scene.

"We're good. Everything okay with you?"

"Did you know Jim moved out and took everything they owned?"

"Yeah. Tiff told me. How did you hear about it?"

"I saw her in town, and we got to talking." He didn't want to tip his hand about the girls' night out, so he didn't confess to stopping by her sister's house.

"Mac," Maddie said, her voice full of suspicion. "What're you up to?"

"Nothing."

"You're going to confront Jim, aren't you?"

How did she always manage to see right through him? While he should probably be annoyed by that skill of hers, he was usually amused by it. "I hope I never have a big secret I want to keep from you."

"Don't even bother trying, buster. I'd know."

Sitting in the dark car, he smiled again at her saucy tone. "I won't be long."

"Don't hit him. Do you hear me?"

"Aw, come on! Why do you have to ruin all my fun?"

"That's my job as your wife."

"I won't hit him."

"Mac . . ."

"What? I'll try not to."

Her delicate laugh stirred him, reminding him of how long it had been since they'd been able to make love. He was better off not thinking about that, since they still had several weeks to go before she'd get the green light to resume activity. Despite his lingering trauma after witnessing childbirth, there was a very good chance he would die of pent-up desire for her before the light turned green.

"Hurry home," she said.

"Will do." He drove to Jim's office on Ocean Road and was glad to see lights on inside. Mac figured his brother-in-law was probably living in the apartment over the office. He scowled at Jim's shiny new Mercedes on the way to the door. Jim had the funds for a fancy new ride but left his wife and daughter in an unfurnished house? Mac would never understand guys who behaved that way. After knocking on the door, he waited several minutes before he heard footsteps bounding down the stairs.

Jim threw open the door, clearly stunned to see Mac. "What're you doing here?"

Though they'd grown up together on the island, the two men had never been friends. They'd been cordial as brothers-in-law. Until now. "You got a minute?" Mac asked.

As usual since returning to the island after college and law school, Jim Sturgil's dark brown hair was perfectly coiffed. His starched dress shirt and pressed slacks screamed, "Look at me! I'm making money now!" He'd left the island a regular guy and had returned a hard-core metrosexual. "I was just heading out."

"This'll only take a minute."

"Fine." Jim turned and led Mac into the reception area of his first-floor office.

The leather furniture looked and smelled expensive. When Mac thought of the way Tiffany and her daughter were living, it was all he could do not to plow his fist into Jim's pretty face.

Hands on hips, Jim said, "So what do you want?"

"I want to know what kind of man leaves his wife and child without a stick of furniture."

Jim's face flushed with anger. "That's none of your damned business."

"You made it my business when you left her high and dry."

"She's neither high nor dry. For years she's been socking away money on the side that she thinks I don't know about. Don't let her play you. She's a master manipulator. I ought to know."

"I promised my wife I wouldn't punch you, but you'd be wise to watch how you talk about my sister-in-law."

Jim snorted out a laugh. "Your bitch of a sister-in-law doesn't even like you, so you're wasting your breath defending her."

Mac decided he'd heard enough. He grabbed a fistful of Jim's starched shirt and jacked him against the wall. "Listen here, asshole. I don't care if she likes me or not, she's in my family and under my protection. If you want your new practice to go to shit overnight, keep talking trash about my wife's sister. I'll ruin you before you even get started, and you'll never know what hit you. Am I clear?"

"Get your hands off me. Right now."

Mac tightened his fist until the shirt was nearly strangling Jim. "I *said* . . . Am I clear?"

"Yeah," Jim muttered.

He released Jim so abruptly the other man nearly lost his balance. "Take care of your wife and daughter, Sturgil, or I swear to God you'll regret it."

"You fucking McCarthys think you own this island," Jim muttered as he attempted to smooth out the mess Mac had made of his shirt.

"No, we don't. But if you think I can't cause you a shitload of trouble around here, try me. Keep your goddamned mouth shut about Tiffany, or else. She has friends here—a lot of friends. I can't say the same for you."

Mac decided he'd made his point and got out of there before he broke his promise to Maddie, along with Jim's nose.

He arrived home a few minutes later to find his wife waiting for him. She wore a long, silky robe that accented her generous curves. Her curly hair was loose around her shoulders, and Mac wanted to throw her over his shoulder and carry her straight to bed.

"Where're your mom and Ned?"

"They went home after they got Thomas to bed."

"Sorry I missed saying good night to my buddy." That was just another thing to be mad with Jim about.

"I told him you'd be here in the morning when he got up. So, did you punch him?"

Mac held out his hands.

She gave each hand a careful inspection. "Thank you for caring about my sister."

"Of course I care about your sister. And your niece."

When she was satisfied there were no bruises, Maddie kissed the back of each hand. The brush of her lips against his skin was all it took to make him hard. Despite his best efforts to hold it back, a small groan escaped from his clenched jaw.

"What's wrong?" she asked, reaching up to frame his face with her soft hands.

The caress of her fingers on his face only made his problem worse. "Nothing," he said, attempting to step back from her.

Holding him in place, she looked up at him with the caramel-colored eyes that slayed him. He wanted to beg for mercy. "Mac . . . Is it Jim? Did something happen that you're not telling me?"

"No."

"Then what is it?"

"It's nothing that three weeks and six days won't cure."

He watched her brows furrow with confusion and then smiled at the way her lips formed the adorable O he loved so much when his meaning dawned on her.

She smoothed her hands over his chest and down his belly.

He sucked in a sharp deep breath when she cupped his painfully hard erection. "Maddie, don't . . ."

"Why not?" She looked up at him with a coy smile as she squeezed and caressed him through his shorts. "You didn't just have a baby. Why should you have to suffer?"

Before he could summon the brain cells to respond, she had unbuttoned and unzipped his shorts, pushed them down over his hips and had him seated on the sofa. When she dropped to her knees in front of him, he nearly stopped breathing. "What're you doing?" He looked around to see if they were truly alone. They were never alone these days. "Kids . . ."

"Are asleep." She wrapped her hand around him and lowered her head to take him into her mouth.

It'd been so long that he nearly exploded at the first tentative touch of her tongue on the sensitive tip. "Maddie," he gasped. "Baby, you don't have to . . . Oh *Christ* . . ." His head fell back against the sofa, and while he knew he should be taking care of her rather than the other way around, he was powerless. She owned him, and she knew it.

"Mmm," she said, letting her lips vibrate against his shaft.

The fingers he'd combed through her hair tightened into fists. "That's enough."

Rather than stop, she took him deeper, and when she added lashing strokes of her tongue, he went off like a rocket, surging into her mouth as wave after wave of powerful release left him drained. "Wow," he said when he could speak again.

Pushing his shirt up as she went, she peppered his belly and chest with soft kisses that fired him up all over again. "I can't wait," she said between kisses, "to be able to . . ." With her lips brushing against his ear, she whispered a blunt description of what she couldn't wait to do.

"Madeline! I'm shocked by your language!"

Chuckling, she said, "No, you're not."

She amused and aroused him like no other woman ever could. "I don't know what's happened to my sweet, innocent wife," he said as he put his arms around her and nuzzled her hair.

"She's become a sex fiend, thanks to you."

"I can't even hear you say the word 'sex' right now," he said as her soft breasts against his chest reawakened his cock.

"There's lots of other stuff we can do, you know."

Of course he knew. She'd done most of the "other stuff" for the first time with him. He brushed the soft hair back off her face and buried his fingers in the silky strands. "You're so tired, honey. I don't want you to feel you have to—"

Her lips landed on his, soft but insistent. "Shut up, Mac."

Since he had no desire to argue with his gorgeous wife, he tightened his arms around her and let her have her wicked way with him all over again.

CHAPTER 12

*E*van held her hand as they walked through town to the restaurant. It was such a small thing, but Grace was thrilled by the feel of his fingers linked with hers. Every woman they passed took a good long look at him as he went by. That he'd chosen to spend this evening with *her* made Grace want to do a happy little jig right there on the sidewalk, but she managed to restrain herself.

How could he know that walking through Gansett's main thoroughfare with his hand wrapped snugly around hers was one of the single most exciting things to ever happen to her? Second only to what had happened earlier in her hotel room.

After a lifetime of self-doubt and yearning to look and feel like other young women, Grace had finally arrived and wanted to enjoy every second of her new life. Almost as if the gods were smiling down on her, the night air was soft and fragrant and exactly the right temperature. Not too warm, not too chilly, but absolutely perfect.

The horn of the last ferry of the day leaving the island echoed through downtown. A few last-minute stragglers rushed past them, sprinting for the ferry landing.

Evan laughed at the melee of people scrambling to make the last boat. "Some things never change around here."

"I can't imagine growing up on an island. It must've been fun."

"Sometimes it was, but it was also horribly confining. Of course, you always want what you don't have. After living away for most of the last decade, I appreciate it more than I used to."

"It's such a beautiful place. I think it would be cool to live here." She sure hoped so.

"You say that now. Wait until the island is buried under two feet of snow or the boats don't run for a week because of rough seas and you have somewhere else you need to be. That's when it starts to lose its charm."

His words struck a note of fear in her as she pondered an isolated winter sealed off from the mainland. She immediately dismissed the thought, refusing to ruin this magical evening with worries or fears.

"Tropical Storm Hailey had us marooned for days," Evan continued. "No ferries, no planes, no nothing. My sister and her new husband couldn't leave on their honeymoon when they were supposed to. We started to run out of gas and food and cash and all sorts of stuff we rely on the ferries to bring over from the mainland."

"That sounds like an adventure to me. I love the idea that once that boat leaves," she said, nodding to the departing ferry, "we're all in it together until tomorrow morning. Anything can happen."

He crooked a rakish eyebrow her way, causing Grace's breath to catch. "And that sounds like fun to you? I knew you had a twisted sense of humor . . ."

She elbowed him playfully. "You have to admit there's a bit of adventure to island life."

"If you say so."

"I say so."

"We've seen a lot of people come and go around here. They come during the summer thinking it'll be so fabulous to live on an island. After one winter, they go screaming for their lives back to the mainland."

Grace swallowed hard. That wouldn't happen to her. No way. She was committed to the pharmacy and her new life plan.

At the Lobster House restaurant, Evan held the door and ushered her inside with a proprietary hand on the small of her back, which set off a flutter of tingles along her spine. Once again, Evan turned every female head in the place as they followed the maître d' to their table. Evan held the chair for her and made sure she was settled before he sat across from her.

The dining room had large windows that looked out over Gansett Sound. With the pinks and purples of sunset lighting the sky, the view was breathtaking.

"What're you in the mood for?" he asked as he perused the menu.

Speaking of breathtaking . . . Grace forced her gaze off him to focus on the menu. "I'm not sure." Since this was the first time she'd been out to a fancy dinner with a man (Trey's pizza dates hardly counted), her stomach was in knots as she tried to figure out what to have. Restaurant portions were notoriously huge, and Grace hated to waste food. But since her surgery, she could consume only small portions.

"They have great scallops, and the fish is really good, too. Most likely caught today in Gansett Sound."

"I'm not that hungry," she said truthfully. "I might just do chowder and a salad."

He eyed her suspiciously. "You're not one of those women who feels she has to eat like a bird in front of men, are you?"

Grace nearly laughed out loud at the irony of that statement. "Hardly. I just have a very small appetite." That was the line she'd learned from a support group she'd attended after her surgery. There she'd learned how to navigate her new reality without feeling like she had to tell everyone she met about why she ate such small portions. If she overdid it, food would get stuck halfway down, which was an uncomfortable situation she went out of her way to avoid.

That was the last thing she wanted to contend with during her perfect night with the perfect man.

The waiter appeared at their table and asked if they'd like to hear the specials.

"Sure," Evan said, winking at Grace.

As the waiter launched into a startlingly detailed description of the specials, complete with balsamic reductions and pretentious French terms that he positively murdered, Grace felt the telltale signs of laughter gurgling in her chest.

When the waiter finally finished his spiel, Grace released a sigh of relief that she had made it through without laughing in his face.

"Grace, did you hear anything that interests you?"

She shook her head and cleared the laughter from her throat. "I'm going to stick with a cup of chowder and a house salad with balsamic," she said, trying not to sputter as the word crossed her lips.

The waiter frowned at her choice. There went his tip. "And for you, sir?"

"I'll do the baked scrod," Evan said.

"And how would you like the fish presented on the plate?"

Stunned by the question, Evan glanced at Grace with wide eyes and then up at the waiter, whose pen was poised on the pad, breathlessly awaiting Evan's decision. "Um, dead would be good."

That did it. Grace erupted into laughter that infuriated their waiter. He grabbed the menus and stalked off.

Amused by her laughter, Evan smiled broadly at her. "What the hell kind of question was that?"

Grace was laughing too hard to respond. As usual during one of her fits of inappropriate laughter, people around her began to take notice. That was the point at which whatever had made her laugh usually ceased to be funny, but this time, she couldn't seem to stop.

She reached for her glass of ice water, forced a sip down her throat and took two deep, cleansing breaths.

"Are you done?" he asked, still smiling.

His smile was a relief and another point in his favor—as if he needed more points. He didn't seem at all embarrassed by her outburst.

"I might be. Just don't use the words 'fish,' 'balsamic reduction' or 'dead on the plate' in any combination."

"I promise to try not to." This was said in an impression of the waiter's murderous French accent that set Grace off again.

"Stop it, please," she begged. "I hurt from laughing."

"Don't hold back. You have a lovely and infectious laugh."

Ridiculously pleased by the unexpected compliment, Grace tried to hide her surprise. "That's nice of you to say. Most people are embarrassed by my propensity to cut loose without warning."

"It's part of your charm. You shouldn't apologize for it."

As Grace was processing yet another stupendous compliment, the waiter returned with the wine Evan had ordered and made a big show of uncorking it and presenting a taste to Evan. His eyes met hers over the rim of the glass, daring her to let go again.

Grace bit her lip in an effort to hold it back as Evan nodded his approval of the wine.

By the time the waiter stormed off yet again, she was in silent hysterics.

This time Evan joined in. "He is just a tad over the top, huh?"

With the napkin pressed to her face to muffle the laughter, Grace nodded. "I can't take it." Hoping she hadn't totally ruined the makeup Stephanie had carefully applied, Grace dabbed gently at her eyes. "Do I have mascara all over my face?"

"Not at all. You look beautiful."

Speechless, Grace stared at him.

"Too much?" he asked with that dimpled grin that made her want to swoon.

"It's all thanks to Stephanie and Laura. They worked their magic."

"You didn't need makeup or magic to be beautiful, Grace." He reached for her hand across the table.

As she took his hand, she felt like she was in a movie watching someone else be charmed and romanced by the incredibly handsome man sitting across from her. This couldn't possibly be happening to her, could it?

He caressed the back of her hand with his thumb, sending sensation to erogenous zones she didn't even know she had. Her nipples hardened, and heat pooled between her legs. Unused to such reactions, Grace struggled to process each new discovery as it occurred. How could the touch of one man's hand accomplish so much? That thought led to another, more disturbing, question. What if he was the only man in the whole world who could set her body on fire with a mere touch? Wouldn't it be just her luck to find that one guy and have him be a commitment-phobe?

Fixated on their joined hands and the riot of emotions storming around inside her, Grace didn't realize he'd spoken until he squeezed her hand.

"Earth to Grace."

Startled, she looked up to find him studying her with arresting blue eyes that made her want to sigh every time he looked her way.

"Where did you take off to?"

"Nowhere. I'm right here."

"I asked where you went to college."

How did she totally miss that? "I went to URI's school of pharmacy."

"I looked at URI. Beautiful campus."

Nodding, she said, "Where did you go?"

"It would be easier to tell you where I *didn't* go. I started out at Rhode Island College, moved to UMass for a year, took a year off that turned into six when I decided college wasn't for me. I finally got a business degree from the University of Tennessee a couple of years ago."

"That's quite a résumé."

"Well, just so you don't think I'm a total dolt, I never would've gone to college at all if it hadn't been so important to my parents. I didn't want to be the one to spoil their perfect record where college was concerned. They were four for five, and I was the lone holdout. I always knew exactly what I wanted to do—play music, write songs, record, tour. I can't ever see myself doing anything else."

"So you write, too? I thought Grant was the writer in the family."

"He's the more successful writer, but I've sold a few of my songs."

"Any I might've heard?"

"Well, you heard one of them that night at the Tiki Bar."

"You wrote that? It was amazing. I had no idea."

Seeming pleased by her praise, he said, "Do you listen to country music at all?"

"Not so much."

"Then you probably haven't heard the others, but I could play them for you sometime."

The thought of getting a private show from Evan McCarthy sent a new shower of tingles down her spine. "I'd love to hear them. How did you get into country?"

"I'm not into country, per se. I'm more of what they call a cross-over artist. I got into a band while I was at UT, and one thing led to another. Next thing I knew, I was playing country and bluegrass and all kinds of stuff I'd never been exposed to before. That's when I started writing my own songs, and apparently they appeal to country artists. I think of myself as a musical mongrel. I do it all."

"And you love it."

"I really do. This last year has been a dream come true. I was signed by a small label, recorded an album that's due out before Christmas, followed by a tour opening for Buddy Longstreet and Taylor Jones. They're—"

"The king and queen of country. Even I've heard of them."

Evan smiled. "You should've seen my reaction when they asked me to open for them on their tour next summer." He grimaced, which only made him more handsome. How was that possible? "I was rather undignified."

"That I'd like to see," Grace said, sharing a laugh with him.

The moment was so charged with desire and awareness that Grace wondered if the whole restaurant could tell they were dying to rip each other's clothes off. Since she'd never had the urge to strip a man naked while in public, she had no idea how one was supposed to behave while having such an urge. The direction of her thoughts threatened to send her into a new fit of giggles, so she took a small sip of wine.

Their waiter returned with their salads, and Grace managed to get through the encounter with nary a snicker.

"He's totally terrified of you," Evan said.

"I feel awful. It's so rude to laugh at someone when they're just trying to do their job."

"You do not feel bad, and he was *way* overdoing his job with the balsamic reductions and the bastardized French."

"You aren't supposed to say those words," Grace reminded him as she cut her salad into tiny bites.

"What words? *Balsamic reduction?*"

"Stop! I've already made enough of a scene."

"What are some of your other trigger words?"

"Do you honestly think I'm going to give you that kind of ammunition?"

"Please? I promise not to use them against you in church."

Grace rolled her eyes at him. "As if you ever step foot in church."

"I've been known to step foot in church."

"Only when Linda holds a gun to your head."

"That may be true, but I might be persuaded to go to church with you, just to see if I can make you laugh."

"Trust me, you could. It doesn't take much at all."

"I may have to take that dare."

His tone was so dirty-sounding that Grace wondered if they were still talking about church.

When their food arrived, he insisted on sharing some of his fish with her. She was careful not to overdo and refused dessert when he offered. He paid the bill and suggested a stroll on the beach in front of the restaurant.

Grace, who would've followed him into traffic at that moment, willingly agreed.

After they kicked off their shoes, Evan slipped an arm around her shoulders, bringing her in snug against him. With the sand coarse against her feet, the breeze light against her face, the moon rising in the sky and his scent surrounding her, Grace knew she'd never forget this. No matter what happened between them, this night would go down in history as the benchmark against which all other dates would be measured.

"What's your favorite color?" he asked, clearly taking her comment about not knowing each other very well seriously.

Amused, she said, "Purple. Yours?"

"Depends on my mood. Some days I'm a red guy, and other days I favor blue. Siblings?"

"Two brothers, both younger. One is in high school and the other in college."

"Are you close?"

"Not really. Not like you are with yours. I was like a second mother to them when they were little."

"My brothers are my best friends, and my sister, who was a royal pain when we were growing up, turned out okay. It didn't hurt that she married a guy we all love."

"That was good of her."

"We thought so, too."

Evan stopped walking all of a sudden and turned to her. Keeping one hand on her shoulder, he brought his other hand to her face.

As she waited to see what he would do, Grace couldn't seem to get air to her lungs.

And then he leaned in and kissed her so softly, so sweetly that she barely had time to react before it was over.

"I couldn't wait another minute to do that," he said, running his thumb over her bottom lip.

"Is there more where that came from?" Grace shocked herself with her own audacity. It was hardly like her to ask for what she wanted, especially from a man.

His eyes heated with desire that she still couldn't believe was directed at her. "Plenty more. Do we know each other better now than we did earlier?"

Grace wanted him desperately. "Much better."

As he took a step closer, his hands moved from her shoulders to her hips, bringing her in tight against him.

She finally ran her fingers through his dark hair and found it to be as silky and soft as it looked.

That seemed to make him a little wild, and he leaned in to take her mouth in a devouring kiss that required her full attention just to keep up with him. His tongue coaxed its way past her lips, exploring and enticing her into cooperating, not that she required much enticing.

Years of reading romance novels and dreaming about this very moment had Grace well prepared to hide her inexperience. Like the heroines in her books, she brazenly sucked on his tongue, which drew a groan from deep inside him. Pleased with her efforts, she did it again.

He tore his lips free and turned his attention to her neck. "God, Grace, you're making me so hot." He cupped her ass and pressed his substantial erection against her belly. Remembering the width and length of him from her earlier explorations, she was suddenly desperate to see and feel him without clothes in the way.

"Can we go back to the hotel now?" Old Grace would've worried about that question making her sound cheap or easy. New Grace didn't care how it made her sound. She wanted him. While she was under no illusions about what might happen between them tomorrow, she was determined to end this perfect night perfectly.

"Are you sure, Grace?" His lips were warm and soft against her ear, sending goose bumps and tingles down her spine.

"Yes," she whispered. "Yes, I'm sure."

CHAPTER 13

*T*aking her hand, Evan led Grace from the beach along a
pathway she never would've found on her own that
brought them out to the main drag. When she started to put her shoes
back on, he told her not to bother.

Knowing he was in a rush only made her more eager to reach their
destination.

They ran across the street and into a side door at the Beachcomber. She had to scramble to keep up with him as his long legs took
the three flights of stairs in record time. By the time they reached her
room, Grace was out of breath for more reasons than one.

Evan took the key from her and had them inside in under two
seconds. Pushing the door closed, he pressed her against it and
thrilled her with passionate kisses that chased away all the worries
and doubts about what he might think of her body. He made it very
clear with his lips and tongue and hands that everything about her
appealed to him. Thankful for the dim glow of a streetlight that gave
them just enough illumination, Grace decided not to worry about
being naked in front of him. He wouldn't be able to see much anyway.

She worked on the buttons to his shirt and pushed her hands
inside, greedy to touch muscles and crisp chest hair and nipples that

hardened under her hands. When she ran her thumbs over them, he faltered.

He tugged at the zipper of her dress, and when it didn't give way fast enough for his liking, he abandoned it and went for the hem, dragging it up and over her hips. His fingertips left a trail of fire on her legs and belly as he pushed her dress up. Finally, he tugged it over her head, leaving her standing before him in the black bra and skimpy panties Stephanie had chosen for her.

"You're a goddess," he whispered reverently as he left a trail of kisses from her neck to her collarbone to the valley between her breasts to the plump portion that spilled over the demi-cups. "So sweet, so soft."

Grace was having trouble standing as he explored her with his hands and lips. With her arms linked around his neck, she played with his hair and gave herself over to him. She wanted to touch him every-where but couldn't handle doing that while he was caressing her.

He took her hand and half walked, half dragged her to the bed. On the way, he tugged off his shirt and dropped his pants, leaving him in silky boxers that bulged significantly at the front. Standing next to the bed, he put his arms around her.

She returned the embrace, breathing in the sandalwood scent she'd forever associate with him and reveling in the soft caress of his chest hair against her over-sensitized skin.

His erection resting against her stomach was an ever-present reminder of where this was leading, which filled her with a healthy dose of anxiety to go with the desire.

"Why did you just get tense?" he asked as he freed her from the bra.

Grace's first impulse was to cover her breasts as they sprang free, but she kept her hands at her sides while he took a good long look.

"You're gorgeous everywhere, Grace." He cupped her with big hands that were never anything but gentle. "Don't be nervous," he said between kisses. "Just relax."

The notion that she could possibly relax while standing all but naked in Evan McCarthy's arms was so far beyond preposterous that she had no choice but to giggle.

He stopped what he was doing, raised his head and stared at her. "What?"

Before her mirth could spin out of control, she shook her head and placed her hands on his chest, hoping the feel of his smooth skin under her palms would stifle the need to laugh, for there was absolutely nothing funny about Evan McCarthy's splendid chest.

"You have to tell me, or I'll think you find me . . . insignificant."

"Now you're trying to make me laugh, and I won't let you."

His grave expression almost undid her. "I could make you laugh if I really wanted to."

"We both know you could, but if I get started, it'll take forever to stop." She stroked his chest in a circular motion. "Wouldn't you rather make me do something else?" This was uttered in the most seductive tone she could muster, and it was, without a doubt, the most scandalous thing she'd ever said in her entire life. In fact, it was so wildly out of character, she wondered for a second if she'd only thought it.

If the smile that stretched across his face was any indication, she'd actually said it, and he wholeheartedly approved of where her thoughts were leading.

He pulled down the covers, helped her get comfortable on the bed and stretched out next to her.

Grace reached for him, bringing his mouth back to hers. Their kisses were deep and sensual. Seeking a better angle, Evan came down on top of her, their limbs entwining, her breasts pressed to his chest as their tongues mated in a dance that made her burn for more of him.

She ran her hands over his back, her fingertips exploring the ridges of his spine. When she reached the waistband of his boxers, she experienced a moment of doubt. Would he think her too forward if she were to slip her fingers under the elastic?

"Touch me, Grace," he whispered, making her wonder if her thoughts were obvious to him. "Nothing you do will be wrong."

She appreciated that he seemed to get she was nervous and was doing all he could to set her mind at ease. As his lips left a trail of fire on her neck, she tucked her hands into his boxers.

Evan gasped as she explored his muscular backside. "Shit," he muttered. "You're making me nuts."

Encouraged, Grace moved her hands to the front.

He raised himself up to give her room to maneuver. This was about the point where it had all gone bad with Trey, before she'd had a chance to touch him like this. Now she was grateful that Evan's penis would be the first one she ever held in her hand. As she ran her fingers over his length, his breathing became choppy and irregular.

"Does it hurt?" she asked.

He shook his head. "Feels too good." Bringing his hand down to cover hers, he showed her how to stroke him.

"Like that?" she asked as she mimicked movements that were far rougher than she would've attempted without his guidance. His skin there was surprisingly soft, and Grace marveled at how he grew harder and bigger.

"*Yes*. Grace, God . . ."

When his hand landed on top of hers again, it was to stop her. His belly muscles rippled, and his jaw clenched with tension. "You're going to finish me off before we get to the best part."

"Are you good for only once?" she asked, again amazed by how uninhibited she was with him.

"Hell, no."

That he sounded downright insulted made her giggle.

"Is that funny?" His hips surged, pushing his cock hard against her hand.

"No," she said, certain her quivering lips were a dead giveaway that she found him highly amusing when he was indignant. She recommitted her efforts to careful, hard strokes that made him moan and groan.

Giving himself over to her, he shifted off her and flopped onto his back.

Grace bit her lip, trying to decide just how brazen she was prepared to be. When she remembered his insistence that this night wasn't leading anywhere, she figured this could be the best chance she'd have to try on him all the things she'd read about in her romance novels.

She released her hold on his erection long enough to help him out of the boxer shorts. The light filtering in from the street was just enough to see the full length and width of him. As she again tried to imagine how *that* would ever fit down *there*, she nearly lost her nerve.

Determined to bring him as much pleasure as she possibly could, she wrapped her hand around him. Settling on her knees, she bent her head to run her tongue over the wide crown.

When that resulted in more tortured moans and groans from him, Grace did it again.

"Take it in," he said in a harsh tone she hadn't heard from him before. His hand pressing on the back of her head told her exactly what he wanted.

While she worried about gagging or choking or other embarrassing possibilities, she did as he asked, wrapping her lips around his thick erection and taking as much as she could into her mouth. The best she could do, it seemed, was only about half, but he didn't seem to mind, especially when she added some tongue action that had his hips rising from the bed to gain a better angle.

"This too," he said, covering her hand with his and showing her how to stroke him while she took him in and out of her mouth. "God*damn*," he said. "Ahh, that's good. So good."

Grace decided that was among the best compliments she'd ever received. In fact most of her best compliments had come from him.

The hand he'd buried in her hair fisted and pulled, gently but hard enough to get her attention.

He jerked himself free of her mouth and erupted.

Grace watched, fascinated, as he came all over his own belly. She dipped a finger into the milky fluid and ran it over his quivering muscles.

"Sorry," he said between deep breaths.

"For what?"

"I wanted to focus on you, but the minute you put your hands on me . . . Sorry."

Amused and delighted to have drawn such a powerful reaction from him, Grace smiled and leaned in to kiss him.

"Let me clean up, and then it's your turn."

His words sent a shiver of anticipation through her entire body, making her nipples hard and needy and the rest of her hot and bothered.

Watching him stroll into the bathroom, Grace took in the splendid sight of his muscular butt. She fell back on the pillows, seeking to calm her wildly beating heart. Pleasuring him had been the most exciting thing she'd ever done, and she couldn't wait to see what happened next.

Evan returned to the bed and crawled right up on top of her, taking her mouth in a heated kiss that had her motor running at full speed in no time at all. She cradled his lean hips between her legs with only a thin strip of satin between them. His reawakened cock moved seductively back and forth, simulating intercourse, and Grace held back what would've been a most unladylike sound.

"It's okay," he said, again tuning in to her in a way that should've freaked her out. Rather it was comforting to know he was paying such close attention to her signals. "We'll do it all, baby. We've got all night."

He'd said exactly the right thing. They were in no rush. They could take their time to fully experience each other. He wasn't Trey. He wasn't going to rush off and leave her alone and unfulfilled.

"That's it," Evan said, as he raised her arms above her head and pinned them to the pillow. "Relax and let me show you . . ."

He kissed from her lips to her jaw to her chest, working his way toward her breasts. Cupping them in his big hands, he teased her nipples with tentative brushes of his tongue over her taut peaks. Grace would've jerked right off the bed were it not for the weight of his lower body holding her still.

It took all she had to keep her hands where he'd put them, especially when he finally tugged her nipple into the heat of his mouth. As he sucked hard, Grace discovered a direct connection from her breast to her womb. Aching for more, she pushed her hips against his cock, letting him know what she wanted.

"We'll get to that," he said as he shifted his attention to her other breast.

The sounds that came from Grace as he licked and sucked and teased would've mortified her if she'd been in her right mind. At the moment, she couldn't have cared less, and apparently neither did he. The more she reacted, the harder he sucked. When his teeth scraped against her nipple, she cried out.

He tended the abused nipple with gentle strokes of his tongue. "Sorry."

"Didn't hurt." She couldn't leave her hands above her head any longer. Burying her fingers in his hair, she held him tight against her breast. "Do it again."

"This?" he asked, rolling her nipple between his teeth.

"Yes," Grace said, gasping as heat and moisture gathered between her legs.

Evan shifted ever so slightly, his lips moving from her breasts to her belly.

Grace went rigidly still as she waited for him to ask about the scar above her belly button, but he skipped right over it and focused on removing her panties.

His hands skimmed over the insides of her legs, opening her as he moved from calf to thigh.

Grace was really, *really* glad she'd listened to Stephanie and Laura and properly prepared for this moment—even if would cost her fifty bucks. She expected him to reach for the condoms he'd put on the bedside table, but rather he held her open and hovered just above the juncture of her thighs. Fighting the urge to squirm, she waited breathlessly to see what he would do next. And then he arranged her legs on his shoulders, and Grace figured out what he had planned.

"Wait a minute," she said, tugging on his hair. "Evan . . ."

"It's okay, baby. Let me taste you. I bet you're so sweet."

All the fight went out of her as she fell back onto the pillows, vibrating with tension.

As he ran his fingers through her slickness, opening her further, Grace bit her lip to keep from screaming. Every nerve ending in her body was on fire, especially the bundle of nerves between her legs that he brushed against on every stroke. Just when she thought she might actually get used to the feel of his fingers, he slid them into her and dipped his head to use his tongue.

Oh. My. God. Nothing she had read could've prepared her for the moment Evan McCarthy's tongue came into contact with her throbbing clitoris.

"I knew it," he said. "So sweet. And so smooth. Mmm."

A surge of need ripped through her body, converging in her aching core, threatening to break at any second. The smooth glide of his fingers demanded a portion of her attention, but then he sucked hard on her clitoris and sent her spiraling into a storm of sensation unlike anything she'd ever experienced before.

"That's it," he whispered, easing her down slowly with less insistent strokes of his tongue and fingers.

As if she was watching the scene from above the bed, she was aware of him lowering her legs and getting up to find a condom. He rolled it on and returned to her.

"Earth to Grace, are you with me?"

Startled out of the dream state she'd slipped into, she was suddenly aware of what was about to happen. Finally.

His brows came together in an expression of concern. "Are you okay?"

Grace reached up to brush away the furrow with her fingertips. "I'm far better than okay. You?"

He grinned down at her. "I'm very good."

Grace took advantage of the opportunity to explore the dimples that had so fascinated her. His jaw was smooth from a recent shave, and he waited patiently for her to discover all the planes and textures of his face.

"You're quite lovely to look at," she said after a prolonged period of silence.

He seemed taken aback by the compliment. "I should be saying that to you."

Grace looked up to meet his gaze in the faint light. "Is there any rule that says we can't say it to each other?"

"None that I'm aware of," he said, kissing her as his cock nudged at her entrance.

Grace sucked in a sharp, deep breath as he worked his way in slowly but surely while continuing to distract her with deep, drugging kisses. Tension vibrated through his big frame, no doubt from the effort it took to go slow.

She would never be able to put words to the exquisite feeling of having Evan McCarthy enter her with such care and concern. This was the way it should be, she thought as she took him in. There ought to be care and concern and emotion and genuine respect between lovers.

Before now, before tonight, she'd been disappointed it had taken her so long to have sex. Now she was glad she'd waited for Evan, because she couldn't dream of doing this with anyone else.

Her hands found their way to his backside, squeezing and drawing another tortured groan from him.

"Feel okay?" he asked, looking down at her.

"Way better than okay." Nothing had ever felt like this. She'd been prepared for pain, but this was all about pure pleasure.

"Good," he said, punctuating the word with another kiss. He flexed his hips, sending his cock even deeper and making contact with a sensitive place inside her.

Grace gasped. "Do that again."

"Do what? This?" He hit the same spot, doing it again and again until the tension built to a boiling point and then burst.

She cried out as she rode a wave of astonishing pleasure.

Evan grasped her hips and moved in and out of her with increasing speed until he threw his head back and came hard before collapsing on top of her.

Grace put her arms around him, stroking his hair and back as his breathing returned to normal.

"That was incredible," he said many minutes later.

"Yes."

"I'm going to want to do that again very soon."

Even though Grace worried that she'd be sore, she was game for another round if it was anything like the first one. "Me, too."

"Give me a minute to recover from the first time, and we'll see what we can do."

That sent a ripple of laughter through Grace.

Evan pushed his hips against her, reminding her he was still embedded in her.

She wrapped her legs around his hips, eager to maintain the intimate contact.

They stayed like that for a long time, until he kissed her and eased his way out of her embrace to deal with the condom. He came right back, slid into bed next to her and covered them with a sheet. Lying with her back to his chest, Grace had never been more content or satisfied.

"You should've told me, you know."

Grace's heart rate slowed to a crawl. "Told you what?"

"That it was your first time."

"Did I do something wrong?"

"No, honey, not at all." His lips on her shoulder added additional reassurance. "I would've been more careful. That's all."

"You were perfect. *It* was perfect." Clutching his hand to her breast, she forced herself to ask the question. "How could you tell?"

"There was some blood on the condom."

For some reason, hearing that embarrassed her, which was ironic in light of what had transpired between them. "I know I should've told you, but there's no smooth way to introduce that into conversation."

"As long as you're okay, I am, too." He tightened his hold on her, which was how Grace felt his cock against her backside.

"That didn't take long," she said with a chuckle.

"We shouldn't do it again. You'll be sore."

She reached behind her to stroke him and felt him get even harder.

"Grace . . ."

She wasn't ready for their perfect night to be over. "I want to do it again. I don't care if I'm sore."

"You'll care tomorrow."

"Are you saying no?" she asked, calling upon the most suggestive tone she could muster as she removed her hand and pressed her backside against his erection. It nestled snugly into her cleft.

"God, Grace, you're hard to resist." He withdrew from her long enough to roll on another condom. "Stay like this," he said with his hand on her hip, arranging her the way he wanted her.

When he entered her from behind, she cried out from the surprise and sheer thrill of the new position.

"Does it hurt?"

"No," she said, reaching for his hand. "It feels amazing."

Encouraged by her words, Evan moved them so she was on all fours and he was poised behind her. Old Grace would've been worried about him seeing her backside, but New Grace couldn't do anything but focus on the exquisite feel of him deep inside her.

Then he reached around her, touching his fingers to her clitoris as he rocked into her, surging deeper with every new stroke.

Grace gripped the sheets, seeking to anchor herself as he took her apart one stroke at a time. She was beginning to fear her perfect night would haunt the rest of her imperfect life. Where would she ever find another man who could make her feel the way Evan did? Cherished and protected and worshiped and adored?

As he slowly stroked her to yet another mind-altering orgasm, Grace began to worry about how she'd ever let him go in the morning.

CHAPTER 14

*A*fter the upsetting call from Justin, Laura wouldn't have
expected to spend most of the evening laughing. Owen had
talked her into sharing a large meat-lover's pizza, arguing that the
baby needed the protein. Laura suspected *he* needed the protein.

On the way back to the hotel, he dragged her into the arcade and
bought a hundred tokens. He insisted they use every one of them
before they could leave. Laura had never done more shooting or
blowing things up or wild driving in her life. She also couldn't
remember the last time she'd laughed until she cried. Blowing things
up, she decided, was rather cathartic, especially with Owen egging
her on.

Laura told herself it didn't mean anything that he kept an arm slung
loosely around her shoulders as they strolled through town on the way
to the hotel. The more time she spent with him, the more confused her
feelings toward him became. In the wake of what she'd just been
through with her husband, the last thing she needed was to become
involved with a man who had no permanent address and liked it that
way. Even if he was one of the most appealing men she'd ever known.

But the thought of not hanging out with Owen anymore made her

132

feel sad, and she was tired of being sad all the time. "You have a gig to get to," she reminded him.

"I've got some time yet."

"Not much."

"You're already sounding like a mom," he said with laughter in his voice.

"Sorry. I didn't mean . . ."

He stopped walking and turned to face her, keeping his arm around her. The new position brought them closer than they'd ever been.

Laura's heart began to pound.

"I was teasing, Princess."

"I know that." Laura was mortified when her eyes filled. Damned hormones!

"Aw, honey, don't . . ."

Laura wanted to kiss him more than she'd ever wanted anything. Alarmed by her reaction to him, she pulled free of his embrace and took off for the hotel, needing some space and distance before she did something she'd regret.

"Laura! Wait!" He ran to catch up with her.

She scrambled up the stairs to the porch. Her hands shook as her stupid key refused to work again.

His hands on her shoulders were nearly her undoing. Dropping her head to her chest, she struggled to regain her composure. She turned to him, planning to apologize for acting so strangely. Before she could find the words, he took her face in his hands, taking her breath away with the intense, hungry way he looked at her. And then his lips were on hers, soft and sweet and undemanding.

Laura put her hand on his chest, intending to push him away, but then he tipped his head ever so slightly, taking the kiss from slow burn to flame.

"I can't," she whispered against his lips. But, oh, how she wanted to! "Owen . . ."

"I'm sorry." He leaned his forehead against hers and seemed to be collecting himself. "I couldn't wait another minute to see if it would be as good as I thought."

Laura knew she shouldn't ask. "Was it?"

Laughing softly, he said, "What do you think?"

"We want different things out of life. I can't set myself up for another disappointment. I just can't."

"I understand."

"Do you? Really?"

"Yes, I really do."

"My life is such a mess right now. I need to be focused on the baby and the hotel. You'll be leaving soon, and . . . I can't do this. I'm sorry."

"I get it, Princess, but I'm not sorry I kissed you."

"It was a good kiss."

He brightened at that. "Yeah?"

She bit her bottom lip and forced herself to meet his gaze as she nodded. "But it can't happen again."

"I know."

"Are we still friends?" she asked, feeling as if her very life depended on the answer to that one simple question.

"Of course we are. You can't get rid of me that easily."

Relief flooded through her, making Laura weak in the knees. "Good."

He reached around her to finagle the key and pushed open the door.

"*How* do you do that?"

"I told you—it's all in the wrist."

"Your wrist, maybe. It doesn't like mine."

"What's not to like about this wrist?" He took her hand and gave it a gentle twist. "Like that."

The brush of his thumb over the pulse point inside her wrist made her breathless and needy and afraid that her wavering self-control wouldn't hold up, so she took back her hand and stepped away from him. "See you in the morning?"

"Yep."

"Have a good night at work."

"You'll be okay here by yourself?"

"I'll be fine. I'd better get used to it, right? Shane won't be here until December," she said of her brother, "so I'll be here by myself for a few months after you leave in October."

His usually sunny disposition turned stormy all of a sudden. "I don't love the idea of you being here alone and pregnant during the off-season."

"You're not changing your mind about offering me the job, are you?" He couldn't possibly do that to her after she'd upended her entire life to move to the island.

"No, silly. The job is yours for as long as you want it."

"How do you know I'll be any good at it?"

"I have no doubt about that, or I never would've told my grandparents to hire you."

"Thanks for the vote of confidence, but the jury is still out on whether an art history major has any business running a hotel."

"I have full faith in you."

"Thank you," she said, humbled by his certainty. "You don't know how much that means to me."

"Go get some sleep, Princess. I don't like those dark circles under your eyes. You've been burning the candle at both ends."

Had anyone ever paid closer attention to her or cared so much about her? Other than her father and the mother she barely remembered, Laura couldn't think of anyone. As she trudged upstairs, it occurred to her that she needed to be very careful where the adorable, sexy, thoughtful Owen Lawry was concerned.

Very careful, indeed.

OWEN WATCHED HER CLIMB THE STAIRS, WISHING HE COULD GO UP WITH her and tuck her into bed. He wanted to stay with her until she fell asleep, until he was certain the demons that chased her during the day would leave her alone to let her get some much-needed rest.

From the first instant he'd seen her at the door earlier, he'd been able to tell by her defeated posture that the last ten days had taken a terrible toll. An aura of fragility surrounded her now that hadn't been there when they'd first met after her cousin Janey's wedding. The deep purple bruises under her eyes were a dead giveaway that she'd had some sleepless nights.

He wanted to go to the mainland, find her deadbeat husband and punch his lights out for putting her through such a horrible ordeal. Any guy who was lucky enough to have Laura McCarthy for his wife shouldn't have any need for other women.

As Owen grabbed his guitar and a sweatshirt and headed out to his van, he thought about the evening he'd spent with her. He couldn't remember the last time he'd had more fun, and they'd done nothing more than eat pizza and play video games.

She was easy to be with, fun, quick to laugh and lovely to look at with her blonde hair, soft blue eyes and flawless skin. And that kiss, *man* . . . He'd be thinking about that for a long time to come. Of course, he got why she couldn't let anything happen between them. He'd made it perfectly clear that he loved his life exactly the way it was, living from one gig to the next with everything he owned fitting inside the old VW van that served as his home base when he was off-island.

He had no interest in shackling himself to any woman, especially one who was pregnant with another man's child. That had "complication" written all over it. What would her husband do when he found out there was a baby? He'd already said he wouldn't sign the divorce papers.

Owen needed to be in the middle of that mess like he needed a hole in the head. By the time he got to McCarthy's marina and set up his microphone on the deck next to the Tiki Bar, he'd managed to talk himself out of wanting anything more with her. A fabulous few hours of fun and one amazing kiss weren't enough to change an entire life.

Except even as he had that thought, the notion of leaving for the winter and not seeing her for months on end made him feel edgy and unsettled. Unwilling to further explore those disturbing feelings, he vowed to shake off the contemplative mood. She wasn't his problem, and it would do him good to remember that.

As he bantered with the rowdy bar crowd and played the opening chords to "Please Come to Boston," he felt sorry for the guy in the song who was pleading with his love to join him in the city of the moment by extolling the virtues of each new place his singing career took him. The guy was pathetic, and Owen would never be him. No way. He was footloose and fancy-free, and he planned to stay that way.

LINDA MCCARTHY WAS ON HER SECOND CUP OF COFFEE BY THE TIME her husband made an appearance downstairs. He'd showered, shaved and combed his wiry gray hair into submission. A closer look at his face indicated that he'd missed a few spots with the razor, not that she'd be foolish enough to mention that to him.

He had a new spring in his step that filled her with optimism as he poured himself a cup of coffee.

"I need you to be ready at six tonight—"

"Grant called—" She stopped when his words registered. "What did you say? Ready for what?"

"I'm picking you up at six and taking you out."

Linda's heart did a silly little jig as she caught a glimpse of the sexy young man who'd swept her off her feet with alarming ease forty years ago. "Where're we going?"

"That's a surprise, but wear jeans and something warm. Don't get dressed up."

"Um, okay. Sure." She was game for anything he wanted if it meant they got to spend some quality time together.

"Now what were you saying about Grant?" he asked.

"He and Stephanie are organizing an impromptu going-away party for Abby tonight."

Big Mac raised a bushy brow. "*Grant* and *Stephanie* are having a party for *Abby*?"

Linda smiled at the way he said that. Yes, it might seem odd that their son and his new girlfriend were having a party for his ex-girlfriend, but Linda also thought it was very sweet of them to give Abby a proper send-off. "I thought the same thing, but he said someone needed to do it, so why not them?"

"They've come a long way in a short time, those two."

"They're madly in love," Linda said with a smile. It did her heart good to see her kids settling down with loving partners. Three down, two to go. "Speaking of madly in love, Evan never came home last night. He told me he was playing with Owen at the Tiki and hanging out with him afterward, but Doro Chase told me she saw him with a woman at the Lobster House. I did a little digging and found out it was Grace, the one who stayed here last weekend. Remember?"

"Of course I remember. Pretty girl."

"*Very* pretty. Grant told me she came out to the island yesterday to pay back the money Evan gave her to get home after her date abandoned her on the island."

"Interesting."

"I'm glad you think so. I liked her for him."

"Now, Lin, don't get ahead of yourself. Just because he had dinner with a gal—"

"And stayed out all night."

"—and stayed out all night, doesn't mean the boy is changing his ways."

"We would've said the same thing about Mac right before he met Maddie," Linda reminded her husband. She couldn't remember the last time they'd had one of their regular conversations that involved her plotting and scheming in their children's lives and him holding her back from doing something she'd regret. "Doro also said she saw Owen and Laura walking arm in arm in town."

"Is that right? Well, good for Laura—and for Owen. He couldn't do any better than my lovely niece."

"I agree, but she needs to get over what happened with Justin before she jumps into something new."

"She's a cautious gal. You don't need to worry about her. At least we know Owen is as straight-up as they come, unlike that douche bag she married."

"*Mac!* Language!" Linda said what he expected from her, but she held back the urge to giggle like a schoolgirl. Her beloved husband was coming back to her, one day at a time.

"Just callin' it like I see it."

"Why did you put your coffee in a travel mug?"

"Mac is picking me up in ten minutes."

"To go where?"

"Can't tell you. It's a secret."

He looked so pleased with himself that Linda had to work very hard to keep the delight from showing on her face. She couldn't wait to find out what he had up his sleeve but was wary of overreacting or doing anything to endanger their fragile accord. "So what're we doing tonight?"

He came over to her chair, propped his good hand on the back and leaned in so he was an inch from her face.

Startled by the almost predatory look on his face, Linda held her breath.

"Nice try, my love, but you'll have to wait and see." He leaned in to give her a lingering kiss.

Wanting to keep him there awhile longer, Linda reached up to curl a hand around his neck and took the kiss to the next level.

By the time he pulled back from her, he was breathing a little harder.

"That was a dirty trick," he said with a sexy grin.

She smiled. "I learned from the best."

That seemed to please him. "Six o'clock?"

"I'll be ready. Did I mention that Grant and Stephanie asked if they could have Abby's party here?"

"That's okay," he said, giving her one last kiss. "We won't be home."

CHAPTER 15

Leaving the Beachcomber before dawn, Evan set out for the bluffs at the island's southernmost point and sat on the grass to watch the sunrise. Hours later, he was still there, trying to figure out what the hell had happened in that small hotel room.

He'd had plenty of sex in his life, but calling what happened between him and Grace "sex" didn't do it justice. With her, the "deed" had bordered on a religious experience. Just thinking about it had him hard and wanting more.

"For crying out loud," he said to the morning breeze. "*Give me a freaking break!*"

Evan felt like some alien force had taken him over without his permission and changed who he was. The unsettling thought only heightened the anxiousness he'd been riddled with since he woke up in her arms earlier.

Upon realizing where he was and who he was with, his very first thought had been to get the heck out of there before this got even more complicated. What had he been thinking, sleeping all night with her? He'd known from the first instant he met her that she was different from most other woman. Not only was she innocent—*truly*

140

innocent, he thought with a groan—but she was too nice and too sweet to be dallying with the likes of him.

A vicious round of sneezing left him dazed as his watery eyes reminded him that in the throes of hay-fever season, the last place someone with allergies like his should be sitting was in a field full of pollen.

With elbows propped on knees, he ran his fingers through his hair as bits and pieces of lyrics danced through his mind. The words were softer and more heartfelt than usual, which only added to his anxiety. One night with Grace and he was spouting poetry, for Christ's sake!

It wouldn't do. It simply wouldn't do. Furious at himself and at her and the pollen that made him so miserable this time of the year, he got up to brush the grass and dirt from his rumpled khakis. As he stormed down the path that led to the road, Evan wondered if she was awake yet. Was she questioning where he'd gone and why? Was she expecting him to call her and make plans to get together again today?

He hoped not, because that was *not* going to happen. There was no way he could spend more time with her, not when he felt so churned up and out of sorts afterward. Did that make him an asshole? Probably, but at least he hadn't abandoned her on an island with no money and no place to stay.

He'd been honest from the beginning about what she could—and couldn't—expect from him. He didn't owe her a damned thing. Just because the sex had been *un-freaking-believable* didn't change who or what he was. He wouldn't allow it to.

Despite the early morning heat and humidity, he walked the long way home to North Harbor, avoiding downtown and any chance of running into Grace. She was leaving tomorrow, and he'd be steering clear of town between now and then. If that made him a coward, so be it. He had no intention of ever seeing her again.

THE SECOND SHE AWOKE, GRACE KNEW SHE WAS ALONE. THAT DIDN'T stop her from sending a hand to the other side of the bed just to be certain. The sheets were cool. He'd been gone awhile. Perhaps she'd dreamed the entire thing. Then she shifted from her side to her back, and every muscle screamed in protest. She definitely hadn't dreamed it.

Releasing a deep sigh of contentment, she relived the extraordinary night with Evan. Although she ached in some delicate places this morning, she wouldn't change a thing about what had transpired between them.

Wondering if he'd left her a note, she got up and pulled on a robe to look around the small but well-appointed room. Through the open window, she heard the horn for the nine o'clock boat from the ferry landing across the street and the squawk of seagulls. When she didn't find a note or any sign that Evan had ever been there, she shrugged off the disappointment and stepped into the bathroom. Eyeing the claw-footed tub, Grace decided a good long soak in the hottest water she could tolerate was exactly what her aching muscles needed.

Floating in the steaming water a few minutes later, Grace wondered if he would call to make plans for the day. She could always call him, of course, but she was old-fashioned that way and decided to wait for him to make the first move. As she thought about seeing him again, her emotions were all over the place—giddy and excited and nervous. Would their easy rapport disappear now that they'd been intimate? What would he say? What would she say? Would she even be able to look at him after what they'd done the night before?

Grace decided she needed a sounding board to figure out what it all meant—and as much as it would embarrass her to admit it, she owed Stephanie fifty bucks. Laura was the closest, right across the street at the Sand & Surf. Hopefully, she was around this morning and available for a chat.

Grace pulled the drain plug on the tub and reached for a towel. While she was reluctant to leave the hotel and possibly miss a call from Evan, who didn't have her cell number, she needed someone to talk to. She also needed to meet with the Golds to discuss the purchase and sale agreement.

In her suitcase, she found a dress she'd bought as part of her new post-weight-loss wardrobe. She'd never worn it before, but as the silky fabric molded to her new slimmer shape, Grace felt sexier than she ever had in her life. Evan had done that for her. Not only had he made her feel beautiful, he'd made her feel cherished and sexy, too.

As she slid her feet into sandals, she couldn't wait to see him again.

OWEN'S FIRST THOUGHT WHEN HE WOKE UP LATER THAN USUAL WAS that he wanted to kiss Laura again—badly. As he lay in bed staring up at a water stain on the ceiling, he went over all the reasons it couldn't happen, but knowing why didn't stop him from wanting more of her. During the long evening at the Tiki, he'd been forced to put aside his plan to stay far away from her and acknowledge the painful crush that had taken him over.

The ten days she'd been gone to the mainland to unravel her marriage and pack up her old life had been ten of the longest days of Owen's life. He'd been tormented by thoughts of what she must be going through and filled with the desire to do anything he could to make it better for her.

Seeing her on the hotel porch yesterday, knowing that she'd finally come back, counted right up there among the best moments of his entire life, which scared the hell out of him. He had no business being so happy to see a woman who was technically still married to someone else, not to mention pregnant with that someone else's kid. He certainly had no business wanting her naked and horizontal under him in his bed. That was for sure!

"Ugh," he groaned as he got up and shook off the cobwebs from a restless night. "Don't even go there. It's not gonna happen, dude."

He took a quick shower, finger-combed his unruly hair, and threw on shorts and a T-shirt. As he took the stairs to Laura's third-floor apartment, he told himself he was only going up to check on her and to make sure they were still friends after he'd crossed the line by kissing her.

All the way up, Grant's words from the day before about not

missing out on the most important thing in life filtered through Owen's mind, making his legs feel like they were made of lead.

On the third-floor landing, he stopped short when he heard telltale retching sounds. Goddamned morning sickness! She was plagued by it.

This morning, however, in addition to the usual retching, Owen heard sobs, too. "Poor baby," he whispered as he realized her pain had become his, too. How and when that had happened was anyone's guess. "No one should have to go through that alone."

Knowing how she hated for him to see her when she was sick, he stood outside the door for a long time, long enough to make a decision he'd probably live to regret. He withdrew the cell phone from his pocket and found the number for the manager of the bar in Boston that had booked him for two nights during the week as well as weekends from Columbus Day to Christmas. It was a good gig and one he usually looked forward to.

"Hey, Jerry, it's Owen Lawry."

"Owen! What's going on?"

"Listen, something's come up, and I'm going to have to bail out this fall. I'm really sorry for the short notice." Owen had no doubt Jerry had a long list of available performers who'd be happy to fill the opening.

"Aw, shit! That's too bad. Our customers love you. Nothing serious, I hope."

As he thought of his fair-haired Princess and the dark circles under her eyes that had so concerned him the night before, he realized he was sunk. "I'm afraid it might be."

"I'm real sorry to hear that. If anything changes, you know where we are. You're always welcome here, Owen."

"Thanks for understanding. I appreciate it."

"Take care."

Owen had no sooner ended the call and stashed the phone in his pocket when panic set in. What the hell had he just done?

~

LAURA COULDN'T TAKE MUCH MORE OF THE MORNING SICKNESS THAT hit her at the exact same time every day. Sometimes it was nothing more than a bout of nausea that eating a few crackers took care of, but on most days, like this one, the vomiting went on for an hour or more. By the time she reached the dry-heave stage, she was so wrung out that she had no choice but to curl up in a ball on the bathroom floor to ride it out.

That was where Owen found her.

Laura suppressed a moan when she realized he was hovering in the doorway. She hated that he'd already witnessed her daily puke-fest once before. That was more than enough.

"Is it over?" he asked.

"For now."

He bent to scoop her up off the floor. "Come on, honey."

Like the rag doll she was, her head flopped onto his shoulder as he carried her to bed.

When he had her settled under the covers, he returned to the bathroom for a washcloth that he dampened and brought back to the bed to run over her face.

Keeping her eyes closed, she said, "You don't have to do this."

"Hush. I don't do anything I don't want to do."

A tear slipped from her closed eye and was wiped away by the gentle sweep of the cloth over her cheek. Laura took hold of his free hand. While she knew she shouldn't be relying on him this way, especially after what'd happened last night, at some point he'd become her rock. She couldn't imagine *not* holding on to him.

"How about some tea? I'll make it nice and weak."

Laura opened her eyes and found him watching her with concern. "That'd be nice. Thank you."

"Sure thing."

She watched him go—tall, broad-shouldered and handsome in the sloppy way she used to disdain when she was busy looking for a clean-cut preppy to marry. Look at how that had turned out. Back then, before Justin, she never would've given a man like Owen a second look. His hair was too long, and he was often in need of a shave, not to mention he was proud of the fact that he lived out of his van and had no permanent job or address.

And yet he was ten times the man her law-school graduate husband was. No, that wasn't giving Owen enough credit. He was a hundred times the man Justin was.

Owen's phone rang, and he took the call while he waited for the water to boil.

Laura couldn't hear what he was saying, but the rumble of his deep voice was comforting. Her eyes grew heavy, so she let them close. When she felt Owen's weight land next to her on the mattress, she startled awake to find him holding the mug of tea.

He helped her to sit up and settled her against a pile of pillows that he arranged behind her.

"You're spoiling me."

He brushed a stray lock of hair back from her face. "You deserve a little spoiling."

"Owen . . . About what happened last night . . ."

"We don't have to talk about that, Princess. It's all good. I promise."

"It's just that . . ." Laura ran a finger around the edge of the mug as she tried to find the words she needed. "I wanted you to know . . ."

"What, honey?"

Everything inside her went soft and needy when he called her honey. He waited to hear what she had to say, as if nothing had ever been so important to him.

Taking a deep, fortifying breath, she said, "I didn't want you to think that I . . . didn't like it. Kissing you." She forced her gaze up to meet his and found him staring hotly at her. "That wasn't the case."

"Oh. Really?"

"If things were different—"

"You know what the good news is?"

"There's good news?" she asked with a laugh.

"There's always good news, and in this case, it's that your situation won't always be what it is today. Who knows what'll happen a month or two from now, six months, a year?"

"True." She could only hope things would get better. It couldn't get any worse, could it?

"That was Grant on the phone. They're having a going-away party for Abby tonight. She's going to Texas to join Cal since he can't come back, with his mother being so ill after her stroke."

"*Grant* is having the party for Abby?"

"Along with Stephanie, apparently."

"Wow, that's nice of them. What about Abby's store?"

"I heard Maddie's sister, Tiffany, is taking over her lease and opening a new store next summer."

"So many changes for everyone."

"That's what I'm trying to tell you. Things change. You know that all too well. You're going through a rough spot right now. No doubt about that, but it won't always be this way. You've got so much to look forward to with a new job and a new baby on the way."

Laura rested her hand on top of his much bigger one. "And new friends."

His smile transformed his face. She wondered if he knew that. "That, too." He cast his eyes down at their joined hands. "So, um, do you want to go to Abby's party with me?" The question was asked with a hint of shyness and uncertainty that touched her.

"Sure, that would be fun."

He seemed relieved that she'd agreed to go with him. "How's the belly?"

"Much better. It always is after I get good and sick. I wish it didn't wipe me out the way it does, though."

"Why don't you take a nap?"

"I need to get to work around here. Your grandparents didn't hire me to nap the day away."

"You've got all winter to get this place whipped into shape. Taking care of yourself and the baby is your top priority."

"You won't tell them I'm slacking?" she asked with a teasing smile.

He brought their linked hands to his lips and placed a tender kiss on the back of hers. "Your secret is safe with me." Releasing her hand, he added, "Get some rest. The party is at six, so I'll meet you down-stairs a little before?"

"Sounds good."

He got up and headed for the door.

"Owen?"

Turning back to her, he raised a brow.

"Thanks."

"Any time, Princess." Owen closed the door behind him. In the hallway, he leaned against the wall and let his head fall back as his eyes closed tight against the desire to rush back in there and take her in his arms, to show her how much he'd liked kissing her.

But he couldn't do that. No, he had to keep his distance. The irony wasn't lost on him. He'd finally met a woman he could picture spending the rest of his life with, and she wasn't available. It was comical, really. Mr. Footloose and Fancy-Free brought low by a woman he couldn't have.

If you'd told him a month ago that he'd be rearranging his life to accommodate a woman who was married to another guy and preg-nant with his kid, Owen would've laughed his ass off. Now he couldn't conceive of a day that didn't include her. Funny, huh?

"Freaking hilarious," he muttered on his way downstairs.

As he landed in the lobby, the hotel's main door opened, and Grace poked her head in. "Oh, hi, Owen. I knocked, but no one answered."

"Come on in, Grace. What's up?"

"I was wondering if Laura might be around."

He glanced at the stairs. "She's in her apartment on the third floor, but she's not feeling too hot this morning."

"Is it the baby?" Grace asked, full of concern.

Owen was surprised to realize Laura had told her new friends about the baby. He'd sort of liked that it was their little secret, which was ridiculous. It had nothing to do with him. "Morning sickness. She's plagued with it."

Grace winced. "That's awful. I can come back later."

"The worst of it's over for today." As if he were some sort of authority on the pattern of Laura McCarthy's morning sickness. "She might welcome the company."

"Are you sure?"

"Yeah. I'm sure she'd want to see you." Because, of course, he was also an expert on what she might want. "Third floor to the right."

"Thanks, Owen."

Sputtering to himself, Owen went off to find his surfboard. He needed to expend some of the energy zinging through his veins before he did something really stupid.

CHAPTER 16

*G*race headed up the stairs, hoping she wouldn't be bothering Laura with her visit. She tapped on the door bearing the word "Manager" engraved on a gold plaque.

"Come in," Laura called.

Grace stepped into the cozy apartment, where Laura was snuggled into bed and chatting on her cell phone.

Smiling, she waved Grace in and patted the bed in invitation.

For someone who'd dreamed all her life of having girlfriends like Laura, the warm welcome was a balm on Grace's lonely soul. She sat on the other side of the bed and listened to Laura's end of the conversation.

"How did you get talked into cohosting a party for Grant's ex-girlfriend?"

When Grace realized Laura was talking to Stephanie, her eyes widened. She and Grant were hosting a party for his ex? Oh, that would be interesting.

"Grace just got here, and no, I don't have any scoop yet."

"Tell her I owe her fifty bucks," Grace said, her cheeks heating with embarrassment.

With a shriek, Laura shared the news with Stephanie and put the phone on speaker so Grace could hear Stephanie's answering shriek.

Grace laughed at their reaction. "What can I say? You were right about the McCarthy powers of persuasion."

"I told you!" Stephanie said.

"Yes, you did."

"So," Laura said, "was it fabulous? And spare me any gory details involving my cousin."

"Totally amazing." That earned more shrieks. "But let me ask you . . . Is it weird that he was gone when I woke up?"

Laura's smile faded a bit at that news. "Did he at least leave a note?"

"No, nothing."

"Oh my God," Stephanie said. "I'll kill him!"

"Why?" Grace asked. "I'm sure he'll call me later."

Laura sent her a sympathetic look.

"He's not going to call, Grace," Stephanie said bluntly as she swore under her breath.

The fruit Grace had for breakfast was suddenly sitting like a brick in her stomach. "Why do you say that? Maybe he had somewhere to be."

"He's freaking out," Stephanie said.

"And he's running away," Laura added. "Typical."

Grace felt like she was watching a foreign language movie without the subtitles. "Would one of you please explain this to me? Because I don't get it."

Laura reached for Grace's hand. "Honey, you must've blown him away. That's the only possible reason for him acting like such an ass."

"He hasn't acted like an ass—yet," Grace said.

"He acted like an ass the minute he left your room without a word to you," Stephanie said. "Must be the day for McCarthy men acting like asses. His brother has a bad case of asshole-itis, too."

Laura grimaced. "Uh-oh. What happened?"

"First of all," Stephanie said, blowing out a deep breath, "we had a huge fight about the screenplay last night. I mean, is it possible that I know better than him what actually happened when my stepfather was accused of kidnapping and molesting me? Was *he* there? *Noooo*. You'd think he'd been right there for the whole thing, since he's such a freaking expert about it all."

"Yikes," Laura said. "That sucks."

"You know it. If I hear one more time, 'But, honey, we have to take some artistic license with aspects of the story if we're going to sell it to distributors,' I'm going to freaking smack him. It's *my* story, and either he's going to tell it the way it happened, or he's not going to tell it at all."

"Um, didn't you sell him the rights to the story?" Laura asked.

"I haven't signed anything yet, and at this rate, I'm not going to."

"How did you end up cohosting a party for his ex?" Grace asked.

"I mentioned to him yesterday, before we had the big fight, that someone ought to do something for Abby. One thing led to another . . ."

"That's rather magnanimous of you," Laura said, grinning at Grace.

"No kidding," Stephanie muttered. "If I don't kill him—and his brother—before the party, it'll be a miracle."

"Don't kill Evan on my behalf," Grace said. "He was very clear that he wasn't interested in anything long-term."

"I don't care if he used the words 'one-night stand,'" Stephanie said, "he still owed you more than waking up to an empty bed, especially after your first time." She paused before she added, "He did know it was your first time, didn't he?"

"He figured it out."

"*Grrrr*," Stephanie said. "Lame."

"She's right," Laura said. "He's my cousin, and I love him dearly, but it was shitty of him to take the coward's way out by leaving before you woke up."

Grace felt like a balloon after all the air had been let out. She'd been sort of okay with what Evan had done until her friends spelled things out for her. "How sad is it that I'm so naïve I didn't even know I should be mad until you pointed it out to me?"

"There's nothing naïve about thinking the best of people," Laura said with a kind smile.

"You guys are coming to the party," Stephanie said. "I need reinforcements."

"I'm not going," Grace said. "This is Evan's turf. It wouldn't be fair for me to show up out of the blue at a party with his family if he's not interested in seeing me again."

"You did nothing wrong," Stephanie said. "Why should you slink off like you have something to be ashamed about? If anyone should be ashamed, it's him! If I have to help throw a party for my boyfriend's ex, I can invite anyone I want to."

"I want to be you when I grow up," Grace said with a sigh.

"Me, too," Laura added.

Stephanie barked out a laugh. "You don't need to be anyone other than who you are—either of you. You're both perfect. Your choice in men, however . . ."

"Listen to her, all full of herself," Laura said to Grace. "You should've seen her mooning over Grant before the I-love-yous. It was downright pathetic."

"That's not nice," Stephanie said.

Laughing, Laura said, "But it's true!"

"Let's talk about you and Owen," Stephanie retorted.

Laura got very still all of a sudden. "What about him?"

"You'd have to be deaf, dumb and blind to miss the sparks between you two," Stephanie said. "So what gives?"

"We're friends. That's it."

"Grace?" Stephanie said. "Is she lying?"

Grace took a good long look at Laura. "She does have a bit of a deer-in-the-headlights look to her."

Laura scowled playfully at Grace. "Traitor."

"Spill it, sister," Stephanie said. "What's up?"

"My ex called last night. He got the divorce papers and was flipping out as if it was some big surprise to him that I want out. He says he won't sign them now or ever."

"Shit," Stephanie said.

"I was upset after the call, and Owen was really great. We went out for pizza and played video games at the arcade. It was . . . It was fun. He makes me laugh when there's absolutely nothing funny about my life right now."

Grace let out a dreamy sigh that made Laura roll her eyes.

"And that's *all* that happened?" Stephanie asked.

"You're a pain in the ass," Laura said, laughing at Stephanie's persistence.

"Yes, I am. Now fess up."

"When we got back to the hotel . . . he might've kissed me."

Stephanie let out another unholy shriek. "I *knew* it!"

"Don't get all excited," Laura said. "I told him it can't happen again."

"*Why?*" Grace and Stephanie asked in stereo.

"Because! Technically, I'm still married to Justin and will be for God knows how long it takes him to sign the damned papers. And when he finds out about the baby . . ." Laura shuddered, as if she couldn't bear to think about that.

"The guy *cheated* on you," Stephanie reminded her.

"He says he never actually cheated."

"Only because the woman he made the date with was a friend of yours seeing if he would keep the date," Stephanie said. "Who knows what else he's been up to?"

"Are you sorry you left Justin?" Grace asked, even though she wasn't entirely comfortable asking her new friend such a personal question. But since she'd told them everything that'd happened with Evan, turnabout was fair play.

"No! I can't even stand the sound of his voice after what he did."

"Then why can't you date Owen if your marriage is truly over?" Grace asked.

"Excellent question," Stephanie said.

"It is truly over. I could never go back to him." Laura fiddled with the blanket, flipping it back and forth between her fingers. "Owen doesn't want the same things I do. He likes his life the way it is, with no commitments or obligations beyond the next gig. I'm going to have a *baby*. My whole life will be about commitments and obligations for the next eighteen years. Besides, what guy wants to be saddled with someone else's kid?"

"Mac took to fatherhood like Thomas was his own child," Stephanie said.

"That's different. Mac was ready for a family. Owen doesn't want a permanent address, let alone a baby that isn't his."

"Is it possible," Grace said, "that what he wants might be changing?"

"A tiger doesn't change his stripes overnight," Laura said.

"That tiger looks at you like he wants to drag you back to his den and have his wicked way with you," Stephanie said.

Grace nodded in agreement. "What she said."

"You guys are nuts. Owen is totally happy with his life. There's no point in talking about something that's not going to happen."

"Whatever you say, tiger," Stephanie said skeptically. "I've got to get back to work. Can I count on you guys having my back tonight?"

"I'll be there," Laura said.

Grace thought about it for a moment and decided Stephanie was right. She hadn't done anything with Evan that he hadn't thoroughly enjoyed. There was no reason to avoid him, especially when someone she hoped would be a good friend in her new life was asking for help.

"Grace?" Stephanie said. "*Come on*, be a pal."

"I'll be there." The words were out of Grace's mouth before she could take any more time to ponder the implications.

"You can come with me and Owen," Laura said.

"Bring that fifty," Stephanie said, laughing as she ended the call.

GRACE LEFT THE HOTEL AND HEADED FOR THE NEARBY FERRY LANDING. Her leg muscles were tired and sore from the workout she'd put them through the night before, and her heart was heavy after her talk with the girls. She could no longer deny the implications of what Evan had done. He'd meant it when he said there couldn't be anything more between them. Grace had to admit that she'd entertained the slightest hope that she might be the exception to his rule. Apparently, that was not the case.

It didn't take years of experience to get that something significant had occurred in that hotel room last night, and knowing that she'd rocked him gave her a measure of satisfaction. If he was too much of a coward to face what'd transpired between them, she had no choice but to get on with her life and file away the experience as something special and magical to remember on lonely nights. That didn't mean she wasn't good and mad about him being a coward, though. While she wanted to nurture the anger, more than anything she was disappointed when she thought of what could've been.

She approached the window where ferry tickets were sold.

"May I help you?" the woman working the counter asked.

"I need to speak to someone about moving household goods to the island."

"That'd be Seamus O'Grady, our general manager. Let me see if he's available."

"Thank you." While she waited, Grace studied the breakwater that formed the northern end of South Harbor. The surf crashing against the rocks sent spray high into the air. Off in the distance, she made out the hulking shape of the next ferry heading toward the island.

"Would you be the lass looking to move to our fair island?" a man asked in a lovely Irish accent.

Grace turned to him and caught herself before she could let out a gasp. What was *with* the men on this island? To call him a redhead wouldn't do him justice. His hair was a rich auburn, his eyes a startling green and his smile full of the devil. In short, he was positively dreamy, a word Grace hadn't used since middle school when she was lusting after Trey. "Um, yes," she said, giving her head a slight shake to regain her focus. "I'm the one looking to move."

"Well, isn't that fortunate for the single men of Gansett?" With a teasing grin, he added, "I call dibs."

Oh my God, was he *flirting* with her? Grace wished she could press Pause, call Laura and get her over here to read the subtitles. She

decided she could at least attempt to flirt right back. It was good practice. "How do you know I'm not married with five kids?"

Feigning shock, he rested his hand over his heart. "Are you?"

"No," she said, laughing at his outrageousness.

With a wink, he said, "Thank God for that. Follow me, lass. We'll
get you squared away."

Grace went with him into the ferry company's main office, located
across the parking lot from the ticket area. Once inside, he gestured
for her to take a seat on the other side of a desk scattered with
binders, coffee cups and stacks of paper. A khaki-colored Gansett
Island Ferry Company ball cap sat on top of the disarray.

From one of the desk drawers, Seamus produced a form and
walked her through the scheduling of a midsize moving truck on the
ferry. "Nothing flammable like propane tanks, for example, can be
packed in the truck," he said, drawing her attention to the list of rules.
He fired up his computer and scanned through a complicated-looking
spreadsheet. "Next available date for a truck of that size is two weeks
from today. You could bring it over in the morning and send it back
the same evening. Would that work for you?"

Grace had already arranged to hire her college-age brother to
drive the truck and help her move in. "That'd be great."

"It's all yours, Gracie, my love."

Yes, definitely flirting. She didn't bother telling him that no one
called her "Gracie," but she liked how the dreaded nickname sounded
coming from him.

"So what brings you to live on Gansett?"

"Can you keep a secret?"

He flashed an offended scowl. "I'll protect your secrets with my
very life. Back in my village in County Cork, they call me 'the Vault.'
Nothing gets past these lips," he said, leaning in closer, "unless you
want it to."

Grace rolled her eyes at the double entendre, charmed by him
despite herself. "In that case, Mr. Vault, I'm buying Gold's Pharmacy."

"You don't say! How exciting for you—and for us."

"I'm thrilled and scared and excited and all sorts of things."

"I can only imagine. Nothing simple about running a business. I ought to know. When Joe Cantrell hired me to run the show for him while his missus is in vet school in Ohio, I figured, how hard can it be? Well, let me tell ya . . ."

"Not as easy as it looks, huh?"

"Not at'all. Forms and inspections and staffing and licenses and more inspections and safety drills and a million decisions every day. Oh my."

"And you love every minute of it."

"Best job I ever had." Flashing a rakish grin, he added, "Did I mention I'm a seafaring captain, among my many *other* talents?"

"No, I don't believe you did," Grace said, suppressing a laugh.

He looked around to make sure no one was listening, even though he was well aware they were alone in the office. "Since we're going to be neighbors," he said gravely, "I'd be happy to show you my license."

Grace made sure to show the proper deference. "I'm sure it's quite impressive."

"Oh, lass, it's very impressive indeed."

By the time they'd ironed out the rest of the details for her move, he had her laughing so hard she was wiping tears from her eyes. Seamus had succeeded in restoring Grace's good mood and her self-confidence. Nothing like a gorgeous Irishman with an overabundance of charm and blarney to make a girl feel good about herself.

"Once you get settled, I insist you let me take you to dinner to welcome you to our fair island."

"That'd be very nice. Thank you for asking."

Seamus took her hand and bowed gallantly before her, kissing the back of her hand. "It'll be my pleasure."

"I appreciate your help with the scheduling."

"Also my pleasure. I'll see you around, Grace Ryan."

"I'll look forward to it."

"Aye. Me, too, lass. Me, too."

With the luck of the Irish on her side, Grace returned to the Beachcomber to freshen up before she headed to Gold's to talk details.

Entering her room, she zeroed in on the phone next to the bed, hoping to see the message light blinking. Nothing.

"That's okay," she said. "Evan McCarthy is hardly the only fish in the sea." As she brushed her hair, she wondered how long it would take—once she mentioned it to Laura and Stephanie—to get back to Evan that Seamus had asked her out. Hopefully, not long. She wouldn't want Evan to think she was sitting around waiting to hear from him. She had far better things to do with her time.

CHAPTER 17

*S*traddling his board and bobbing in the late afternoon chop, Evan watched a new wave grow about two hundred yards offshore. With four-foot rollers breaking on the island's west side, he'd expected a mob scene at his favorite surfing spot, but he had the place to himself. Under normal circumstances, he didn't surf alone. But nothing about this day was normal, and he needed the mindless escape surfing always provided.

Evan paddled out a little farther, eyeing the cresting wave and moving into position. Grabbing a ride on a wave was all about timing. Balance and coordination played a role, too, but primarily it was about timing the collision of board and wave just right.

Growing up on the island, surfing had been one of Evan's favorite things to do. Whenever he needed to clear his head, he'd grab his board and head for the west side. Surfing was also the one athletic pursuit he'd been better at than his brothers, and he never missed a chance to remind them of that.

As the wave started to peak, Evan paddled furiously, skimming along the top until the force of the water grabbed him and sent him hurtling forward. Evan scrambled to his feet for the wild ride to shore, crouching into a turn that gave him another hundred yards of speed before he bailed out into shallow water.

"*Awesome.*" He climbed back on the board and took a minute to catch his breath, drifting in the smaller waves that broke closer to the shore. Other than his parents and family, he missed riding Gansett waves most of all when he was in Nashville.

When he lived here, Evan had surfed year-round, much to his mother's dismay, but on this trip, one thing after another had kept him out of the water. His sister's wedding, the tropical storm that made the conditions too dangerous, the birth of his niece and helping to run the marina while his brother was busy with a new baby and his father was recovering from a head injury had left little time for surfing.

As he paddled out in search of the next wave, Evan's mind raced a mile a minute. He thought about his parents and their current struggles as well as his new niece, Hailey. Thinking of his sister, Janey, he wondered if she and Joe were settling back into their home in Ohio for her second year of vet school. He'd have to give them a call this week to see how things were going.

No matter where he was or what he was doing, Evan made a point to speak to each of his siblings every week. The phone calls kept the five of them connected, which was important to him—and to them.

Speaking of phone calls, he needed to return the call from his manager that he'd received while he was out last night with Grace—

"No!" His heart kicked into gear at the thought of her. "You're not thinking about her. So don't go there. It was *one* night. No big deal." The whole point of surfing was to *not* think about her. He'd already spent enough time thinking about her. He was all done with that subject.

Facedown on the board, he paddled hard, the muscles in his arms burning from the effort. Despite his iron will to think about anything other than her, the erotic interlude ran through his mind like one of those loop videos that played over and over again. Every detail was burned indelibly into his memory, as vivid as it had been in the moment.

Every moan, every sigh, every stroke of her soft hands . . .

"Stop it!" he screamed at the surf. *"That's enough, goddamn it!"* Just stop! There's nothing special about her! She's a nice girl, and we had a good time. That's the end of it!" He eyed a new wave with the potential to be bigger than the last and paddled into position to wait for it.

The closer the wave came, the bigger it got. Adrenaline cruised through Evan's body, feeding the high he could only get from surfing. Nothing was quite like riding atop the perfect wave, except perhaps an exquisite night in the arms of the perfect woman.

"Oh, for fuck's sake," he muttered, summoning all the concentration he needed to ride the monster that was barreling down on him. As the undertow sucked him out from the shore, Evan moved into position. He eyed the roller, measuring and calculating, waiting for the break that didn't come.

"Shit," he whispered as it peaked right under him, lifting the board and shooting it forward. He'd timed it all wrong. Getting his balance, he stood for the ride, whipping over the surface of the water so fast that the shoreline blurred. Realizing the wave was going to break very close to the beach, it occurred to Evan that being out here alone might not be the smartest thing he'd ever done.

The board flew out from under him, but the ripcord fastened to his ankle kept it attached to him. The wave dragged him down and slammed him into the bottom. He couldn't get his hands down in time to keep his face from grinding into sand and shells and rocks. Knowing better than to fight the currents, he gave in to the will of the water and eventually broke the surface, gasping for air.

"Holy shit," he whispered, ducking beneath another wave as the ripcord pulled and tugged at his ankle. Trying to catch his breath and unscramble his brain, Evan floated on his back, letting the board drag him along behind it. The salt water burned his abraded face, and Evan wondered if he was bleeding, which led to thoughts of sharks. Just as he was about to swim for shore, a strong arm encircled his chest.

"Jesus H. Christ," Owen said, breathing hard. "Are you okay?"

"I think so."

"That was one hell of a wipeout. Scared the freaking shit out of me."

"Where'd you come from?"

"I was on the stairs coming down when I saw you misread that one, big-time."

He'd been misreading everything lately. "I'm okay," he said when his feet connected with sand.

Owen released him but stayed close. "You're sure?"

"Yeah." Picking up his board, Evan walked on wobbly legs and dropped down in the sand.

Owen landed next to him and handed him a towel. "You're bleeding like a stuck pig."

Evan pressed the towel to his face and winced from the sting of terrycloth meeting raw skin.

"That's gonna be nasty looking."

"It's not that bad." Evan withdrew the towel and was stunned by how much blood there was. "Is it?"

"It's pretty bad. You're gonna want to get that cleaned up so it doesn't scab over when it's all sandy."

Returning the towel to his face, Evan reclined on the sand and looked up at the blue sky. "And this day goes from bad to worse."

"I take it things didn't go well with Grace last night?"

Owen's question struck him in the sensitive area just above his rib cage, leaving an ache that demanded his full attention.

"Ev?"

"It was okay."

"Just okay?"

Evan wished he could share his thoughts on the matter with Owen, but since he couldn't explain his unusual reaction to Grace to himself, how would he explain it to someone else?

"What's with you? It's like pulling teeth to get a word out of you."

"It was probably the best date I've ever been on."

Evan could tell that he'd shocked the shit out of his friend. "Is that right? Wow. So what now?"

Evan shrugged. "Nothing. We had a good time. What else is there to say?"

"So let me get this straight—it was the best date of your life, but you're not going to see her again?"

Why did it sound so awful when Owen put it that way? "That's about right."

"You're screwed up, man."

"There's a news flash."

"I don't get why you're so anti-relationship. You grew up with two parents who wrote the blueprint for successful marriage. So how does the son of Big Mac and Linda McCarthy run from anything that might, someday, down the road, *in the distant future*, lead to marriage?"

Because he had no answer to Owen's very good question, Evan went on the offensive. "How am I any different from you?"

"My parents were nothing like yours."

Since Owen rarely talked about his family or his upbringing, Evan was intrigued by the rare insight. "How were they different?"

Owen hesitated for a long moment, as if deciding how much he wanted to share. "My dad, the general, was kind of a dick. Everything was his way or the highway, you know? We all breathed easier when he was deployed, including my mom."

"He didn't, you know . . ."

"Knock us around? Sometimes. Mostly we went out of our way to avoid him. I went out of my way to keep him away from my younger brothers and sisters."

Having never heard any of this before, Evan marveled at how he'd known Owen most of his life but didn't know him as well as he'd thought. He'd come to the island every summer to see his grandparents, but he'd never talked much about what went on the rest of the year. "So you bore the brunt."

Owen stared straight ahead at the ocean. "Something like that."

"I'm sorry. I had no idea."

"It was a long time ago." Owen flashed the grin that was far more his speed than the somber expression. "He wouldn't dare look at me cross-eyed now."

Evan smiled. "I bet sometimes you wish he would."

"I'm not above that level of pettiness, but I don't live my life looking backward. No point in that."

"So you don't ever see yourself with a wife and kids?"

"I never said that."

Evan studied his old friend. "Why are you acting all smug, as if you've got a big secret or something?"

"No secrets."

"What's up with you and Laura?"

"Nothing."

"Why do I not believe you?"

"I don't know what you want me to say. We're friends. I like her. I think she likes me. We have some laughs. Nothing more to it than that."

"Who're you trying to convince? Me or you?"

"You're really not going to see Grace again?"

Evan had to give Owen credit for successfully deflecting the conversation. "What's the point, O? She lives in Connecticut. I'm going back to Nashville soon. I don't want to get into something I can't handle right now. I've got enough to deal with."

"I suppose that makes sense. I'm sure she'll understand—as long as you didn't sleep with her or anything."

As the comment scored a direct hit, Evan continued to stare up at the sky.

"Aw, jeez, man. You didn't sleep with her, did you?"

Evan let his silence speak for him.

"Shit," Owen said. "That changes everything."

Wasn't that the truth?

CHAPTER 18

*W*ith Grant and Stephanie preparing for Abby's party and arguing about every detail, Linda decided it would be better to wait for her husband outside. That way she could resist the temptation to get in the middle of the screenplay dispute that had spilled into the party prep.

Linda hoped they would work out their differences, because she loved Stephanie and adored the two of them together. She'd never seen her second son as happy and content as he'd been in the last few weeks since he decided to stay with her rather than return to LA. They belonged together but working together was no easy task.

She ought to know. Linda and her husband had done it for the first eight years of their marriage, before they discovered life was much more harmonious with him running the marina and her handling the hotel.

They also learned that not spending so much time together during the day made for sweeter nights. Thinking about those days as young parents with so many responsibilities and so little time to call their own made Linda smile when she remembered all the creative ways they'd made up for lost time.

The closer the sun got to setting, the chillier the air became. As she snuggled into her sweater, she realized she was nervous. It seemed like a lot was riding on this evening, and she didn't even know where they were going.

The rumble of a motorcycle engine caught her attention because it sounded like her son Mac's bike. If he was riding that death trap he loved so much with two babies counting on him, Linda would shoot him. Of course it could be Evan, too, since he'd borrowed the bike from his brother last week. Linda wished she'd sent the damned thing to the junkyard when she'd had the chance.

She got up and headed down the stairs as the motorcycle crunched to a stop in the crushed-shell driveway.

When the rider removed his helmet, Linda gasped at the sight of her husband. "What're you *doing*? You shouldn't be on that thing! What if you fall off or hit your head again or—"

"Lin," he said, smiling despite the note of warning in his tone. "I'd like to take you on a little adventure. Are you game?" From his perch on the motorcycle, he held out a hand to her.

What was she supposed to do? Of course she was game, but she hated that stinking motorcycle. Every time Mac had driven off on it as a teenager, she'd been convinced he'd be killed. Now her husband expected her to actually *ride* on it?

"Why don't we take my car?"

"Because there's nothing adventurous about a VW bug."

She scowled at the insult to her beloved yellow bug. "How can you operate that thing with a cast on your arm?"

"I cut off the hand part with a hacksaw." With the boyish grin that still made her knees weak, he held up his arm to show a cast that now began at his wrist and ended just below his elbow. He looked so darned pleased with himself that Linda fought back a smile that would undercut her disapproval.

"Really, Mac, you can't honestly expect me . . ."

He got off the bike, unhooked the spare helmet and placed it on her head. "I expect you to trust me. You know I'd never risk your safety." Securing the strap under her chin, he made sure it was good and snug before he framed her face with his big hands and gently compelled her to look up at him. "Trust me?"

"Of course I do, but—"

He kissed the words right off her lips. "No buts. Hop on."

"Mac . . ."

"You'll love it. I promise. There's nothing like it."

The last thing Linda wanted was to start this night off on the wrong foot, so she reluctantly slid her leg over the seat and settled behind him. He wore a long-sleeved denim shirt that was one of her favorites because of the way it set off the vivid blue eyes he'd passed down to each of their sons.

"Put your arms around me, babe, and hold on tight."

Since there was nothing she'd rather do, Linda snuggled in close to him, and as she caught a whiff of the cologne he applied after every shave, she realized he must've showered and changed at the marina. He'd put a lot of thought into this evening, which filled her with hope and anticipation.

He fired up the bike and had them on their way before Linda had the chance to chicken out.

She'd never been on a motorcycle, and it didn't take long to discover she'd been missing out, especially as the ripple of her husband's muscles under her hands reminded her of how much she loved being close to him. After such a rough couple of months, she was thrilled to be going somewhere—*anywhere*—with him.

Linda closed her eyes and gave herself over to him and his adventure.

They rode for a long time, through town, up and down hills, past the bluffs and the southeast lighthouse. Finally, he downshifted and turned into a driveway she recognized. He brought the bike to a stop in front of Luke Harris's house.

"What're we doing here?" she asked when he cut the engine.

"You'll see." After he helped her off the bike and stashed their helmets, he produced a flashlight and held out a hand to her.

Linda took his hand and followed him to the stairs that led to the beach below. "Where's Luke? Does he know we're here?"

"I imagine he's probably over at our house by now for the party, and yes, he was happy to loan us his beach for the evening."

As they took the stairs to the secluded stretch of shore, Linda's heart began to race with excitement. He knew how much she loved the beach, and it meant a lot to her that he'd taken that into consideration.

"Careful now," he said as he led the way.

Linda held on tight to his hand and followed the faint beam of the light on the stairs. When they landed in the sand, they kicked off their shoes and stashed them next to the stairs. The sand was cool against her bare feet, the breeze soft on her face and the moon bright upon the water.

"Madame," he said, bowing before her and extending his arm.

Linda settled her hand into the crook of his elbow and walked along the shoreline for a short distance until they ducked into a secluded inlet between two dunes.

"Wait here for a sec, hon," he said.

A minute later, a fire striker flared to life, and he went around lighting a ring of tiki torches, ending up at a fire pit that he also lit. The flames shot high into the sky, casting a glow upon him that took her breath away. He was still, without a doubt, the sexiest guy she'd ever laid eyes upon, and he was holding out his hand to her.

Linda went to him, taking in the open-sided tent that had been staked to the sand. Underneath were two lounge chairs and a cooler. "When did you do all this?" Linda asked, astounded by the effort he'd gone to.

"I can't take credit for the beach camp. It belongs to Luke and Syd. I guess they had Mac, Maddie and Thomas over for a cookout earlier in the summer. Mac told me about it and helped me get the cooler down here."

"So Mac knows that things have been . . ."

He put his arms around her, drawing her into a hug. "Off." The feel of his lips on her neck sent shivers cascading through her. "Things have been off between us, and I hate that. I hate that it's my fault. I hate that I've been an ass to you, and I hate that our kids have noticed that we're not getting along the way we usually do."

Linda blinked back tears as his softly spoken words registered. "They've noticed that?"

"Apparently, there's been some talk in the ranks about what's going on between Mom and Dad. They've been worried about us."

"*I've* been worried about us."

"I hate that most of all."

Linda pressed her face to his broad chest, listening to the strong beat of his heart and delighting in the caress of his fingers on the back of her neck. No matter how difficult things had been since the accident, she was so very thankful he'd survived. What would she ever do without him?

"In my whole damned life," he said gruffly, "you're the one thing I got totally right."

Moved to tears, Linda said, "You did a pretty darned good job with those kids of ours, too."

"Maybe so, but it all comes back to you." He drew back to look down at her. "Do you have any idea how much I love you?"

"I think so."

"You couldn't possibly know, because there're no words to tell you what you mean to me, what you've meant to me for so long."

"Mac . . ."

"We've been so lucky, you and me. I could've whisked you off to Paris on a private jet tonight if that's what I thought you'd want."

"I've never wanted anything like that—and besides, you'd hate leaving the island. We both would. What fun would that be?"

"I used to worry, you know, about whether you'd take to island life. You were such a city girl when I met you, all polished and pretty. I worried for five long years after I brought you here that you were going to tell me one day you couldn't take it anymore."

"I had no idea! You've never told me that before!"

"I was afraid to say it out loud, but I was constantly watching for signs of discontent."

"I've never been unhappy here. Not for one minute. I feel so bad you worried about that. All that mattered to me, all that's ever mattered to me, was being with you. I wouldn't have been happy anywhere else without you."

He brought his lips down on hers for a soft, sweet kiss that made her heart pound the way it had the first time he kissed her, the moment she'd known for sure that he was the one for her.

"What would you have done if I told you I couldn't handle island life?" she asked.

"I would've moved to wherever you wanted to go."

"I can't picture you anywhere but here."

"Neither can I, but I would've gone anywhere in the world if it meant I got to be with you."

Linda snuggled into his warm embrace. "I can't believe we've never talked about this before."

"I hope you always knew that if there was anything you wanted that we didn't have here, I'd find a way to get it for you."

"Of course I knew that. You got me my bug, right?"

"That silly car," he said, shaking his head with mirth, the same way he had on the day he drove it into the driveway as a surprise for her birthday.

"What more could I want, with you, five wonderful kids, two adorable grandbabies, our friends and the business? Heck, even my sister and her family ended up here after they came to visit and fell in love with the place."

"Which gave you someone besides me to bicker with every day."

Linda snorted out a laugh. "So true." She ran a hand over his chest and looked up at him. "I want to tell you something I'm sorry about."

He raised an eyebrow. "What do you have to be sorry about?"

"The day of the accident . . . That morning . . . I was late for a hair appointment, and you were in the shower. I left without even saying good-bye. All I could think about during the long hours at the clinic was what if that was the last chance I'd ever have to talk to you, to kiss you, to tell you I love you, and I'd missed it?"

"We'd both gotten complacent about that stuff. I was just as guilty about coming and going without a thought as to what might happen."

"We can't do that anymore. If we've learned nothing else from the accident, it's that we never know what's going to happen. I think about that call from Stephanie . . . You could've been taken from me so suddenly . . . I may never get over that."

"I'm right here, and I'm fine." He kissed her forehead, her nose and then her lips. "We'll get back on track, babe. I promise."

"I've missed you so much, Mac. I never imagined I could be so lonely for you when you were right there next to me."

He released a deep sigh filled with regret. "I wish I could tell you it's going to be fine from here on out—"

Linda pressed a finger to his lips. "You don't have to tell me that. All I need to know is that whatever happens, we'll deal with it together."

"That much I can promise." He kissed her again, more intently this time, and the passion they'd always shared roared back to life. "How about some dinner?"

Linda slipped her fingers under his shirt, making him shiver when she caressed his back. "Remember what we did after we got Mac and Grant through the chicken pox?"

"Vaguely."

"We were so relieved to be getting a break from sick kids. We hired a babysitter, got a pizza and went to the beach to celebrate surviving the siege."

"I do remember that night. As I recall, there was also a bottle of wine and skinny-dipping."

"Among other things. How about a do-over?"

"It's kinda chilly for skinny-dipping tonight."

She ran a finger straight down the center of his chest and hooked it on the waistband of his jeans. "We could skip that part and go right to the *other* things."

He seemed somewhat scandalized by her suggestion, which she loved. "*Here?*"

"Why not? We've got a houseful at home—just like the old days. We've got to be creative, the way we used to be."

"Linda McCarthy, you never cease to surprise me," he said as he tugged the sweater over her head and reached for the button to her jeans.

"I hope I never do." As he urged her down onto a blanket he produced from the darkness, Linda was overcome with relief and desire and love. He was the best thing that'd ever happened to her, and as he made love to her for the first time since the accident, she felt like he'd finally come home to her.

CHAPTER 19

"I thought Mr. and Mrs. McCarthy would be here," Abby said.

The women had gathered in the family room while the guys wandered onto the deck to drink beer and swap stories. Tiffany tried to concentrate on the conversation, but all she could think about was the argument she'd had with Jim when she'd dropped Ashleigh off with him earlier. Once again, she'd had no luck engaging him in civilized conversation.

"They're out on a date," Maddie said of her in-laws. Baby Hailey slept in her arms as Maddie rocked her. It was their first outing since Hailey's birth. Abby's party had messed with the plans for a girls night out, so she and Mac had decided to postpone it until Hailey was sleeping better and Maddie wasn't so tired.

"Isn't that so sweet?" Stephanie said. "I've never known anyone who's been married as long as they have, and they're still gaga over each other."

"They've had a rough time since the accident," Maddie said. "Mac said his dad had this night already planned so they could reconnect. Otherwise, you know they'd be here, Abby."

"I totally understand," Abby said.

"Speaking of reconnecting," Sydney said, "I saw the most hilarious thing on TV this morning. They had this couple on who had reconciled after nearly divorcing. You won't believe what she did to get his attention."

"What's that?" Grace asked as everyone hung on Sydney's next words, especially Tiffany.

"She handcuffed herself to him and wouldn't take the cuffs off until they worked out all their issues. She said it took three hours of fighting and crying and talking and compromising, but they finally scored a breakthrough. After she told one of her friends about it, the story ended up on Facebook, which led to the interview. Isn't that great?"

Long after the others had discussed the lady with the handcuffs and moved on to other topics, Tiffany was thinking that if Jim were cuffed to her, he'd have no choice but to listen. She'd have all the power.

Tiffany grew more enamored of the idea with every passing moment. *Where can I get a pair of handcuffs on this island?* Just as she had the thought, Blaine Taylor stuck his head into the room. Speaking of handcuffs . . .

"I'm looking for the guest of honor," he said, zeroing in on Tiffany rather than Abby. Per usual, he wore the sex-on-a-stick uniform that made her want to drool.

Under the heat of his intense gaze, Tiffany felt like he'd burned off her clothes, leaving her naked and vulnerable.

Abby got up to give him a hug, which broke the spell he'd cast over Tiffany. She took a couple of deep breaths to calm her raging hormones. The reaction she had to that man every time she saw him was positively indecent.

"Thanks for coming, Blaine," Abby said. "I really appreciate it."

"I couldn't miss the chance to wish you well."

"Let me get you a beer."

"I got it." Stephanie jumped up to take Blaine's arm. "Stay with your friends, Abby."

"Thanks, Stephanie."

~

STEPHANIE LED BLAINE INTO THE KITCHEN, GOT A BEER AND OPENED IT for him. Once she'd sent him outside to join the other guys, she refreshed the food and cleaned up discarded plates and cups. Since "the big fight" with Grant, she'd focused on staying busy so she wouldn't lose her mind.

Last night, she'd been so furious over what he wanted to do with the story that she'd said some things she probably shouldn't have, and so had he. It'd gotten quite ugly and heated, and they'd gone to bed mad. The incident had her questioning everything she'd come to believe about them.

She was terrified that their fledgling relationship would come unraveled. What would she do then? He'd become essential to her, as critical as air and water and food. If they broke up, she'd have one hell of a time rebuilding her life once she got past the devastation of losing him. She'd do it if she had to. It wasn't like she hadn't done it before, but the thought of being without him made her ill.

Stephanie rested her hands on the sink and let her head fall forward, stretching out the tension that had gathered in her shoulders during the long day. She had no idea how long she'd been there when strong, capable fingers began kneading the knots from her muscles. She'd know those particular hands anywhere. If she traveled around the world and back again, she'd never find anyone whose touch affected her like his did.

"What's the matter?" Grant's lips skimmed over her neck from behind as he continued the heavenly massage. "Is this too much for you? Hosting a party for my ex-girlfriend?"

"No, it's fine. Everyone's having a good time."

"Everyone but you."

"I'm having fun. I always do with this group. You know that."

Turning her to face him, he ducked his head to force her to meet his gaze. "Talk to me, Steph. Are you upset about what happened last night?"

Because she couldn't lie to him, she nodded.

"Aww, baby, come on." He hugged her tight. "It'll be okay. We'll figure it out."

Her hands landed on his hips. "What if we don't? What if it all falls apart—"

"That's not going to happen. We won't let it."

"You don't know that for sure."

"Yes, I do." He rested his forehead on hers. "I love you more than anything. I can't remember what my life was like without you to argue with. I love everything about us, even the fighting."

That drew a reluctant laugh from Stephanie. She never got tired of hearing him tell her how much he loved her.

"You know what's the best part about fighting?" he asked, his lips vibrating against her ear.

"There's a best part?"

"Mmm-hmm. Making up."

She linked her arms around his neck, molding herself to him in a move that had become as natural to her as breathing. They fit together so perfectly, like two halves of a whole. "Is that what we're doing now?"

"Hell, no. That's what we'll do when we get home later."

She closed her eyes and relaxed into his embrace. It was going to be okay. "I'm already home. You're home."

"Does that mean you love me, too? Even when you think I'm unreasonable and pigheaded and stubborn?"

As he tossed out all the words she'd thrown at him the night before, Stephanie smiled. "Despite your many negative traits, I do love you."

"Good," he said, sounding relieved.

It occurred to her that he'd been worried, too.

"Steph?"

"Hmm?"

"I don't want you to worry about us breaking up, okay?"

One of the things she loved best about him was that he always seemed to know exactly what she needed to hear. "Okay."

"It's not going to happen."

MARIE FORCE

"You don't know that for sure."

"Yes, I do."

"Get a room," Evan muttered as he came into the kitchen wearing board shorts and a ripped T-shirt.

Stephanie pulled free of Grant and let out a gasp. "What happened to your face?"

Grant turned to his brother. "Holy creature from the black lagoon! What the hell, Ev?"

"A little surfing accident. Face versus the bottom."

"Ouch," Grant said with a grimace.

Stephanie guided Evan to a chair at the kitchen table and went to get some wet paper towels. "Is there a first aid kit somewhere?" she asked Grant.

"I'll get it."

"It's no big deal," Evan said. "I'll grab a shower and clean it up in there."

Stephanie kept a hand on his shoulder to stop him from getting up. "You need something more than soap and water on that mess."

"Is it really that bad?"

"It's worse than bad."

"Gee, thanks a lot."

"I'm seriously pissed with you, by the way."

Startled, Evan looked up at her. "What'd I do?"

She made an effort to keep her voice down. "You spent the night with Grace and then split this morning without a word." Stephanie didn't mention that she'd done the same thing after the first night she spent with Grant, because that was different. It hadn't been the first time for either of them.

"How is that any of your business?"

"Because she's my friend, and I expected better from you."

"That's where you made your first mistake."

"You need to fix this. She's not someone you use and discard. For reasons you can't *begin* to understand, what you did was the worst possible thing you could've done to her."

"What does that mean?"

"I'm not at liberty to say."

As Evan glowered at her, Grant returned with the first aid kit and handed it to her.

"Don't leave me alone with her, bro," Evan said. "She's in a mood."

"You're on your own, pal," Grant said with a laugh. "I've got to get more ice."

"There's some in the garage freezer," Stephanie said. To Evan, she said, "This might hurt." She did her best to clean the huge scrapes on his face without hurting him, but he winced more than once.

"Oh my God," Grace said when she came into the kitchen and stopped short when she caught a look at Evan's battered face. "What happened?"

Evan went completely rigid.

"Man versus surfboard," Stephanie said. "Surfboard won."

Grace came in for a closer look. "Are you okay?"

Stephanie stabbed Evan in the back with her fingernail, hoping to snap him out of his stupor. She really wanted to smack him upside the head!

"I'm fine," he said without looking at Grace.

Reaching into the first aid kit, Grace found a particular tube of ointment and handed it to Stephanie. "Use this. It's antibacterial."

"Why don't you take over?" Stephanie said. "I've got stuff in the oven I need to tend to."

Evan started to get up. "Wait a minute."

Stephanie reseated him with a hand to his shoulder. Bending down close to his ear, she said, "Man up."

As she walked away, she felt his stare burning holes right through her.

EVAN WOULDN'T HAVE BELIEVED THIS DAY COULD GET ANY WORSE. THE last person he'd expected to see at his parents' house was Grace.

As she dabbed ointment on his wounds, she went out of her way to avoid eye contact. He wanted to ask her why she was there, but he assumed Stephanie had invited her. Or maybe she'd come hoping to see him again? And how did he feel about that?

His every nerve ending felt like it was on fire and not because of his injuries. No, it was *her*. She was doing it again—whatever it was that she did to him. It was like a spell or something. She only had to touch him and he forgot all about his plans and his rules and his aversion to anything that even resembled a relationship.

"Just so you know," she said as she dabbed at his wounds, "I'm here because Stephanie asked me to be, and not for any other reason."

"I never thought otherwise," Evan said, lying through his teeth.

"Good. I wouldn't want you to think it had anything to do with you, because it didn't."

Well, he thought, *that wasn't very nice*, but it was probably the least of what he deserved. He sat still for as long as he could before he grabbed hold of her hand and withdrew it from his face. "That ought to do it." He tried to ignore the current that traveled through him like lightning when his skin came into contact with hers.

"But there's a whole area—"

"It's fine."

She shrugged and tossed the ointment into the first aid kit. "Suit yourself."

The potentially awkward moment was diffused by the arrival of Dr. David Lawrence, Victoria Stevens, the nurse practitioner-midwife at the clinic, and Seamus O'Grady, who made a beeline for Grace.

Evan watched in stunned amazement as Seamus greeted Grace as if she was his long-lost best friend, making a big production out of hugging her and kissing her cheek.

And Grace! She giggled like a schoolgirl. What the hell was that about? How did they even know each other?

"Gracie, my love, help me find a beer," Seamus said in the ridiculous accent that made the women swoon. *Whatever!* "This has been the longest day in the history of long days."

He thought *he'd* had a long day? And her name was *Grace*, not *Gracie*. Why didn't she tell the bloody bloke that?

Seamus tucked Grace's hand into the crook of his arm and

whisked her away. She never so much as glanced at Evan as she took off with the Irishman.

After what they'd shared just twenty-four hours earlier, who did she think she was, flaunting another guy right in front of his face? Apparently, she was pissed he hadn't called her. Maybe he hadn't called her *yet*. Had that occurred to her?

Couldn't a guy take a few hours to get his head together after a woman turns his well-ordered world upside down? And what was with her telling her friends about what'd happened between them? As if a guy could do that and get away with it. Total double standard!

Grant handed him a beer. "Looks like you could use this more than me."

"What's the latest protocol on next-day phone calls?" Evan asked his older brother. He kept an eye on Grace and Seamus, who were standing far too close on the back deck. She was wearing a dress that showcased her abundant curves, and Evan rolled his hands into fists to keep from going out there and dragging her away from that Irish charmer.

"What do you mean?" Grant asked.

"You go out with a girl, have a good time and want to see her again. How long do you have to call her, before you've officially blown it?"

"Define 'have a good time.'"

"You know. A good time."

Grant sighed with exasperation. "*Sex* or no *sex*?"

Evan wished he'd never started this conversation. "Option A."

"With sex, I'd say a day. Two at the most."

"So I'm not a jerk because I left before she was awake and didn't call her today. I knew it."

"Wait, *whoa*. You left *before* she was awake, and you didn't call her *all day*?"

"You just said—"

Grant looked at Grace, who was laughing at every word Seamus had to say. To Evan, her laughter had never been more inappropriate.

"I hate to say it, but you might've blown it, bro."

Hearing his brother say those words, Evan wanted to hit Rewind and undo this entire day. Everything he'd done had been wrong. He wanted to be there when she woke up, share breakfast in bed with her, entice her into the shower and spend the entire day with her. He couldn't have blown it beyond repair. Not yet.

He stood and headed for the deck.

"Evan!" Grant grabbed his arm. "Wait! Don't go out there spoiling for a fight. Think about what you're doing."

Evan tried unsuccessfully to shake off his brother's iron grip. "I want to talk to her."

"She's talking to Seamus right now. Bide your time. Wait until she's alone."

"I don't want her talking to Seamus," Evan said, consumed, for the first time in his entire life, by a fit of jealousy so fierce it stole the breath from his lungs.

Grant, that son of a bitch, threw his head back and *laughed*. "Welcome to the club, my friend."

Infuriated by his brother's laughter, Evan said, "What club? What the hell are you talking about?"

"It's a super-secret club for guys who've lost their minds over a woman. I'm a new member, but Mac, Joe and Luke are veterans. They can probably advise you better than I can."

"Keep your damned club. I haven't lost my mind or anything else over her."

"Then why do you look like you want to go out there and disembowel poor Seamus?"

"I do not look like that."

Luke hobbled up to them on his crutches. "Whoa," he said when he got a good look at Evan's battered face. "Definite improvement."

Evan scowled at Luke.

"Don't mind him," Grant said. "He's pissed because his lady is talking to someone else."

"He has a lady?" Luke asked as Mac joined them with Hailey asleep in his arms.

"Who has a lady?" Mac asked

Grant nodded to the deck. "Evan."

"*Evan* has a *lady*?" Mac asked, incredulous.

"I like Grace," Luke said. "Syd and I met her on the ferry. She's great."

"Everyone likes her," Grant said. "Especially Evan. Right, Ev? Apparently, Seamus likes her, too. That's making our boy *good* and mad."

Since he wasn't allowed to talk to her at the moment and didn't feel like listening to any more of his brother's bullshit, Evan headed upstairs to take a shower.

Their laughter followed him all the way up.

CHAPTER 20

$\mathcal{E}$merging from the shower, Evan blotted water from his face, which was starting to seriously hurt. He threw on shorts and a T-shirt and sat on the bed in his childhood room. Everything was just as he'd left it—surfing posters, trophies, photos of Cindy Crawford, his first celebrity crush, posters of the metal bands he'd loved back then, and the mystery novels he'd devoured as a kid. When was the last time he'd read a book? He couldn't remember.

Looking to kill some time before he returned to the party (because he refused to hide out *and* he wanted to know if Grace was still talking to Seamus), Evan picked up his cell phone to return the call from his manager, Jack Beaumont.

"Evan," Jack said, sounding relieved. "I'm glad to hear back from you."

Jack's unusually somber tone put Evan instantly on alert. "What's going on?"

"I'm afraid I've got some bad news."

Evan sat perfectly still as he listened to Jack's recitation of how Evan's recording company, Starlight Records, had filed for bankruptcy over the weekend and how all its assets—including Evan's record—were tied up in the legal proceedings.

He should've known. It had all been too perfect. From the first meeting with Starlight to the recording process to the demos, it had been too smooth. Something was bound to go wrong, because it would've been too much to hope that the album would be released on time and launch the career he'd worked so hard for all these years.

"There is some good news," Jack was saying when Evan tuned back in. "Are you still with me? Evan?"

Clearing the lump from his throat, Evan said, "Yeah, I'm here."

"Word is that Buddy Longstreet's company, Long Road Records, has been in touch with the attorneys for Starlight. Buddy wants to buy your record from them and put it out under his label. If that happens, you're totally golden—even more so than you would've been with Starlight."

He didn't have to tell Evan that. Long Road was one of the top dogs in Nashville, whereas Starlight was small potatoes. Nonetheless, Evan had been thrilled to ink a deal with them after years of trying to get noticed in the business. "And if it doesn't?"

"Well, then I guess you're fucked until the bankruptcy proceedings wind through the courts."

Jack didn't have to tell him that would take years.

"What would that mean for the tour?"

"I haven't heard anything for certain, but I assume there's no tour without the album. We'll have to wait to hear from Buddy's people."

As he tried to frantically process the implications, Evan's head spun and his stomach churned.

"I know this is a huge disappointment to you," Jack said. "Hell, it is to me, too. But there's still a chance it'll all work out. Say your prayers."

"I'll get right on that. Would it help anything if I came there?"

"Nah, sit tight and let the suits figure it out. I've got our attorneys working the phones. I'll let you know as soon as I hear anything more. I'm real sorry, Evan."

"Me, too." As he ended the call and tossed the phone aside, Evan wished he'd never bothered to return the call. Ignorance was truly bliss. After a day this crappy, there was really only one thing to do—get good and stinking drunk.

With that goal in mind, Evan got up and headed back downstairs.

GRANT GATHERED EVERYONE INTO THE FAMILY ROOM, KEEPING A watchful eye on Stephanie. He'd been shocked when she suggested they host the party for Abby. It was awfully good of her to be so generous toward his ex-girlfriend. When he'd said as much to her, she'd replied, "She's no threat to me. She's in love with Cal." Grant smiled, remembering how he'd added, "And I'm in love with you."

Watching Stephanie interact with his family and friends as if she'd been part of their lives for years rather than months, Grant was filled with excitement about all they had to look forward to. In a few months, after they got her stepfather out of jail, Grant would ask her to marry him. Since she'd been denied so much in her life, he wanted to give her everything, including a proposal she'd never forget.

But tonight was all about Abby, so Grant gave a short whistle to quiet the boisterous group. When he had their attention, he turned to the woman who'd been at the center of his life for close to a decade, until she got tired of waiting for him to pay attention to their relationship. Grant was thankful they'd been able to maintain their friendship after they broke up.

"Abby, we've all come here tonight to wish you—and Cal—well in your new lives in Texas. We want you to know we'll miss you both, and we hope you'll get back here to visit once in a while. We're also pulling for Cal's mom to make a full recovery."

"Hear, hear," Ned Saunders said.

With tears in her big brown eyes, Abby stood to hug Grant. "Thank you, Grant—and Stephanie—for hosting this lovely party," Abby said, wiping her eyes as she spoke. "I'm so happy to be able to see everyone before I leave but also sad to know it'll be a while before we're together again. Please know how much I love you and how much I'll miss you. Any time you feel like getting off the island, come on down to Austin. Our door will always be open."

As Abby handed out hugs to her friends, Grant noticed Evan had reappeared and was hovering in the doorway. Immediately, his brother zeroed in on Grace, who was sitting next to Seamus on the sofa. Evan, the poor bastard, looked like he'd been hit by a bus. Grant wondered if he'd looked that pathetic when he'd been fighting what he felt for Stephanie. With hindsight, he could see what a stupid waste of time that had been.

Watching her hug Abby as if they were old friends, Grant decided if he'd been pathetic, it was well worth it. *She* was well worth it.

THE PARTY WAS STARTING TO WIND DOWN WHEN SOMEONE POUNDED ON the front door.

"I'll get it," Mac said. On his parents' front porch was a man he'd never seen before. He was tall with gray hair and a scowl on a face that might've once been handsome. "Hi, there. Help you with something?"

"I'm looking for Francine Chester and her daughters, Maddie and Tiffany. Someone told me they might be here."

Instantly on alert, Mac stood up a little straighter. "Who wants to know?"

"None of your business. Just answer the question."

Mac pushed open the screen door and stepped onto the deck, pulling the inside door closed behind him. "Since this is my family's home and one of the women you're looking for is my wife, I'd say it's very much my business."

"So you're the McCarthy kid Maddie married."

The statement was said with such disdain and condescension that Mac chose not to dignify it with a response. "And you are?"

"Your father-in-law."

Even though he was shocked, Mac went out of his way to deny

Bobby Chester the satisfaction of the big reaction he so clearly wanted. "I don't have a father-in-law."

"You do now. I want to see my wife and daughters. Immediately."

"They don't want to see you."

"And you speak for them?"

"You bet I do. The only thing they want from you is a divorce so Francine can marry the man she loves—the man she's always loved."

Bobby's eyes narrowed. "What the hell does that mean?"

Mac caught a whiff of liquor on the older man's breath. "It means, you son of a bitch, you can't come back here thirty years after you left them and think you can pick right up like nothing ever happened. You're *nothing* to them. In fact, you're less than nothing."

Bobby's right hand rolled into a fist.

"Don't even think about it."

"You've got a lot of nerve talking to me like that. This is none of your business."

"Anything that affects my wife and her family is my business. Now, I want you to turn around and get the hell out of here before I call my friend the police chief to come out here and take out the trash."

The inside door swung open. "Mac? Are you out there?"

"Go back inside, Maddie. I'll be right there."

"Does the little woman always do what you tell her to do?"

It took all the self-control Mac possessed not to deck the guy.

Despite Mac's overwhelming desire to protect her from ever having to see her deadbeat father again, Maddie came outside. She rested a hand on Mac's arm, which had an instant calming effect on him. He had no idea how she did that.

"What do you want?" she asked her father.

"I want to talk to you and your mother and your sister."

"We have nothing to say to you. You should go now."

Bobby crossed his arms over his chest in a mulish gesture that reminded Mac of something Thomas might do. "I'm not going anywhere until I talk to the three of you."

"Come on, Mac," Maddie said, taking Mac's hand. "Let's go back inside to our friends."

"Don't you dare walk away from me, young lady," Bobby said.

"Why not?" Maddie amazed Mac with her calm when he knew she had to be falling apart inside. "Isn't that what you did to me?"

Mac could see that her comment scored a direct hit with her father.

"I need to talk to you," Bobby said, sounding more desperate than belligerent now. "Please."

"I'm sorry," Maddie said, unfailingly polite even when she had no reason to be. "But that's not going to happen."

"Until you and your sister spend some time with me—and I'm talking more than five minutes—there'll be no divorce."

With that, Bobby finally got Maddie's attention. She stared at him, agog. "You can't be serious."

Mac slipped an arm around her, wanting to shield her from the pain and hoping to hold himself back from physically harming her father, since he knew she wouldn't appreciate that.

"I'm dead serious. If I give her the divorce, I'll never see any of you again."

"You lost the right to see us when you walked away without a word."

"I was young and stupid and overwhelmed by the responsibility."

Maddie's entire body stiffened. "Do you think I'm not overwhelmed by the responsibility for my children? Do you think I wasn't overwhelmed when my son's biological father left me without even knowing I was pregnant? I never once, during the most difficult years of my life, considered *leaving* my child. Not once."

"It's different for mothers—"

"Like hell it is," Mac growled. "We've heard more than enough. You do what you have to, but stay away from my family. You've got nothing we need." Squeezing her shoulder, he said, "Come on, babe. Let's go in."

The second they were inside the house, she began to tremble uncontrollably, which infuriated Mac. He should've smashed the guy's face in when he had the chance.

"Come here, baby," Mac said, bringing her into his embrace. "It's okay. Everything's okay."

She clung to him. "Why would he come here? Why does he want to see us? I don't get it."

"He's feeling guilty, and he's probably all alone."

"Which is his own fault."

"I'm sure he knows that."

"God, Mac, what if he meant it when he said he won't give Mom the divorce unless Tiffany and I—"

"Unless you and Tiffany do what?" Francine asked.

Mac and Maddie broke apart and turned to her.

"Nothing, Mom. It's nothing."

"Was your father here?"

Maddie seemed to be weighing what she should say to her mother. Mac reached for her hand, nodding in encouragement.

"He . . . um, he said he wants to spend some time with Tiff and me or—"

"Or there's no divorce," Francine said. "Right?"

"Something like that."

"Then there'll be no divorce."

"But then you and Ned can't get married!"

Francine shrugged. "We'll still get to spend every day together for the rest of our lives. We don't need a piece of paper to make it official."

Ned came up behind Francine and put his arm around her. "That's right, doll. Fuck him and his divorce."

As the other three laughed at Ned's bluntness, Mac was filled with affection for the man who'd been like a second father to him and his siblings. He'd said just what the women needed to hear.

Francine embraced her daughter. "No matter what, you're not spending any time with him. I'd never ask you to do that on my behalf."

"What about me?" Tiffany asked as she joined them. "Do I have any say in the matter?"

"Honey," Francine said, reaching out a hand to her younger daughter. "You don't have to see him, either."

"What if I want to?"

Francine was clearly caught off guard by the question.

"I have nothing of him," Tiffany said. "Not a single memory. I know what he did was horrible, but I can't help being curious about him."

Francine considered that for a long moment. "Then you ought to see him if that's what you feel you need to satisfy your curiosity."

"And you wouldn't mind?"

"Whatever you want to do is fine with me."

"I don't know if I'll actually do it," Tiffany said, "but it's good to know you wouldn't mind."

"I'm ready to go home," Francine said to Ned. "Let's go say our good-byes to Abby and the others."

"Lead the way, doll."

Tiffany went with them, leaving Mac and Maddie alone in the front hall.

"So if Tiffany sees him and gives him what he wants, then it would just be me standing in the way of my mom and Ned being able to get married," Maddie said.

The dull, flat tone, which was so out of character for her, pained Mac. This whole situation pained him. Why did her father have to show up now, when she was finally happy and settled and at peace with the past?

"You certainly don't have to do anything you don't want to, babe."

"I know." She went up on tiptoes to kiss him. "Thanks for what you did out there."

"Any time."

"Let's get our kids and go home."

As Mac followed her into the family room where his cousin Laura kept watch over their children, he was filled with worry over what his wife might be willing to sacrifice to ensure her mother's happiness.

CHAPTER 21

*I*f it hadn't been for the fact that she couldn't take her mind or her eyes off Evan McCarthy, this would've been one of the best nights of Grace's life. In addition to the abundance of attention she'd received from Seamus, she was now engaged in a fascinating conversation with Gansett's sexy police chief, Blaine Taylor.

His brown hair was streaked with blond highlights, and his skin was deeply tanned from hours in the sun. He had soft brown eyes, what her mother would call "kind" eyes, and they'd been focused on her for the last fifteen minutes.

They were talking about OxyContin and the problems pharmacies were having with people breaking in, looking to steal the pain medication to feed their addiction.

"I was on a task force on my old job," he said. "It's a real problem in the cities."

"We've seen it in our small town, too." Grace appreciated the way he gave her his full attention rather than that half-hearted, patiently indulgent thing guys often did when they couldn't care less about what a woman was saying. She'd been on the receiving end of that treatment far too often when she was heavy.

"At the hospital where I work, we have all sorts of special protocols for keeping that—and some of the other more popular addictive prescription drugs—locked up where no one can get to them even if they manage to breach the pharmacy itself," she said. "We've also been involved in a lot of community outreach projects with the local high schools."

"Remember the good old days when cocaine and heroin were our biggest problems?"

Grace laughed. "Those were the days."

He lowered his voice. "Did I hear a rumor in town about you and Gold's?"

"Wow, news travels fast around here."

"I saw the transfer in ownership on the docket for the town council meeting next week."

"Mrs. Gold tells me it's just a formality, to make the council aware of the change. I don't even have to be there."

"Should be no big deal." He touched his beer bottle to the glass of wine she'd been nursing all evening. "Congratulations."

"Thanks. I'm looking forward to the challenge."

"Maybe we can work together on a program for the kids at the island school. We don't have a lot of drug issues here, but most of the kids will be leaving the island for college, and it would be good to send them out into the world prepared for what they might face."

While there was nothing overtly flirtatious in Blaine's words or expression, Grace sensed that he might be interested in getting to know her better. At least she thought she might sense something. What did she know about such things? "I'd love to do that."

"Great," Blaine said with a smile that would've made her swoon before she knew Evan McCarthy was in the world. Damn him! Had he ruined her for all other men? Was that her fate after one night with him? "Give me a call at the station after you get settled, and we'll get together for dinner to work out the details."

Okay, that sounded an awful lot like a date. Where had all these lovely men been hiding before she met Evan?

Laura came up to them. "Sorry to interrupt, but Owen is giving me a lift back to town before he goes to work. Are you ready to go, Grace?"

"I'll stay for a bit to help Stephanie clean up. I can get a ride from someone."

"I'll take you, Gracie," Seamus called from across the room, waggling his brows suggestively at her.

Grace's face heated with embarrassment. "Thank you, Seamus."

Laura leaned in to whisper in Grace's ear, "Keep it up. Evan is *seething* with jealousy."

"Keep what up?" Grace said out loud. "He is not!"

"Is too," Laura said, kissing Grace's cheek. "Give me a ring tomorrow before you leave." She pressed a slip of paper into Grace's hand. "Here's my number."

"I'll do that."

"What was that all about?" Blaine asked after Laura had left with Owen.

Since she couldn't very well mention to Blaine that she was apparently making Evan jealous by talking to him, she said, "Laura is just being silly. I'm going to give Stephanie a hand with the cleanup, but I'll be in touch when I get back to the island."

"I'll look forward to hearing from you. It was nice to meet you, Grace."

"You, too."

Grace went into the kitchen, where Stephanie was up to her elbows in soapsuds.

"Look who it is," Stephanie said. "Miss Congeniality. The *belle* of the ball."

Grace took a garbage bag someone had left on the counter and started collecting empty beer bottles. "What's that supposed to mean?"

"All the single guys at the party have chatted you up."

"So what? They're just being friendly."

"Uh-huh. Whatever you say, Miss Gansett Island." Stephanie raised her chin to draw Grace's attention to the window that overlooked the deck. "Poor old Evan. He's *dying* out there watching you work the room."

"He couldn't care less what I do."

"Oh, trust me, he cares, Grace. That's his problem. He has no idea what to do about it because it's never happened before. He's skated through life without a care in the world until he met you and fell flat on his face. I hope you can excuse his bad behavior today and chalk it up to male stupidity."

Grace leaned against the counter, contemplating what Stephanie had said. "You're saying I should give him a second chance?"

"Only if you want to. I'd say the ball is firmly in your court."

Grace took a moment, choosing her words carefully. "I went through a lot of rough years to get where I am today. Just wearing this dress," she said, gesturing to the silky, slinky fabric, "is a big deal for me. I never imagined I'd get to the point where I'd feel comfortable showing off my arms. I spent years—literally *years*—in a gym trying to reinvent myself. After all that work, I want a real man, not a boy pretending to be a man."

Stephanie dried off her hands and turned to face Grace. "I have a feeling there's a really good man in there trying to get out. If you had it in you to be a little patient and maybe a bit indulgent, you might find he's everything you could ever hope for."

"Is that what you did with Grant?"

"I guess I did," Stephanie said, smiling. "When we met, he was still hung up on Abby and determined to get her back any way he could."

"That must've been hard to deal with, especially if you were interested in him yourself."

"I wasn't so much interested in him at the beginning as I was attracted to him. I'm ashamed to admit that when I first met him, I was totally wowed by how he looks." With a sheepish grin, she shrugged. "What can I say? I'm only human, and he's hot."

Grace laughed. "I've got the same problem with Evan. I look at him and go stupid in the head."

"You'll be glad to know that passes after a while. They become less godlike and more like mortal men. That's when the trouble starts."

"Are you guys still fighting?"

"Not at the moment. I'm sure we will once we get back to work on" the screenplay, but he assures me that all the fighting in the world won't change how he feels about me."

"That's very sweet."

"Isn't it? He knows all my insecurities and goes out of his way to reassure me."

"Speaking of insecurities, I never got around to telling Evan about the surgery."

"Maybe you should."

"I've been annoyed with him all day for blowing me off, but I wasn't exactly an open book with him, either. I also never mentioned the deal with Gold's. I didn't want him to think it has anything to do with him, you know?"

"That's perfectly understandable. If I were you, I wouldn't write him off yet. If he's anything at all like his brother, and I think he might be, he's well worth the effort to make him civilized."

As Grace laughed at Stephanie's statement, Evan came into the kitchen and made a beeline for the fridge. He withdrew a beer, popped off the cap, downed half of it in one swallow and followed it with a loud belch.

That sent Grace and Stephanie into a fit of laughter, which made him scowl.

"What's so funny?" he asked.

Was it Grace's imagination or was he going out of his way not to look at her?

"You are, you uncivilized beast," Stephanie said.

"Gracie, my love, are you ready to go?" Seamus asked as he came into the kitchen. "I'm on the eight o'clock boat in the morning, and I need my beauty sleep."

"No, you don't." Grace played along with Seamus's outrageousness, enjoying that Evan was, in fact, seething, now that she noticed. "You're beautiful just the way you are."

Staggering backward, Seamus rested a hand on his heart. "Are you teasing me, Gracie? Because if you are, I don't think I'll survive it."

"Oh my freaking *God*," Evan muttered as he slammed his way toward the deck. "I think I just threw up in my mouth."

"Where else would you throw up?" Stephanie called after him. "In your armpit?"

The whole situation struck Grace as ridiculously funny. She was still laughing when Seamus escorted her out of the McCarthy's home and into his company truck for the short ride back to town.

AFTER SEAMUS DROPPED HER OFF WITH A FRIENDLY PECK ON THE CHEEK, Grace took a shower and pulled on the robe provided by the hotel. She brushed her hair and teeth and then stared at her reflection in the mirror. How was it possible that everything had changed and she still looked exactly the same?

Surely after all that had happened in the last few days there ought to be some sort of outward sign to tell the world this wasn't the same Grace Ryan who'd arrived on the island yesterday. That Grace had been hesitant and uncertain. This Grace was confident and ready to take on the world.

No matter what happened from here on out, there was no going back to who she used to be, and she had Evan to thank for part of her transformation. He'd made her feel beautiful and sexy and desirable, and she'd never forget him for that.

She startled when someone pounded on her door. Her heart skipped a few beats as she checked the peephole and found Evan was staring furiously at her.

"Grace!" More pounding. "Open the damned door. Is he in there? Did you let him in? Grace, come on . . . Open the door." In a quieter, more urgent tone, he said, "Please."

Worried about disturbing her neighbors, Grace unlocked the door and opened it.

Reeking of beer and something stronger, he leaned against the doorjamb. His poor face . . . It had to be hurting something fierce by now. His eyes traveled the length of her, pausing at the V over her breasts where the lapels of the robe came together, before moving down and then back up to her face. All he'd done was look at her, but Grace felt like he'd stripped her naked.

"Is he here?" he asked, trying to see around her.

"Who?"

"Your new boyfriend."

What was he talking about? "I don't have a boyfriend."

"Did that Irishman kiss you?"

"Maybe," Grace said with a coy smile. Of course when his face fell with dismay, she immediately felt bad for being intentionally mean to him. She pointed to her cheek. "He kissed me right here."

At that, Evan brightened considerably. "Can I come in?"

"Why do you want to?"

"This has been the worst day ever. I need a friend."

"Are we friends?"

"Grace . . . I'm sorry. I shouldn't have left this morning. I was . . . I was confused."

"Are you still confused?"

"Yes. No. I don't know."

Her lips began to quiver. He was entirely too cute for his own good. His wounded look didn't help to quell the brewing laughter.

"Are you going to laugh at me?" he asked.

"I'm trying not to."

Before she could gauge his intent, he leaned forward, buried his lips in the curve of her neck and destroyed her resistance. "Can I come in?" he whispered. "Please?"

"As long as you know nothing is going to happen."

"By nothing, do you mean—"

"*Nothing.*" She took his hand and led him into the room, closing the door behind them.

"Grace." He pulled her close and wrapped his arms around her.

Smiling at how adorable he was, even when he was more than half drunk, she returned his embrace, stroking a comforting hand over his hair. "I'm sorry you had such a rough day."

"It's all your fault."

Once again, she found herself choking back a laugh. *"How* is it my fault?"

"You've cast some sort of spell on me. That's the only possible explanation."

"For what?"

"For the fact that I can't stop thinking about you. I think about you all the time. I don't understand it." He raised his head and met her gaze. "Tell me the truth—did you cast some sort of spell over me? Did you slip me some pharmacy thing that rebooted my computer?"

Grace shook with silent laughter.

"It's not funny! You're making me into a lunatic!"

"Tell me you didn't drive here."

"Of course I didn't," he said, full of indignation. "I don't drink and drive."

Grace led him to the bed and pushed him down. Knocking his flip-flops off his feet, she lifted his legs onto the bed and settled his head on the pillow.

"Grace . . . Come here with me." As he held out his hand to her, his eyes fluttered closed. "Tell me what you did to me. Whatever it is, you can undo it, right?"

Grace took his hand and crawled onto the bed next to him. "I don't think it can be undone."

Evan moaned. "So what am I supposed to do? How am I going to stop thinking about you every second of every day?"

Grace had never been more amused—or aroused—by a conversation. "I'm sure it'll pass in time. Just like a fever or a virus." She smoothed the hair off his forehead, the silky strands gliding through her fingers. "Give it a few days. You'll feel better."

He opened his eyes and turned his head to look at her. "I don't think it's going to pass."

They stared at each other for a long, breathless moment. Right then he could've asked her for the moon, and she would've found a way to get it for him. *Remain calm*, she told her racing heart. *He's not himself. Nothing he says tonight should be taken too seriously.*

"My record company is bankrupt," he murmured as his eyes closed again.

"What? *Evan!* What did you say?"

"It's all gone to shit. The company's bankrupt, and my album is caught up in it."

"Oh God." She pressed her lips gently to his abraded cheek. "I'm so sorry."

"Just as well." He reached for her. "Cuz I get stage fright. Did I tell you that?"

"No, you didn't," she said, touched to be in on a secret that she suspected he didn't share with just anyone. Moving closer to him, she rested her head on his chest and her hand on his belly while trying to process everything he'd said.

"Why do you let him call you Gracie?" His fingers combed through her hair rhythmically.

"Who?" Grace asked, trying to keep up with the ever-changing conversation.

"That Irish charmer. He's trying to take you away from me."

"I'm not with you. How can he take me away from you?"

The fingers in her hair tightened into a fist. "You are with me. You *have* to be with me. I can't stop thinking about you, about what we did. Right here. Last night."

Grace's entire body flushed with heat at the reminder.

"It was so good, wasn't it, Grace?"

"Yes."

"Why did you pick me to cast your spell on?"

"Because you're so handsome, and I love dimples. You didn't stand a chance."

"You did this to me," he said, his voice starting to fade as sleep beckoned. "You have to stay with me until we can fix it."

She wondered if he'd remember any of this in the morning.

"Grace? You gotta promise me. You'll stay with me, won't you? I need you."

Her heart contracted, and the breath got caught in her lungs. If only . . . "Yes, Evan, I'll stay with you. Tomorrow will be a better day. Don't worry."

"Grace," he said on a sigh the instant before his body slackened into sleep.

Grace was awake for a long time thinking about what he'd said, watching him sleep and listening to the strong beat of his heart.

CHAPTER 22

*P*ain woke Evan early the next morning. His face was on fire, and an entire drum corps had taken up residence inside his skull. As long as he didn't move or breathe, he might survive. And then he opened his eyes to blinding sunlight streaming in through the blinds.

He quickly closed his eyes as pain ricocheted through his brain. It was official—he was never drinking again.

Somehow he'd ended up in Grace's hotel room. He had vague memories of pounding on her door and hugging her, but he didn't remember much else. And while the idea of moving was unimaginable, his tongue was stuck to the roof of his mouth and he needed to pee. Urgently.

Moving as slowly as he could, he sat up and waited for the pain to catch up to the movement. When it did, it took his breath away and left him hanging on the precipice as his stomach reacted with a surge of nausea.

"Christ have mercy," he muttered as he stood up and headed for the bathroom.

The door was closed, but not all the way, and Grace was talking to someone.

When he nudged the door open, she winced at the sight of him (he must be quite a sight), and gestured for them to switch places, giving him the bathroom.

After he took care of business and washed his mouth out with water and toothpaste, he tuned in to her conversation.

"I've applied for a ninety-day temporary license with the state of Rhode Island, so we should be good to go when I get back in two weeks. Since I'm licensed in Connecticut, they said the temporary wouldn't be a problem. I've applied with NABP to take the MPJE, so that's all set, too."

What the heck was she talking about?

"I've got a reservation on the ferry for two weeks from today. Will that give you enough time to vacate the apartment?" She paused to listen. "That sounds good. So you'll schedule the closing with Jim for that afternoon?" Another pause. "Perfect. I'll see you then. In the meantime, you have my number if anything comes up."

By the time she ended the call, Evan had started to put two and two together, but nothing was adding up. "Something you want to tell me?"

"Good morning. How're you feeling?"

"I feel like shit. What's going on, Grace?"

Her face flushed, and just like that, he wanted her. While his first impulse was to get the hell out of there, he'd done that once before. Today, he was going to stay and somehow rid his system of the madness she'd inflicted upon him. Maybe then he could get on with his life without thoughts of her tormenting him morning, noon and night.

"I was going to tell you . . ."

He realized that whatever she needed to tell him was making her nervous. "Tell me what?"

"I'm buying Gold's."

The statement hung in the air between them like a live wire. He had no idea what to say.

"Before you totally freak out or think this is a nefarious plot to trap you in a godforsaken relationship, let me set your mind at ease. This has nothing at all to do with you."

"I know that." Was it possible for a head to explode? If so, his was about to.

She went into the bathroom and returned with two painkillers that she dropped into his hand. "I hope so, because this was in the works before I saw you on Saturday. For all I knew, I was going to pay you back the money I owed you and go on my way without ever seeing you again."

Appreciating that she took care of him without even seeming to think about it, he popped the pills into his mouth and washed them down with the glass of water she gave him. "And was that what you wanted?" He stepped closer to her, drawn to her like a magnet to steel. He couldn't be in the room with her and *not* touch her. The discovery, like so many others in the last few days, was unsettling and worrisome. "To never see me again?"

"We want different things, Evan. You're still sowing your wild oats, and I'm looking for someone who wants to be with just me."

"I want to be with just you." The words were out of his mouth before he had fully considered the implications. As long as he was on a roll, he might as well go all the way. "And I don't want you with anyone else."

"Evan, you don't know what you're saying—"

"I know exactly what I'm saying." The thought of her with another guy did him in. With his hands on her hips, he tugged her in tight against him and took her mouth in a kiss that should've been sweet and innocent, like her. But the instant her lips met his, he lost his mind after the long day of dreaming about her. The kiss became fierce and demanding. He fisted her hair to keep her right where he wanted her as he set out to weaken her defenses with passionate kisses.

When he finally came up for air, they were both breathing hard. Her brown eyes were focused on his mouth, and when she ran her tongue over her bottom lip, he nearly came in his pants. He tugged on the belt holding her robe together and about swallowed his tongue when he realized she was naked under there.

"Wait, Evan . . ." She grabbed hold of his hands before they could venture inside the robe. "We need to talk."

"We will." He pressed his lips to the spot on her neck that he already knew rendered her helpless and pushed the robe off her shoulders.

"*Evan . . .*" She tilted her neck to give him a better angle.

Sliding his hands from her hips over her ribs, he cupped her breasts and ran his thumbs over the pebbled tips. The aching drum-beat in his head was nothing compared to the throbbing need that surged straight to his groin when her soft hands ventured under his T-shirt to pull it up and over his head.

Returning his hands to her breasts, he backed her up to the bed and came down on top of her, lowering his head to taste one of the pink-tipped crests. He took his time, determined to savor every inch of her before he sated his own overwhelming desire. While his free hand pinched and rolled her other nipple, he sucked hard on the one in his mouth.

Her hips launched off the bed, seeking him.

Evan pushed his erection into the V of her legs, simulating what he wanted more than his next breath. While everything in him was urging him to hurry, he didn't. He licked and sucked and squeezed, reveling in every sigh and moan he drew from her.

"Evan. *Please . . .*"

"What do you want, love?" The word rolled off his tongue, as if it was the most natural thing in the world for him to use such an endearment.

Her eyes flew open and connected with his, leaving no doubt that she'd heard him.

It occurred to Evan that he could still put a stop to this whole thing. He could stand up, utter his apologies and get the hell out of there before she succeeded in totally changing his life. Or he could stay. He could try his best to be the guy she wanted and deserved. The choice was his, and the time was now. The one thing he knew for sure was that if he made love to her again, there'd be no going back and no running away. Not this time.

Watching him study her, Grace furrowed her brows in confusion. "Is something wrong?"

Say it. Tell her there's something very wrong. Tell her you can't do this. It's not your thing. She deserves better. Say what she needs to hear so she'll know it's you, not her.

She ran her fingers through his hair and then gently over the wound on his face. "Are you in pain? Evan? What is it?"

"I . . . I don't want you to see anyone else but me." Now where in the hell had that come from? That wasn't what he'd planned to say! Oh, who was he trying to fool? If he walked away from her, she'd haunt him for the rest of his life. She'd be with him everywhere he went, and he would never escape the yearning for more of her.

Her face slackened with shock at his declaration. "What're you saying?"

He kissed her again, a tongue-tangling kiss that went on for what felt like forever. "I'm saying," he said, kissing her face, the end of her nose, each eyelid and then her lips again, "that I don't want you to do this with anyone but me."

Kissing his way down the front of her, he paid homage to each breast before continuing to her belly. He could tell by her gasp that he shocked her again when he delved his tongue into her belly button. Looking up at her, he said, "Is that going to be a problem?"

She made him wait a long, breathless moment before she said, "No."

With that single word, she sealed her fate—and his. Using his shoulders to push her legs apart, he settled between them, teasing her with his fingers as he left openmouthed kisses on her hips and then her core.

"*Evan!* Oh my God." Her voice hitched on what sounded like a sob as he teased her with his tongue for a long time before he sucked hard on her clitoris and sank two fingers deep into her. The abrasions on his face hurt like a son of a bitch, but he wasn't about to let that stop him from bringing her the ultimate pleasure. She came apart under him, thrashing and crying out.

Reluctant to leave her, even for a minute, Evan reached for the condoms that were still on the bedside table from the other night and rolled one on. Returning to her, he said, "Hey, are you still with me?"

She opened her eyes and looked up at him with affection that touched him deep inside, in a place no one else had ever reached. "Barely."

Did she have any idea how cute and sexy and sweet she was when she looked at him with amusement and affection in her eyes?

"I need to be inside you." With his elbows propped on either side of her head, he used both hands to brush the hair back from her face. "Are you sore from the other night?"

"Not anymore."

He pressed the head of his cock against tender flesh that was slick and ready for him. "So you were? Yesterday?"

She raised her hips, seeking him as she caressed his back in gentle strokes that somehow managed to calm him when he was feeling anything but calm. "A little."

"I'm sorry about that. I should've been here to make sure you were okay." Capturing her bottom lip between his teeth, he ran his tongue back and forth over it. "It was wrong of me to leave the way I did yesterday morning. Do you forgive me?"

"No," she said, breathlessly, grasping his ass with both hands to encourage him to take her.

"Grace . . . Come on! I'm being serious. Tell me you forgive me."

"I shouldn't."

"No," he said, kissing her again because he couldn't help himself. "You really shouldn't, but you will, won't you?"

"This one time." She looked up at him, as if to ensure he understood what she was saying. "Not a second time."

"I've learned my lesson. Don't worry." Relieved, he flexed his hips and entered her slowly, carefully, holding his breath until he was deep inside her. "Grace . . . Ah, you feel so good." Letting his forehead drop to her chest, he tried to summon the control he needed to make this good for her.

The light stroke of her fingers on the back of his neck was nearly his undoing. Every time she touched him, it was like the first time all over again.

"Wrap your legs around my hips," he said.

Watching him with a mixture of awe and trepidation, she did as he asked.

The new position allowed him to go deeper, which made her gasp in surprise and then moan with what sounded like pleasure.

"Good?"

She nodded and dragged his head down for another of those kisses that made him so crazy—sweet and hot at the same time.

He hooked his arms around her legs, opening her even further. "Touch yourself," he said, his voice harsh from the effort it took to hold back and wait for her.

Her face turned bright red, which he found utterly charming. "I . . . I can't do that."

"Yes, you can." Reaching for her hand, he placed it between them and used his fingers on top of hers to stimulate her most sensitive place. The combined action of their two hands made her entire body flush with heat, turning her rosy nipples a darker shade. Her lips parted, and her back arched into him.

He picked up the pace, pumping into her with abandon. When he felt her legs start to quiver, he bent his head and sucked hard on her nipple.

As her internal muscles clamped down on his cock, she cried out, and the combination sent him with her into the single most exquisite release of his entire life. His body was racked with shudders as he came for what felt like forever.

Breathing hard, he rested on top of her, mindful of not crushing her with his weight. At least he knew now that what'd happened the other night wasn't a one-time thing. A bead of sweat rolled into his eye, forcing it to close against the burn.

He started to move off her, but her arms tightened around him. "Not yet," she said.

Settling into her loving embrace and breathing in her enticing scent, Evan acknowledged that his goose was good and truly cooked.

~

For Grace, that morning was something out of a dream. They made love again, slowly this time, and she couldn't help but notice something had changed. She wasn't sure what, but the first time they were together, he'd been lighthearted and amusing. Now he was serious, almost reverent, as if what they were doing together was the most important thing he'd ever done.

Grace wasn't complaining. This new Evan was someone she could see herself spending a lot of time with—if he was here to stay. And wasn't that the big question? If they spent another night together, which Evan would she wake up to tomorrow morning? The one who ran for his life at the first sign of something that smacked of commitment? Or the one who was so tender and attentive?

"I'm starving," he said, his voice muffled by her breast.

"I'll order some breakfast."

He kissed the side of her breast and left a trail of kisses to her lips. "I'll do it. What do you feel like?"

"An English muffin and some fruit would be good."

Turning up his nose, he said, "That's not enough for a bird."

She needed to tell him why she ate so little, but not now. "It's more than enough for me."

"If you say so." He got up to prowl around the room in the nude.

With her head propped on her hand, Grace watched his every move as he called room service and ordered enough food for ten people.

"Who's going to eat all that?" she asked when he crawled back into bed and pulled her close to him.

"I am." He nibbled on her neck, sending shivers down to her toes. "I need to keep up my strength so I can keep up with you."

"*Right*," she said, laughing. "Because it's all about me."

"It certainly is." He ran a finger lightly over her face, tucking a strand of hair behind her ear. "Everything is suddenly all about you."

"Why?" she asked, unnerved by the intensity of his gaze and the sincerity of his words.

"For one thing, you're beautiful—inside and out. But of course you already knew that."

She shook her head. "Not until you said so."

"Come on! What's wrong with the guys in Mystic? Are they blind?"

"They . . . I . . ." *Tell him! Say it!* "I don't know." Trying to redirect his attention, she rested her hand over the scabs on his face. "Does it hurt?"

"Not so bad. That's also your fault, you know."

"How in the world is your surfing accident my fault?"

"I was thinking about you when I should've been paying attention to the wave."

Touched by his confession, Grace brought his face down closer to her and placed soft kisses on the wounds.

"That makes it all better."

She smiled at him and rolled her eyes as he snuggled into her chest, seemingly his favorite place to be when they weren't making love. "You're full of it, McCarthy."

"So I've been told."

"Have there been a lot of them?"

"A lot of who?"

"Women." Grace was already sorry she'd asked because she didn't really want to know. Well, she kind of wanted to know.

"None that mattered." He brought her hand to his lips. "Until recently."

They were quiet for a long time before she said, "Evan?"

"Hmm?"

"Last night, you said something about your album and the record company being bankrupt. Is that true?"

Releasing a deep sigh, he said, "I'm afraid so."

"What will happen to your album?"

"That's a very good question. There's some talk about Buddy Longstreet's record company trying to buy it from Starlight—that's the company I signed with. If that happens, I'm saved."

"And if not?"

"I don't want to think about that. It'll mean years of litigation that'll totally screw my career before it even starts."

"I hope that doesn't happen. You've worked so hard. I want to see you get your big break."

"Even if it means you'll be here and I'll be God knows where most of the time?"

The question was asked somewhat flippantly, but there was nothing flippant about the way he looked at her, as if his very happiness depended upon her answer.

"If this is what we both want, then we'll make it work. Somehow."

"And is this what you want, Grace? Am I what you want?"

"I, ah . . ." She was afraid of appearing far too eager if she blurted out her true feelings on the matter.

"I've put you on the spot. I'm sorry."

"No, no." Before she could say anything more, there was a sharp rap at the door.

"That'll be breakfast," he said, bounding out of bed and heading for the door.

"Evan! Put some pants on!"

"Oh, hell, I knew I forgot something," he said as he pulled on his shorts.

Grace was seized by a fit of laughter as she tugged the covers up and over her shoulders, mortified by the idea of the waiter seeing her in bed.

Apparently, Evan had thought of that because he took the tray at the door and didn't let the waiter in. With a great flourish, he presented the meal to her in bed, tucking the rose from the tray behind her ear. "Coffee?"

"Absolutely," she said, ridiculously pleased by the romantic gesture.

"I take it you're addicted?"

"Completely and totally. I normally can't function without my first cup."

"You functioned just fine without it this morning."

The comment made her blush, which seemed to please him.

"Cream and sugar?"

"Both, please."

He handed her the mug and watched her take the first sip, awaiting her verdict.

"Perfect," she declared. In fact, coffee had never tasted better. She watched his brows furrow with concentration as he spread butter over her English muffin.

"Jelly?"

"Grape."

When he was satisfied with the distribution of condiments, he held it up for her to take a bite.

"You need to go ahead and eat," she said, "before it gets cold."

"If you insist." He handed the rest of the muffin to her and dove into the eggs and pancakes he'd ordered for himself. Sitting cross-legged on the bed, he looked like a little boy who'd had a particularly nasty crash on his two-wheeler the day before. But when he looked over at her with intent in his eyes, he was every bit the man. "You never answered me, you know."

Of course she knew exactly what he meant. "What was the question again?" she asked with a coy smile.

"The question, as you know darned well," he said, leaning over the tray to bring his face in close to hers, "is . . . am I what you want, Grace Ryan?"

CHAPTER 23

*a*t ten o'clock, Owen took the stairs to the third floor two at a time. Sure enough, the sounds of violent retching greeted him. Right on schedule, he thought grimly, hating that she had to go through this every day. Wondering how much longer the morning sickness would continue as a daily event, he stepped into Laura's suite and went to the kitchen to fill the kettle.

Leaving the tea to steep, he waited until the vomiting finally stopped before he went into the bathroom to collect her off the floor. After he helped her to rinse out her mouth and brush her teeth, he scooped her up.

"We've really got to stop meeting like this," she murmured as she looped her arms around his neck and rested her head on his chest.

Amazed that she could be so droll when she was clearly miserable, Owen chuckled. Her good humor in the face of so many daunting challenges was just one of the many things he was coming to love about her. *Love?* Yes, he thought with a sigh. At this point, it would be foolish to deny that he was falling fast and hard.

"Why the big sigh? I keep telling you that you don't have to do this."

"And I keep telling you I don't mind." Rather than take her back to bed, he settled into one of the upholstered armchairs, keeping her on his lap, next to the table where he'd set her tea.

"Owen—"

He rested his hand on her head to keep her snuggled into his chest. "Relax, Princess. I've got you."

Her entire body went lax as she released a deep, shuddering sigh of her own.

"Do you want your tea?"

"Not quite yet." When she flattened a hand on his chest, he wondered if she could feel the effect her nearness was having on his heart rate. "You've really got to stop waiting on me hand and foot. What'll I do without you when you leave?"

"I'm not going." He hadn't planned to tell her for a while yet, because he knew she'd protest. But the words were out of his mouth before he could contemplate the consequences of tipping his hand too soon.

She raised her head and met his gaze. Those dark circles under her eyes bothered him more than they should. He'd get rid of them if it was the last thing he ever did. "What do you mean you're not going? Of course you are! It's the great gig in Boston that you do every year—"

Owen placed a finger over her lips. "I'm not going."

"Why?"

His face twisted into a wry smile. "You know why, Princess."

Incredulous, she stared at him for the longest time, during which he hadn't the foggiest idea what she was thinking. It suddenly occurred to him that maybe she didn't want him around, and perhaps he'd made a huge mistake in judgment. Before that unsettling thought could take hold, she cupped his face with her soft hand, making his heart stagger.

"None of this is your problem, Owen."

"You know, it's funny, I keep telling myself that, but it doesn't seem to matter."

"You're really staying?"

"I'm really staying."

"Because of me?"

"No, because of Evan. He needs constant supervision." Owen cuffed her chin. "Yes, because of you, silly. Someone has to pick you up off the floor every morning. It may as well be me."

"Oh."

"Is that okay?"

"You really don't have to . . ."

Burying his fingers in her soft blonde hair, he pressed his lips to her forehead. "I want to, Laura. I really want to."

"I can't."

"What can't you do, honey?"

"I can't allow myself to depend on you."

"Why not?"

"Because this isn't the life you want. You don't want to be settled and domesticated, and I'd never ask you to change for me. You'd hate me for it someday."

"First of all, I could never hate you. And second of all, you're not asking me for anything. All I know is I can't go off and leave you here all by yourself. I don't *want* to go off and leave you here."

"How long will it be before you're itching to get out of here, before the open road beckons and you feel trapped by responsibilities that shouldn't even be yours?"

As much as he wanted to argue otherwise, she made good points. "I have an idea."

"I'm listening."

"Let's spend this winter together. I'll stay until the baby is born, and then we'll see what's what. How does that sound?"

"It sounds like just long enough to ensure that I'm completely attached to you and unable to imagine a single day without you in it."

Which was exactly what he wanted, he realized with sudden clarity. "The idea of being domesticated no longer horrifies me."

She laughed, which he'd hoped she would. "That's something, I guess."

"Give me a chance, Laura. That's all I'm asking for. You have to know I'd never hurt you."

"You'd never hurt me on purpose."

"All I know is being where you are is way more appealing than being anywhere else."

"I don't know that I've ever received a nicer compliment," she said, smiling warmly at him.

That smile filled him with a kind of joy he'd never experienced before.

"I've been wanting to do this for the longest time." She reached out to bring order to his unruly hair. Rolling her bottom lip between her teeth, she was the picture of concentration. "There," she said when she was satisfied. "All better." She dropped her gaze to meet his.

He'd promised her he wouldn't kiss her again, but hadn't they just brokered a tentative agreement to give this thing a whirl? "Laura . . ."

"Yes?"

"I really want to . . . That is, would it be okay if . . ."

She put him out of his misery by drawing him down to her and pressing her lips to his in a sweet, chaste kiss that affected him more profoundly than any kiss ever had. When she started to pull back from him, he stopped her with a hand on the back of her head.

"Do it again."

With her hand on his cheek, she kissed him again. This time, her lips parted, ever so slightly, and her tongue skimmed over his bottom lip. Nothing in his entire life had ever been more erotic or electrifying.

"If being domesticated means more of that, I think I'm going to like it," he said, smiling at the shell-shocked look on her face. His own expression had to mirror hers, because he felt as shell-shocked as she looked. "Do we have a deal, Princess? We'll give it the winter and see where we stand?"

She took his hand and brought it to her lips, placing a soft kiss on the back. "We have a deal."

∾

GRACE WATCHED THE CLOCK EDGE CLOSER TO NOON. "I HAVE TO CHECK out soon."

Evan released her, turned over and reached for the bedside phone. "Hi, there. I'm in room 320, and I'm wondering if I can reserve it for another night."

"Evan! I'm leaving at five!"

"It's available? Great. I'm going to use a different credit card for tonight, so I'll bring that down later." After a pause, he added, "You can tell housekeeping we're all set. Thanks." He hung up the phone and turned back to her.

"What're you doing? You're wasting your money—"

He shut her up with a kiss that cleared her brain of every thought that wasn't about him. "It's not a waste if it buys me four more hours right here," he said, kissing his way to her breasts.

"Evan . . . This is depraved. We can't keep doing . . ." His mouth closed over the tender tip of her breast, and all she could think about was the exquisite feel of his lips and tongue on her sensitive flesh.

"You still haven't answered my question," he said as his tongue made circles around her nipple, denying her more.

"I can't think when you're doing that."

He stopped what he was doing, lifted his head to make eye contact and raised a brow in question.

"You know I want you. Why do you need me to say it?"

"Because it'd be nice to know we're on the same page here."

"Haven't we been on the same page all morning?" she asked with a smile, hoping to diffuse some of the tension.

Shifting onto his back, he stared up at the ceiling.

Grace put her hand on his chest. "Evan—"

His cell phone rang, breaking the uneasy silence. "Sorry," he said as he got up, "I've got to take this with everything that's going on."

"Go ahead."

"Oh, it's Grant. Hey, bro, what's up?" Evan listened for a minute and then turned to look at Grace. "Let me ask her." Holding his hand over the phone, he said, "Stephanie's new lawyer, Dan Torrington, managed to get the hearing for her stepfather's case moved up to

Wednesday. They need to get a car off the island ASAP so they can spend tomorrow with Dan going over her testimony, but the ferries are booked for the rest of the day. Is there any chance—"

"Yes! She can have my spot. Of course she can."

"They can get you on the eight o'clock boat in the morning, so you'd only be a little late for work."

"It's fine. Tell her I said no problem and good luck."

"Thanks, Grace."

While Evan worked out the particulars with his brother, Grace thought about Stephanie and how excited and nervous she must be. Her mind also raced with the implications of another night with Evan. By the time she left the island, she'd be completely in love with him, a thought that would've terrified her before the morning they'd spent together.

In the last few hours, she'd gotten a good glimpse at the man Stephanie had told her might be inside the overgrown boy. While she was thrilled to have more time to spend with the man, she was worried about whether the boy would return and ruin everything.

"How about a shower?" he asked when he'd stashed the phone in his shorts pocket.

"Go ahead."

"I meant together."

"Oh."

His face lifted into a sexy half smile as he held out a hand, inviting her to join him. Despite the intimacy they'd shared, it still took an act of courage for her to throw back the sheet, get out of bed and walk across the room naked.

He watched her every move, his eyes heating with desire as she came toward him. "Go start the water," he said. "I'll be right there."

When he joined her, he placed a condom on the soap dish.

Grace's belly took a dip when she tried to picture how sex in the shower would work.

"Don't go all tense on me," he said as his lips skimmed her neck and shoulder from behind. As the warm water created a blanket of steam around them, he cupped her breasts and teased her nipples with talented fingers while his erection found a home in the cleft of her ass. He reached for the bar of soap, lathered up his hands and ran them all over her until her legs quivered and threatened to give out from under her.

"Let me turn around so I can touch you," she said.

He stepped back and handed her the soap.

She started with his shoulders, continued with his chest and belly, playing with his nipples before venturing to his rigid cock. With soapy hands, she explored his shaft and balls, loving the way his head fell back in utter abandon.

Thinking of what he'd done to her earlier, she dropped to her knees and let the water rinse him clean before she tentatively ran her tongue over the tip. She stroked and licked, marveling how he got even harder.

"Grace . . ."

"Hmm?"

"Stop teasing," he growled.

Laughing, she took him into her mouth, lashing him with her tongue and stroking him the way he'd shown her. If his tortured groan was any indication, Evan seemed to like that. He also liked when she sucked on him.

"Shit," he muttered. "Stop. Grace, *stop*." He helped her up and crushed his mouth to hers, plundering her mouth with his tongue as his fingers dug into her hips.

"Did I do it right?" she asked when he shifted his focus to her neck.

"If you did it any better, you would've finished me off."

"I'd like to do that sometime."

"Finish me off?"

As she nodded, her face heated with mortification. "In my mouth."

"Christ, Grace, when you say things like that, it's the hottest thing ever."

"Why?"

"Because I know you've never said it to anyone else, and I like that. I like it a lot." He kissed her softly and reached for the condom. "This way." Turning her so her back was once again to him, he said, "Put your hands on the wall and trust me. I've got you, babe."

When he put his arm around her waist and slid into her from behind, Grace couldn't stop the cry that slipped through her parted lips.

He kept up a slow but steady pace that had her quickly on the verge of release. And then he let the hand he'd rested on her belly slide down to where they were joined to stroke her into a shattering climax that powered through her with lightning speed.

His fingers dug into her hips to anchor her for his fierce possession until he too cried out his release. For a long time afterward, he remained inside her as they throbbed with aftershocks. Only when the water started to cool did he finally withdraw and turn her into his embrace.

"You're amazing," he whispered, "and one more night isn't going to be enough."

"For me either."

He reached for towels, handed one to her and then led her back to bed when they were dry.

Grace snuggled into his embrace, using his chest as a pillow. His chest hair was soft against her face as she traced a finger along the path that led to the thicker patch of hair that surrounded his penis.

"I need to ask you something," he said.

Grace was immediately on alert. "Okay."

"Last night, Stephanie said something that's been bugging me."

Since there were any number of things Stephanie could've said, Grace's mind whirled with possibilities. "What's that?"

"She said that for reasons I couldn't possibly understand, you were the last person I should've snuck out on after having sex. Other than the obvious that it was your first time, what did she mean by that?"

In the scope of a second, Grace thought of a dozen things she could say but decided to go with the truth. She took his hand and brought it to rest on the faded ridge of scar above her belly button. "Feel that?"

"Yeah. What about it?"

"I had what they call lap-band surgery about eighteen months ago. Do you know what that is?"

"I've heard of it, but I can't say I know the particulars."

Grace swallowed hard and forced herself to look at him, wanting to see his reaction. "For most of my life, I was significantly over-weight. I tried every diet, and I spent so much time at the gym that the owner said he should give me stock in the company. But nothing worked."

Evan's expression was unreadable as he listened intently.

"In fact, the muscle made me *gain* weight rather than lose, which made me nuts. So I decided to take drastic measures and had the surgery. The band is a ring around the upper part of my stomach that makes me feel full with much smaller portions."

"Which is why you eat like a bird."

"Yes. If I overdo, it can be really unpleasant."

"I'm sorry if I made too big a deal out of the way you eat."

"It's okay. You didn't know." With her fingers on top of his, she pressed on the port that lay below the scar. "If I feel like I'm eating too much or gaining weight, I go to the doctor and have the band adjusted."

"How does that work?"

"It's done with a needle to the port under my skin, which doesn't hurt at all. It's just a pinch and a pop." She tried to keep still while he investigated the area. "I want you to know that you're the first person I've let touch it."

His eyes widened with surprise. "Really?"

She nodded.

"Will you always have the band?"

"I suppose so, unless something better comes along. I've lost a hundred and thirty pounds since the surgery. I've got about twenty to go—"

"No," he said, startling her with his vehemence. "You don't need to lose any more. You're perfect just the way you are."

"That's kind of you to say, but I could stand to lose a bit more." She ran her fingers over the stubble on his jaw. "You can't know what it means to me that you find me appealing—stretch marks and all."

"Appealing? Jesus, Grace, that's hardly the word for it. You're sexy and gorgeous and curvy and *beautiful*. You're a freaking goddess."

His every word went straight to her heart. "You never would've looked at me before I lost the weight."

"You don't know that."

"Yes, I do. Guys like you . . ."

"Like me? What does that mean?"

"You've spent your whole life looking like a movie star and having your pick of women. You would've looked right past me before."

"I like to think you're wrong about that, but I guess we'll never know." He ran a hand over her hair, letting it slide through his fingers. "That guy you'd been with when I met you . . ."

"Trey the douche bag."

He laughed at the description. "You knew him before the surgery?"

"I'd known him most of my life, which is why it was so hurtful when I realized he was only going out with me because he had a bet with his stupid friend that he could 'nail the Whale.'"

"*What?*"

"That's what they called me in school—the Whale."

"Oh God, Grace. That's awful."

"Yeah, well, kids are awful." She caught a glimpse of something on his face that looked a lot like guilt. "What? Are you going to tell me now that you were one of those kids?"

He seemed to be trying to decide what he should say.

"Evan? What is it?"

"I was involved in something once that was kind of similar," he said in a regretful tone. "You know my sister-in-law, Maddie?"

She'd loved meeting Mac, Maddie and their children at Abby's party. "What about her?"

"She developed really early, and all the boys were fascinated with her . . . attributes. This one guy I was friends with, Darren Tuttle, he'd been trying to cop a feel for months, but she wouldn't let him anywhere near her. He finally got pissed and made up a story that Maddie had fooled around with the lot of us at the beach one night. He started calling her Maddie Mattress, and the name took off like wildfire."

Grace stared at him, astounded. "Tell me you didn't go along with that."

"I'm deeply ashamed to say that I allowed peer pressure to get the best of me."

"Oh, Evan . . . That's awful! What you guys did to her . . ."

"We did a terrible thing. I had no idea just how terrible until Mac started dating her and cued me in that until she got together with him, she'd had sex twice in her life and managed to get pregnant with Thomas one of those times. People in town had branded her a slut, and it was all because of a teenage prank gone wrong. He made everyone involved write letters to the *Gansett Gazette*, confessing that we made it all up."

"Good for him."

"I want you to know I was ashamed over the whole thing long before Mac ever called me out on it."

"I should hope so. You guys nearly succeeded in ruining her life."

"Believe me, I know that, and I hate that I was a part of it." He reached for her hand and linked their fingers. "Have I totally ruined any good feelings you might've had for me by telling you this?"

Grace studied his earnest face. "You didn't have to tell me. That counts for something."

"In light of all you've been through, I wouldn't want you to hear about it from someone else. That would've been worse."

"Yes, it would've."

"I'm not that guy anymore, Grace. I swear to you. I learned from that incident, and I deeply regret having been a part of it in the first place. Having to face my father after he heard about it was one of the low points of my life."

"What did he say?"

Evan blew out a deep breath. "I expected him to rant and yell. Rather, his voice was icily calm when he said, 'I was disappointed to hear you were part of such a thing. I raised my sons to be better men than that.'"

Grace winced. "Brutal."

"Totally."

"Thanks for telling me. It means a lot that you shared that with me, knowing it could've changed the way I feel about you."

"And how do you feel about me?"

Laughing, Grace said, "I walked right into that one, didn't I?"

He smiled, but his eyes were serious.

She ran her fingers over the whiskers on his jaw. "I feel so many things where you're concerned that I don't know how I'd ever put them into words."

"Try."

Grace drank in the sight of him, still so handsome in spite of his injury. "I like you a lot, and I want to spend more time with you, but I worry that we may be setting ourselves up for a difficult path. I'm putting down roots here on the island just as your career is taking off."

"That remains to be seen," he said bitterly.

"It'll happen. Maybe not right when you thought it would, but eventually."

"I wish I was so certain."

"Don't forget that I've seen you perform. I know you've got what it takes to succeed."

"I appreciate your faith in me, and I get what you mean about the difficult path. All I know is I want you in my life, Grace. I want to see what might happen if I take a chance on . . ."

"On what?"

"Love," he said, seeming stunned that he'd actually said the word. "I've never used that word in relation to any woman before. Ever."

"Evan . . ."

"Do you think you could maybe someday possibly . . ."

Grace dissolved into laughter.

"Oh my God! I *cannot* believe you're laughing right now! This is the most inappropriate laughter *ever!*"

His indignation only made her laugh harder. When she was finally able to control the outburst, she had to look away from his injured pout or risk starting all over again. "Evan, you're just so cute. Can't you see that I'm already more than halfway there?"

His mouth fell open. "You are?"

She nodded.

"Since when?"

"Since the night you rescued me and risked your reputation as a bad-ass confirmed bachelor by taking me home to Linda."

"Aw, Grace." He hugged her and pressed his lips to her forehead. "I think it's going to turn out that you're the one who rescued me."

CHAPTER 24

*T*iffany moved carefully to secure the handcuff around her sleeping husband's wrist. The police-issue cuffs had been rather easy to find in the island's toy store, although why any parent would allow their kid to have actual cuffs was beyond her. What did she care, though? They had two links and a key, which was all she needed. She cringed at the loud clicking noise the cuff made as it locked into place.

Jim shifted onto his back but didn't wake up. That he slept like a dead man was a critical part of her plan, as she was leaving Ashleigh with her mother and Ned for the night.

She released the breath she'd been holding. He couldn't wake up until she was ready, until everything was in place—especially her.

Moving fast, she stripped off her clothes, took another deep breath to calm the butterflies in her belly and slid between cool sheets. Right away, the warmth of his sleeping body reminded her of the overwhelming desire they'd once shared, before he got tired of her and their marriage.

This time, he was going to listen to her, even if she had to take drastic measures to keep him from walking away—again. Clicking the other cuff to her own wrist, Tiffany studied Jim's sleep-softened face.

A rough layer of dark stubble lined his jaw. His soft lips moved in his sleep, something she'd found so endearing back when she had reason to believe he was dreaming of her. Strands of dark brown hair fell over his forehead, giving him a boyish appeal. Awake, he was a life force, always in motion, always thinking, dreaming, reaching for more. Asleep, she'd always thought he became even sexier, if possible.

Suddenly, the tension of the last few months didn't matter. The angry words and long silences were immaterial. All that mattered was saving her marriage to the man she had loved for as long as she could remember. She'd been with him through college, law school, the bar exam, the birth of their daughter, setting up his practice and the many day-to-day challenges that came with being married. After all the time she'd invested in their family—in *them*—she couldn't let him go without a fight.

The last time she'd seen him, when she'd dropped off Ashleigh before Abby's going-away party, he'd accused her of being unfaithful to him, among other things. None of it was true, and if he'd only listen to her, she was certain she could convince him of that.

The recent reappearance of her own long-lost father had only cemented Tiffany's resolve that Ashleigh would grow up in a home with both parents surrounding her with love and attention. *I'll be damned if I'm going to give up on us now*, she thought, taking one last look at his face before she reached out to rest her free hand on his belly. Her heart beat so fast she feared it would burst through her chest.

Jim's abdominal muscles quivered under her hand. Encouraged, she continued south, taking the sheet along for the ride as her fingers encircled his semi-erect penis.

Tiffany licked her lips. It'd been a long time, maybe even a year, since they'd last had sex, and she was more than primed. The sight of his nude body made her want to take him into her mouth. When she thought of how many times she'd done just that, only to be rejected by him . . .

This isn't the time for those thoughts, she chided herself. *This is the time for action.*

227

Rising to her knees, she bent her head and went for broke.

Jim sat up so quickly he threw her off balance, causing her jaw to contract and her teeth to sink into some very important flesh.

He howled and tore at her long dark hair. *"Let go! What the hell, Tiffany? Let go!"* All at once, he realized he was cuffed to her and roared as he jerked hard on their joined arms.

His penis popped out of her mouth as she fell forward and landed with a pointed elbow to his chest, her knee catching him squarely in the balls. *This is not going according to plan.*

Moaning and gasping for air, he began to fight like a wild animal to get free of her. *"Are you serious? What is wrong with you?"*

Tiffany struggled to keep him on the bed, which was the only place she had a prayer of getting his attention. "I need to talk to you."

Pushing at her, he said, "I have nothing to say to you, so get your knee out of my balls, and *get the hell off me!*"

Suddenly, she was falling and reached out for anything she could get her hands on. Before she hit the floor, her finger sank into something wet and squishy.

Jim shrieked. *"You poked my freaking eye out!* Oh my God! *You blinded me!"* He dragged her with him, the carpet burning her ass and her boobs bouncing all around, when he reached for the phone.

"Who are you calling? What're you doing?"

Keeping his injured eye closed, Jim used his free hand to dial three numbers.

Tiffany's stomach dropped. *Uh-oh.* "Jim, please. Don't. I just want to talk to you."

"I'd like to report a break-in and assault at my home," he said in the no-nonsense tone he usually reserved for the courtroom. Glancing down at her with disdain, he said, "Yes, I know her." He rattled off the address of his Ocean Road office and hung up the phone. From the end of the bed, he grabbed a pair of boxer shorts and winced as he used his unshackled hand to settle them against his injured testicles.

"I'm sorry I hurt you," she said. "You wouldn't talk to me, you wouldn't listen—"

"I told you weeks ago that I'm all done talking and listening to you. Where's the key for these goddamned handcuffs?"

"In my car."

Tears from his injured eye wet his face as he stared at her sprawled out on the floor in all her glory. "Well, then, let's go get it." He headed for the door.

Tiffany resisted, cringing when the carpet further abused the burned skin on her bottom. "You can't drag me out there stark naked!"

"Oh no? You have some nerve telling me what I can't do when you sneak into my house, handcuff me, nearly bite my dick off, and poke my eye out of my head." Jerking hard on their joined arms, he headed for the door.

Tiffany fought him with everything she had, throwing him off balance.

He came down hard and landed on top of her. Their bodies would've been perfectly aligned for lovemaking had she not raised her knee in defense at the last minute, catching him once again right where he lived.

All the air left his body in one long gasp of pain. *"Jesus Christ, son of a bitch,"* he muttered, his face gone pale and chalky.

"Sorry," she muttered weakly. *Had a plan ever gone so totally wrong?*

Moaning, he lay next to her for several minutes, and for a brief instant, Tiffany thought she'd hurt him to the point where he might actually be willing to talk to her.

Then he rallied, rose to his knees and then to his feet. The murderous look in his one working eye had Tiffany shrinking back from him, despite their joined arms.

"Let's go," he snarled.

A knock on the door saved her from being paraded on Ocean Road in the nude.

Jim reached for it with his free hand, but she jerked him back. "Let me at least put some clothes on first!"

"In your dreams," he growled, throwing open the door.

"Chief Blaine Taylor, Gansett Police. You called about a B and E? I was in the area when the call came through."

"That's right." Jim stepped aside to admit the officer.

Oh, no, she thought. *Not him. Anyone but him!* Tiffany closed her legs and struggled to cover all the important parts with the arm that wasn't attached to Jim. Her full breasts spilled over the top of her forearm, giving Blaine a view of her nipples. She gasped and shifted to cover them. As always, he was totally hot in his dark brown uniform pants and crisp white shirt. His sun-streaked hair was mussed from a long day of work and his brown eyes were locked on her breasts.

After taking a good, long look, he cleared his throat, diverted his gaze away from her and focused on the cuffs. "Um, listen, folks, I don't know what's going on here, but if you're having some sort of personal problem . . ."

"It *is* a personal problem! My ex-wife—"

"I'm not your ex yet!"

"She broke in here when I was sleeping, cuffed herself to me and attacked me!" Jim gestured to his face. "Look what she did to my eye!"

Placing his hands on lean hips, Blaine leaned in. "Ouch."

"Want to see the teeth marks on my dick?"

Blaine winced. "Thanks, but I'll pass." Glancing at Tiffany on the floor, Blaine said, "Is this true? Did you break in here and attack him?"

"I didn't intend to *attack* him," she said in a meek tone, painfully aware of the picture she must be making sitting naked on the floor, handcuffed to her irate husband. "I just wanted to talk to him. Every time I try to talk to him, he leaves." Tears welled up in her eyes, but she blinked them away. It was bad enough that she was sitting naked on the floor while her soon-to-be ex-husband berated her in front of a guy she'd secretly lusted after for months. She wouldn't give Jim the satisfaction of seeing her cry, too.

"So you figured if you locked yourself to me, I'd have no choice but to listen to your lies?"

"They're not lies! Why do you say such awful things about your own wife? I've never been anything but faithful and devoted to you!"

"How'd you get in, ma'am?" Blaine asked, his handsome face tight with irritation. Nothing in his rigid stance gave away that they knew each other. She supposed he had no choice but to keep things professional in light of what she'd done.

"The door was unlocked. He never locks it."

"I will from now on," Jim snapped.

"The Mercedes outside," the chief said, "with the four flat tires—"

"*You did not*," Jim hissed through clenched teeth.

"I didn't want you to leave before we had a chance to talk."

"I want her arrested."

"*For what?*" Tiffany cried. "Wanting to talk to my own husband?"

Without looking at her, Jim said, "Breaking and entering, assault, vandalism." Raising his handcuffed arm, he added, "Kidnapping."

Blaine reached for a ring of keys on his belt, unlocked the cuffs and handed them to Tiffany.

Jim made a big show out of rubbing his wrist. "I need medical attention. I can't see a goddamned thing out of my eye, and she crushed my balls—twice."

Blaine didn't even try to hide his disdain for Jim as he keyed the microphone on his shoulder and called for paramedics. "Mrs. Sturgil, why don't you put some clothes on? I'm afraid I have to take you in."

Gasping, Tiffany looked up at him. "You're not serious."

Blaine glanced at Jim, whose face was set in a hard and unyielding expression.

What did I ever see in that face?

"Get dressed, ma'am."

With her arm still clutched to her chest, she said, "Look away, will you please?"

Hours later, Tiffany sat in the island's only jail cell, a place she'd managed to avoid during her entire wild-child youth, with only the handcuffs to keep her company. The bruises on her wrist and the burning skin on her rear end reminded her of how badly her last-ditch plan to win back Jim had failed. This time, it was really over.

For a minute, she indulged in a fantasy about sexy Blaine Taylor and the heated look he'd given her when he entered the apartment to find her naked on the floor. In the instant before he remembered his official duties, he'd been nothing more than a man—a man who wanted her. She had no doubt about that, and for some reason, the knowledge comforted her.

Passing the cuffs back and forth between her hands, Tiffany thought about the girl she'd been before she married Jim at age nineteen. Full of ambition and dreams and lists of things she wanted to accomplish by twenty-five, thirty, thirty-five, she'd had her life all mapped out.

Somewhere along the way, she'd allowed *his* goals and plans to become hers. "Huh. Well, that wasn't too smart now, was it?" Other than the dance studio, which fed one of her passions, and the day-care center that served a practical purpose after she'd had Ashleigh, she'd fulfilled none of those many goals she'd once had.

What did *she* need? What did *Tiffany* want? Thinking back to those lists, one thing came to mind, the one thing that had topped every list she'd ever made—the desire to have her own store. Not just any old store, but a specialty shop for women. Lingerie, lotions, candles, massage oils, maybe even some sex toys . . . A nervous tingle rippled through her when she thought about her plans for such a business in the heart of conservative Gansett Island.

And imagining Jim's reaction when he realized the owner of the island's new sexy lingerie shop was the wife he'd discarded? Well, that gave her the giggles.

BLAINE STOOD OUTSIDE THE JAIL CELL AND WATCHED TIFFANY TALK TO herself. Why a woman who looked like her had to stoop to cuffing herself to a guy to get his attention was beyond him.

She tucked a strand of dark hair behind her ear, exposing the long, elegant column of her neck. Her vulnerability tugged at him. Nothing about her was fragile, yet she seemed so alone that Blaine couldn't help wanting to help her. However, he'd promised his friends and family that he was done with "projects"—women who needed protecting, bailing out or just downright fixing. This one had trouble written all over her, and he'd already had more than his share.

If only he could get the vision of her naked and sprawled on the floor out of his mind. If only he hadn't caught a glimpse of raspberry nipples on the most spectacular breasts he'd ever beheld—and he'd spent a lot of time in the last few months dreaming about what Tiffany Sturgil's breasts might look like. Reality had far exceeded his fantasies. Forgetting what he'd seen in that apartment wouldn't happen overnight.

Steeling himself to deal with her, he unlocked the cell door.

Her head whipped up, and her green eyes connected with his.

Blaine felt the impact from the top of his head to the bottom of his size-thirteen feet. The surge below his belt caught him off guard. Clearing his throat and attempting to rid his mind of naked Tiffany pictures, he stepped into the cell.

She tensed, and right away Blaine's heart went out to her.

You can't save the world one woman at a time, he heard his mother saying. *Enough is enough, Blaine.*

"Do I have to spend the night?" she asked in a tiny voice.

"No."

Her sigh of relief echoed through the small cell. "I've been here a long time."

"I was at the clinic, speaking to your husband."

"*Ex*-husband."

Blaine was ridiculously proud to realize she'd moved on at some point in the last few hours. Using his best stern cop voice, he continued. "I managed to talk him out of pursuing the B and E, assault and kidnapping charges, all of which are felonies."

Tiffany swallowed hard. "Thank you."

"You do have to make restitution on the tires, and he's demanding a restraining order, requiring you stay at least five hundred feet from him except for when you're dropping off or picking up your daughter."

"Bastard," she whispered. "That rat bastard." Her big eyes shone with tears.

Damn it. If there was one thing Blaine couldn't handle, it was a woman's tears. Without giving himself time to think about the implications, he sat next to her on the narrow bunk. "Mind if I ask you something?"

She swiped at a tear as if it was pissing her off. "Sure."

"What's a nice girl like you doing with a tool like him?"

The snort of laughter seemed to take her by surprise. "Gee, Chief, don't hold back."

Pleased that he'd succeeded in turning her tears to laughter, he shrugged. "It's an honest question and one I've had for a while now."

"I have no idea," she said without an ounce of guile. "At first I thought he was cute, sexy . . ." She glanced at him. "You know?"

"I'll have to take your word for it. He doesn't do it for me."

When she laughed again, a coil of desire heated Blaine from within, making him wish he'd taken off his jacket. "He doesn't do it for me anymore, either." Gathering a thick handful of hair, she twisted it into a knot that exposed the exquisite stretch of neck again.

Blaine wanted to drag his tongue from the shallow hollow of her collarbone all the way to her delicate earlobe. He could only imagine how sweet she'd taste. Shifting to relieve the growing pressure in his lap, he forced himself to pay attention to what she was saying and not what she was doing.

Once again, she turned those green eyes on him, and something stirred deep inside, in the place he'd vowed to never go again.

"You really think I'm a nice girl after what I did tonight?"

Touched that his opinion mattered to her and mesmerized by the movement of her full, lush mouth, Blaine chose his words carefully, not wanting to give her the wrong impression. "I think you did what you felt you had to."

"It was stupid."

"Maybe."

"More than anything, I hate that he thinks I'm so desperate to get him back that I'd resort to what I did tonight."

"You didn't consider that in the planning for this mission?"

"I really thought it would work," she said, defeat radiating from her. "I did it more for Ashleigh than me. I wanted her to grow up in a normal family, you know?"

Blaine resisted the urge to put his arm around her and offer his shoulder to lean on. *No more projects, Blaine.* Clutching his hands together, he tried to process his overwhelming reaction to her. *It's because you saw her naked,* he rationalized.

Then how do you explain the way you've obsessed about her for months? She'd been on his mind from the second her sister first introduced them when he'd gone to the clinic to see Big Mac McCarthy after the accident at the marina.

"Are you all right?" she asked, jarring him out of his thoughts.

With his face hot, his skin itchy, his cock hard enough to pound nails, Blaine stood, hoping if he moved away from her and her bewitching scent, he could get himself under control. Leaning against the cell door, he watched eyes full of curiosity travel the length of him, stopping at the halfway point and widening with surprise. "So what happened between you guys?"

She tore her eyes off his crotch and met his gaze. "I wish I knew. When we moved back here after I helped him get through law school, it started to go bad."

"That's not fair."

"Life's not fair. After I waited *forever* for him to have time for me, he checks out of our marriage like I was never more than a meal ticket to him."

The defeated slump to her posture touched him. "Do you want to call your mom or your sister?"

"God, no. I don't want anyone to ever know about this."

He didn't mention the police log or the *Gansett Gazette* reporter who checked it every day. Maybe he could "forget" to file a report on this one. "Let me give you a ride home."

"I can call a cab."

Let her. Walk away and say good-bye. As always, his brain and his mouth had a significant communication problem. One of these days, he had to do something about that. Before his brain could overrule his mouth, words that couldn't be taken back were being spoken. "It's no problem."

"Thank you. I'd appreciate that."

"Don't forget your, um, cuffs."

"I'm not expecting to have much use for them."

"You never know." Now where did that suggestive comment come from?

Her face flushed to an appealing rosy shade. Realizing he'd embarrassed her, Blaine gestured for her to lead the way out. After she signed a few forms acknowledging her culpability in the vandalism and agreeing to make restitution, Blaine helped her into his police department SUV.

Once inside the truck, he further recognized the error of his ways. Her scent, a combination of sexy spice, sweet woman and strawberries, filled the small space, reawakening his libido. *What was it about this woman?* Blaine could hardly concentrate on driving when his cock throbbed painfully in the tight confines of his uniform pants.

"Do you know where you're going?" she asked, startling him.

Shifting in an effort to find some relief, he glanced over at her. "Your address was on the report." She didn't need to know that he'd known where she lived for months.

"Oh. Right."

Her voice, her scent, that hair—how he yearned to see that hair raining down on him as she rode him hard—her creamy white skin, those raspberry nipples, the memory of the dark strip of hair at the juncture of slender thighs . . . A groan escaped from between his clenched teeth.

"What's wrong?" she asked, alarmed.

"Nothing. Just a headache." His head was aching all right, just not the one sitting on his neck.

She shifted in her seat to take a closer look at him.

Great.

"Did you take something for it?"

They hadn't yet made the pill to cure what ailed him. "I will when I get home. After my shift."

"When is that?"

"Midnight. I'm filling in for one of my officers who's on vacation."

"The chief does that?"

"There're only six of us. We all cover for each other."

"You shouldn't have to wait four more hours to take something for your headache. I'll get you some pills when we get to my house."

"Thanks, but I can stop at the store and get some." No way was he stepping foot inside her house. Nope. No way. Not happening.

"After everything you've done for me, I insist."

Blaine wanted to groan again, but held it back this time. How about what he wanted to do *to* her? They arrived at her house a few minutes later.

"Nice place."

"Thanks." She stared at the house for a long time. "It's been in Jim's family forever. My mom and Maddie and I bounced from place to place all my life. This is the first real home I've ever had."

"Then you should fight for it."

"I have been, but I'm starting to wonder if it's worth it. After tonight, I just want to be rid of him. If that means giving up the house, so be it. It's hardly worth holding on to now anyway."

"What do you mean?"

"Come see for yourself." Before he could protest, she got out of the car.

Tell her you can't. Fabricate a call. Come up with something. Anything.

Turning to see if he was following her, she shot him a questioning look that went straight to his already over-involved heart.

With a deep sigh, he reached for the handle and opened the door. Following her inside, Blaine took in the empty living and dining rooms.

"Come in," she said, her voice echoing through the cavernous space. She led him into a modern kitchen with a gaping space in front of a bay window that might've once housed a table. The view of South Harbor during the day would be quite spectacular from that window.

In the living room, a single easy chair sat in front of a small television propped on a cheap stand. Blaine wanted to go find Jim Sturgil and beat the living shit out of him for doing this to his wife. *Project alert!*

"I ... ah ... really ought to be going."

"Let me get you the pills." Going up on tiptoes, she reached for a shelf in one of the maple-colored kitchen cabinets.

Blaine's mouth went dry as he watched tight jeans hug her shapely ass.

As she bustled around the kitchen getting him a tall glass of ice water to go with the medication, her full breasts swayed under a hot-pink T-shirt.

When she handed him the glass, her fingers brushed against his, and once again he went hard as stone. Not since his teenage years had his big brain fought such an unsuccessful battle with his little brain. After downing the water and the pills he didn't really need, he placed the glass on the granite countertop.

"I have to go."

"Okay."

Except neither of them moved. Instead, they stared hungrily at each other, the crackling tension threatening to consume him. Okay, it was official. He'd never wanted a woman more in his life. Operating on autopilot, he reached for her. Before he could process what he was doing or the potential implications, his tongue was plundering her mouth as his hands traveled from hips to breasts and then back down so he could lift her into his tight embrace.

A moan erupted from her throat as her tongue dueled with his in a fierce battle and her arms tightened around his neck. Months of heated looks and barely concealed desire exploded into passion the likes of which he had only heard about but never experienced before now.

He turned them, leaned her against the counter and pressed his erection into her soft center. When she pushed back, he almost lost control—again for the first time since his horny teenage years. He'd never tasted anything sweeter than Tiffany Sturgil's soft, supple mouth. However, he had a feeling he'd find even sweeter treats elsewhere on her lean, lithe dancer's body.

Tearing his lips free of hers, he indulged in the opportunity to finally taste her sweet neck. A tremble rippled through her, feeding his ravenous desire. He pushed her shirt up and tugged on her bra, gasping as her breasts popped free from the tight confines of hot-pink lace.

Hands overflowing with soft breasts, he dipped his head and laved at one of those raspberry nipples he'd thought of constantly since he first saw them hours earlier. Groaning when her fingers burrowed into his hair, Blaine licked and tugged and then sucked as hard as he dared.

She cried out, and her pelvis ground against his rigid length, almost daring him to take more, to take everything.

"Blaine," she whispered through lips swollen from torrid kisses.

The sound of his name coming from her sent a new surge of tenderness and desire right through him. Suddenly, he needed more of her. He needed all of her. Running his hand down over her belly, he tugged at the button to her jeans, fought the zipper down and plunged his hand into silky panties.

Tiffany let out a surprised squeal but opened her legs and tilted her hips in invitation.

Combing his fingers through damp curls, he parted plump lips to find her drenched with desire. "Oh my God," he said softly. He lifted her to pull the jeans down over her hips to gain better access, his entire world reduced to the tight nub of her clitoris, which pulsed under the finger he slid over it. Her thighs quivered and clenched around his questing hand.

"Don't stop," she begged, panting and tightening her grip on his hair.

Since stopping wasn't on his agenda, he wondered if he'd have a bald spot by the time this was over. And how would it end, exactly? Had he thought that far ahead? Hell, he'd never expected to have his lips wrapped around her nipple or his hand in her panties, so what did he know?

Unable to bear her mewling whimpers or his own pounding desire for another second, he pushed two fingers into her while sucking hard on her nipple.

Tiffany came with a shriek, going wild in his arms.

As he watched her, feeling her tighten around his buried fingers, Blaine's resolve crumbled, and he vowed to do whatever he could to help her get her life back in order. Project or not, she was unlike any woman he'd ever known, and after giving her a quick but intense orgasm on her kitchen counter, he needed more of her. Much, much more.

"That was amazing," she said softly, releasing the death grip on his hair. With a coy smile, she said, "Now what about you?"

Just as he was about to tell her exactly what she could do for him, his radio crackled. As if hit by a bucket of ice water, Blaine snapped out of the sex-induced stupor to listen to the call for assistance at a multicar accident on Southeast Lighthouse Road. The moment he heard the dispatcher's voice, his raging boner shriveled up and died along with his resolve to help this troubled woman. Moving fast, he withdrew his hand from the moistness between her legs and helped her sit up.

In a self-conscious gesture, she tugged her T-shirt over whisker-abraded breasts.

"I'm sorry," he said, aware all at once that he'd crossed multiple lines—both personal and professional. "That shouldn't have happened."

"You're probably right, but I'm not sorry it did." She pulled up her jeans. "That was the single best orgasm I've ever had in my life."

Taken aback by her candor, Blaine could only stare at her. *Trouble*, he reminded himself, the big empty house a further indication of how much trouble she had the potential to be. A second more urgent call for help came over the radio.

"I've got to go."

"I know."

Since they both knew he wouldn't be back, she didn't ask and he didn't offer.

"Thanks for the ride—both of them."

Blaine's cheeks heated with uncharacteristic embarrassment. "Sure."

Her jeans still gaping open, she followed him to the front door. "And for everything else tonight. With Jim."

"No problem."

When they reached the door, he turned for a long last look at her gorgeous face, now flushed and whisker-burned. He wished he had it in him to be what she needed. "Good luck with everything, Tiffany. I hope you find what makes you happy."

"Oh, I will. Don't worry."

The glint in her eye would've made him nervous had he planned to stick around. Blaine took her by the chin and raised it so he could see her big green eyes. "He's not worth mourning over."

"I know that, too."

He studied her for another long moment. "If you'd cuffed yourself to me and wrapped those beautiful lips around *my* dick, I would've been calling for mercy, not the cops. You can bet on that." Pressing a soft kiss to her cheek, Blaine reveled in the tremble that rippled through her. "Take care of yourself."

He wouldn't soon forget the image of her delectable mouth hanging open in surprise.

CHAPTER 25

*E*van was awake long before the alarm they'd set for six thirty
went off. As Grace's departure time drew near, panic set in.
He worried it was a huge mistake to let her leave. What if he never
saw her again? What if she changed her mind about Gold's or the deal
fell through or she changed her mind about him?

They'd never made it out of the cozy hotel room the day before.
Rather they'd stayed in bed, snuggling and talking and laughing and
making sweet, sexy love until they'd run out of condoms. It had been,
without a doubt, the best day of Evan's entire life.

He thought about what she'd told him, about her surgery and the
weight loss as well as the pain of growing up heavy in a world that
catered to physical perfection. In his eyes, she was as close to perfect
as any woman could ever be, and all at once it became critical to him
that she know that.

"Grace," he whispered as he sprinkled kisses on her face and neck.
"Wake up."

"Hmm. Not yet."

"Yes, now. I need to talk to you. I need to tell you . . ." What? What
did he need to tell her?

Her eyes opened, and she blinked a few times. "What's wrong?"

"I can't let you leave without telling you . . . That I really want . . ."

"What, Evan?"

"I want you. I want us. I want it all. And I'm afraid if you leave, if I let you go, we'll never get a chance to see what this might be."

She took his hand and brought it to her chest, flattening his palm over the strong beat of her heart. "In two short weeks, I'll be back, and we'll get to see what this is."

"That's a really long time." As a new idea occurred to him, his desperation lessened. "I could come with you. There's nothing keeping me here now that Mac is back to running the marina, and Owen can handle the last couple of weekends at the Tiki without me. It's his gig anyway."

Grace was shaking her head. "I need some time to process everything that's happened and to prepare for the move. I won't be able to do that if you're there distracting me." She brought his hand to her lips. "I think we should both take the next two weeks to make sure this is what we really want."

"It is what I want."

"Then it'll still be what you want in two weeks."

"What if you change your mind when you have time away from me to think?"

"I don't think that'll happen."

"Will you at least call me while you're gone so I can make sure you don't forget about me?"

She smiled at him. "If you want me to."

"I really want you to."

"Come here." She held out her arms to him, and Evan sank into her soft sweetness, breathing in the scent that would forever remind him of her. "It's going to be okay. I promise."

"You're awfully calm to say that you've managed—in just forty-eight hours' time—to upend my entire life."

"I'm not calm on the inside. Believe me. Think about it from my point of view—I came out here to pay you back, and look at what happened."

"Best weekend ever."

"By far."

"You're really coming back?"

"I'm really coming back."

~

EVAN WAS RATHER PROUD OF HOW HE GOT THROUGH THE FIRST WEEK after Grace left. He kept himself busy writing songs, performing with Owen and practicing his craft. According to Jack, it was looking more likely that Buddy Longstreet's company was going to strike a deal to separate Evan's album from the bankruptcy proceedings. While he was cautiously optimistic, Evan refused to get his hopes up until it was a done deal.

Under normal circumstances, the drama unfolding in Nashville would've consumed him. It would've been on his mind every minute of every day, and it would've kept him awake at night. But worry over his career wasn't what kept him awake at night.

No, when he lay awake most of every night, it was Grace he thought about. He'd relived their time together at least a million times and had spent hours on the phone talking to her about everything and nothing.

By the end of the tenth day, he began to wonder if he was losing his mind. Had two weeks ever gone by so slowly?

Naturally, his brothers had tuned in to his agony and were ragging on him every chance they got. Grant and Stephanie were still high off the thrill of victory in court. Her stepfather, Charlie, had been released from prison after fourteen long years behind bars for a crime he hadn't committed. They'd talked him into coming out to the island until the media circus that accompanied his release died down.

Ned had squared Charlie away with one of his rental properties, and Mac had promised him a job that winter when Mac and Luke's off-season construction company would be renovating the Sand & Surf Hotel.

Everything was falling into place for everyone, except him, Evan decided after another long dinner with his family at which he'd been the butt of every joke. The only one who seemed to understand what he was going through was Owen, who'd been making some rather dramatic changes in his own life lately, also thanks to a woman.

Evan loved the idea of Owen and his cousin Laura together and was pulling for them to make it work. Her ex-husband was making all sorts of threats that didn't sit well with any of them, and Evan didn't envy them the road they had ahead.

During dinner, Evan had been counting the minutes until his self-imposed deadline to call Grace. When he'd last talked to her, two endless days ago, he'd asked her if she missed him. She'd teasingly said that since he called her every night, she hadn't had time to miss him. So he'd waited two hellish days to call her again, hoping that maybe he'd hear from her in the interim. But there'd been no call, no text, no nothing. And he was slowly going out of his mind from missing her and worrying that she might've changed her mind about him.

When Grant and Stephanie finally went home, Evan helped his mother clean up the kitchen.

"Everything okay, Ev?" she asked as she wiped the countertops.

Startled, he was immediately on guard against whatever form of inquisition she might be preparing to mount. "I'm fine," he said, loading the last of the plates into the dishwasher.

"If you ask me, your brothers are being rather hard on you."

"It's fine. Nothing I didn't do to them."

"When they were falling in love with Maddie and Stephanie, you mean."

Trapped, he stared at her as he tried to think of some way to wiggle out of this conversation.

"It's okay," she said. "I know what you're going through."

"Oh, you do, huh?" he asked, amused by her when he knew he should be running for his life away from her.

"Sure, I do. I went through it once myself, don't forget."

"You're not going to share details about you and Dad that'll scar me for life, are you?"

Linda laughed and tossed the dishrag at him.

He caught it and dropped it into the sink.

"You know how Uncle Frank introduced me to Dad. I went to a party at Frank's house with Aunt JoAnn when she and Frank were dating."

"I don't remember much about her," he said of his cousin Laura's mother, who'd died young.

"No, you wouldn't," Linda said sadly. "She and I were friends from school, and we lost her far too soon. Anyway, Dad and I met the day before he closed on the purchase of the marina. Of course, I'd heard about Gansett, but I'd never been here. To hear Dad talk about it that first day, it sounded like paradise."

Evan couldn't help but be intrigued by parts of his parents' story he hadn't heard before.

"He talked me into coming over with him to see it the next day, and I totally fell in love."

"With the island?" Evan asked in a teasing tone.

"Among other things." Smiling, she looked up at him. "I know that feeling of wanting someone so badly and seeing nothing but obstacles in the way of making it happen."

Evan was reluctant to say too much to the woman they called Voodoo Mama for good reason. "Well, it certainly worked out well for you."

"And there's no reason to believe it won't work out just as well for you."

"I guess we'll see, won't we?"

She put her hands on his shoulders. "You're a terrific guy, Evan McCarthy, and any woman would be lucky to win your heart. It certainly wouldn't break *my* heart if that woman was Grace."

Evan smiled. "You liked her, huh?"

"Very much so."

"I'm glad. That matters to me."

She went up on tiptoes to kiss his cheek. "It's all going to work out. Try not to worry."

Big Mac strolled into the kitchen. "Are you badgering that boy, Lin?"

"For once, I'm not," she said with a wink for Evan that made him laugh.

"She's on best behavior," Evan confirmed.

"Well," Big Mac said, "that's a first."

"She might just be growing up," Evan said.

Linda rewarded that comment with a middle finger aimed at both of them.

Laughing, Big Mac slung an arm around his wife. "Let's go for a walk. I need to burn off that amazing dinner you made."

"I'd love to. We'll be back in a bit, Ev."

"Take your time."

They were holding hands and whispering to each other by the time they walked out the door, and Evan was relieved to realize they'd apparently patched up whatever differences had come between them. His love life would probably be the topic of their conversation on the walk, and whereas that once would've bothered him tremendously, it didn't anymore. Apparently, he was doing a piss-poor job of hiding his torment over Grace.

The moment he was alone, he rushed upstairs to his room and shut the door to make the call he'd been dying to make for days now. By the fourth ring, he was convinced she wasn't going to pick up, so when she did, he was too tongue-tied to even say hello. What a fool she'd turned him into!

"Evan? Hello?"

"I'm here."

"Are you okay?"

"I'm just great," he said, his tone rife with sarcasm. "You?"

"I'm tired. Moving is hard work. The furniture I ordered for my new apartment arrived today. We had to move it to the truck I'm bringing to the island. Thank goodness my brothers were able to help me. But every muscle I have is screaming."

"When you get here, I'll give you a massage."

"That'll be nice." She paused for a moment. "I was worried when I didn't hear from you. Is everything okay?"

"I wanted to give you time to miss me. Did it work?"

"Maybe," she said, laughing at him the way she always did. "I was going to call you, but I figured you were playing at the Tiki with Owen. I didn't want to bother you."

"Grace, honey, any time you want to talk to me, call me. I'll never be too busy for you."

"That's very sweet of you to say."

"What're you wearing right now?" The question was met with silence. "Grace?"

"Why do you want to know?"

"Because I do."

"It was really hot today, so I just took a shower and changed into a T-shirt and panties."

"Why is it that when you say the word 'panties,' I get hard as a rock?"

Her nervous laughter traveled through the phone and wrapped around his heart like a warm blanket. "Maybe because you're a fifteen-year-old trapped in a thirty-two-year-old's body?"

"It's because of the spell you cast over me that makes everything about you sexy."

"*Everything?*"

Evan smiled when he realized she was enjoying tormenting him. Well, two could play at that game. "Take your shirt off."

"Evan! Why?"

"Just do it."

"You're nuts."

"Is your shirt off yet?"

Sighing with exasperation, she said, "Hang on."

He could hear her moving around before she returned to the phone. "It's off. Are you happy now?"

"Not quite yet. Is your room near anyone else's?"

"I've got the garage apartment."

"Good, put the phone on speaker."

"Evan . . ."

"Grace . . . Do what you're told."

"Fine. It's on speaker. I think you've lost your mind since I last saw you."

"I know I have, and that's your fault, too."

"Everything is my fault."

"I'm glad you realize that. Are your nipples hard?"

"Um, yeah, I guess."

"Roll them between your fingers."

"I'm not doing that."

"Yes, you are. Are you doing it?"

"If you insist."

"I do. Tell me how it feels."

"It feels . . . I don't know . . ."

"Close your eyes and pretend it's me doing it instead of you. Is that better?"

"Yeah." She was starting to sound a little breathless, which made him even harder, if that was possible.

"Tug on them."

"If I have to do this, so do you. Take off your shorts and stroke yourself."

"Really, Grace, I love it when you talk dirty to me."

"Do what you're told."

Laughing at her saucy tone, he stripped off his shorts and boxers.

"Are you hard?" she asked.

"Extremely. Put your right hand inside your panties."

"Evan, really, that's enough," she said with a nervous laugh. "We don't have to—"

"Are you wet?"

"Extremely," she said, sounding resigned.

His cock surged at that news. How he wished he could bury himself in her slick heat. "I'm never going to survive four more days."

"Neither am I."

"Let your legs fall open and rub your clit."

"Oh God, Evan, *seriously*?"

"Do I sound like I'm kidding? Are you doing it?"

"Yes!"

"Keep it up and tell me what you want to do when you see me again."

Without hesitation, she said, "I want to get naked in bed with you."

"What do you want to do?"

"I want to have sex."

"Surely a girl with such a dirty mouth can do better than that."

"I want to fuck," she said tentatively.

"That's more like it," he said, laughing. "Are you blushing?"

"What do you think?"

"I can picture it. I bet your nipples are dark red by now. That's how they get when you're turned on. Did you know that?"

"No," she said, panting now.

"Pinch your left nipple."

She let out a moan. "Are you participating over there?"

"You bet your ass. Speaking of your ass, have I mentioned how much I love it? I can't wait to kiss you there when you get back."

"Evan . . ."

"Do you want to come, honey?"

"Yes, *yes*."

"Not quite yet."

She let out a tortured moan that nearly undid him.

"Tell me how you want to do it when you get back. Do you want to be on top this time?"

"I don't care how we do it as long as we do it."

"We'll do it every way we can think of. Does that sound good?"

Her reply was rather inarticulate.

"Do you want to come now?"

"*Yesssssss*."

"Let's go together, and don't you dare be quiet about it."

Her cries of fulfillment did him in, too. For a long time afterward, the only sound was that of ragged breathing on both ends of the phone.

"Do you miss me, Grace?"

"God, *yes*, I miss you so much it's not even funny."

"And have you thought about what you want?"

"I've hardly thought about anything but you since the second I left you."

Evan's smile stretched from ear to ear. "That's what I needed to hear."

"Have you thought about me?"

"A little. Here and there. Nothing much." When she laughed, he said, "I'll tell you what I've been thinking when I see you, okay?"

"Okay."

"I can't wait to see you, babe."

"I can't wait, either."

ON THE DAY OF GRACE'S RETURN, EVAN WAS UP EARLY TO SHOWER AND shave. Studying his face in the mirror, he was glad that the last of the abrasions had finally healed. At least he no longer looked like a creature from the black lagoon, as Grant had said at least a dozen times since it happened.

He walked into town two hours before Grace's ferry was due in and killed the time drinking coffee at the South Harbor Diner. Evan spent so much time studying the horizon, willing the boat to appear, that his eyes began to play tricks on him. So when the ferry actually appeared, he wasn't sure if it was real or an illusion.

"You need to get it together, freak show," he muttered as he crossed the street.

"Talking to yerself now, boy?" Ned asked from his usual post in the line of cabs awaiting the next boat. The guy owned half the island and drove a cab for fun. Go figure.

Embarrassed to have been caught talking to himself like a lunatic, Evan was suddenly mad at Grace. This, as well as the torture of the last two weeks, was entirely her fault. Before he met her, he didn't lie awake all night thinking about a woman or talk to himself in public places.

"Ahhh, boy," Ned said with a delighted chuckle. "Ya've got yerself a bad case, now don'cha?"

Since Evan could no more deny that than he could his own name, he didn't try.

"I heard she's coming back today and puttin' us all outta our misery."

"What misery have you been in?" Evan asked indignantly.

"Watchin' ya suffer ain't no picnic for any of us that love ya."

"Aww, jeez. Don't be nice to me. I can't take that right now."

Ned reached out to squeeze his shoulder. "Follow yer heart, boy. It'll lead ya home. If ya love this girl, tell her so. Don't let her wonder."

Fortified by Ned's pep talk, Evan nodded.

"Good luck to ya."

"Thanks." He walked down the hill to the ferry landing and watched the boat clear the breakwater to South Harbor. Had it ever taken longer for a ferry to make a one-eighty and back into its berth? Evan looked up at the rear controls and wasn't surprised to see Seamus O'Grady at the helm. *Figures.* Had Grace spent the passage chatting with her good pal?

A burst of jealous rage made Evan feel like an even bigger fool than he already was.

When the ferry was finally secured, cars and trucks came off first, including a rental truck that Evan realized was probably Grace's.

As he watched it go by and strained to see inside, someone tapped him on the shoulder. He spun around, and there she was, wearing a big smile and looking thrilled to see him.

She threw herself into his arms.

For a second, he was almost too stunned to react, but then he scooped her up and swung her around.

"It's about damned time you came back to me," Evan said. "I was this close to losing my mind."

"How close?" she asked playfully, sounding as if she was enjoying his torment.

"If you laugh right now, I swear to God . . ."

Of course, she laughed, and he did the only thing he could to make it stop—he put her down and kissed her until he was sure she'd forgotten all about what she found so funny.

"Missed you," she whispered. "So much."

"I missed you more." He stared at her, drinking in every detail. "Did you think long and hard while I was gone?"

"So long and *so* hard," he said, his tone rife with double meaning.

She smacked his arm. "I'm being serious."

"So am I." He took her hand and led her away from the maelstrom of people and cars and bikes. Behind the ticket office, he pressed her against the wall and kissed her senseless again.

With her arms linked around his neck, she said, "What did you decide?"

"I decided I'm no good without you. I decided I'll do anything I can to keep you in my life." As he'd practiced this declaration over and over during the last few interminable days, he'd expected this last bit to be the hard part. But with her in his arms, looking up at him with her heart in her eyes, he found it wasn't hard at all. "And I decided I love you."

"That works out perfectly," she said with the cheeky grin he so adored. "Because I love you, too."

The relief at hearing that and being with her again was so overwhelming, so consuming, it was all Evan could do to remain standing. Holding on to her was the only thing that kept him upright. "Come on," he said after he held her for a long while. "We need to get you moved in, and then we've got a lot of plans—and a lot of love—to make."

She took his hand and smiled up at him. "Let's get to it."

EPILOGUE

"*Y*ou are absolutely *not* having dinner with him," Evan said as he secured a corner of the fitted sheet on his side of the bed. The move-in crew he'd organized and fed with pizza from Mario's were long gone along with her brother Craig, who'd taken the truck back to the mainland on the five o'clock boat. She was exhausted from the hard work but exhilarated by the way her things had fit into the apartment, as well as the warm welcome from her new friends—not to mention being back with Evan. That was rather exhilarating, too.

"Why not?" Grace was getting a kick out of tormenting him as she tucked the top sheet in on her side. "We're just friends. I'm allowed to have friends, aren't I?"

"That bloody Irishman isn't interested in being *friends* with you. He wants to get his hands on you, and it's not happening."

Knowing this was her moving day, Seamus had come by to help and had flirted shamelessly with her, which had driven Evan wild. With a houseful of people—including his parents, brothers, Stephanie, Owen, Laura, Maddie and the kids—helping her move in, she and Evan had been forced to keep their hands to themselves for hours.

The tension had slowly built to a boiling point, aided by Seamus's blatant blarney.

"I don't think I like your attitude," Grace said indignantly, fully aware that she was throwing gas on a fire.

"Too bad. You need to let him know you're taken. Off the market. Whatever you have to say so he gets the message."

Grace put lavender cases on the feather pillows she'd bought for her new place. "And what message is that?"

It was a good thing she was looking right at him, or she might've missed the moment he finally snapped. He stalked around the bed, took the pillow from her and tossed it aside. Pulling her roughly against him, he captured her mouth in a savage kiss that would probably leave her lips bruised and swollen tomorrow. Not that she cared in the least, because she'd been longing for him for weeks now. She fisted her hand in his hair and gave as good as she got.

"The message," he said when he came up for air many minutes later, "is you're mine. Mine, mine, *mine*. I don't want him anywhere near you."

"You're being somewhat ridiculous. You know that, don't you?

"I don't care. Tell me you won't go out with him."

"I won't go out on a *date* with him. I will have dinner with him—as a friend."

"*Grace* . . ." He dropped his head to her shoulder. "You can't encourage him! He isn't capable of telling the difference!"

"I'll tell him I'm involved with someone."

Evan lifted his head to meet her gaze. "Really? Will you tell him who?"

As if the whole island didn't already know! Nodding, she pushed her lips together to suppress the laughter that she knew he wouldn't appreciate just then.

"Are you trying not to laugh at me?"

Tears filled her eyes as she shook her head.

"You're really quite awful."

"I tried to warn you about that the night we met."

"It's a wonder I love you this much when you're so mean to me."

She went up on tiptoes to kiss him. "Say it again."

"Say what?"

"You know what."

"I love you?"

Nodding, she rested her forehead against his chest. "Does it feel weird to say that?"

"Not to you." He reached for the hem of her T-shirt and pulled it over her head. "I've been dreaming about touching you, holding you, loving you."

"I have, too." She unbuttoned his shorts and pushed them and his boxers down over his hips, freeing his erection. As she touched and stroked him, Grace was filled with relief to be back with him again. "I have a surprise for you."

"What's that?" he asked as he released her breasts from the sheer bra she'd worn with him in mind.

"I saw my doctor about birth control right after I got home."

Raising his head, he stared into her eyes. "And?"

"It's already effective, so no more condoms. If you're okay with that."

"*If I'm okay with that?*" His eyes nearly bugged out of his head, and his voice was oddly high-pitched and strained. "What do you think?"

Grace smiled up at him and helped him out of his T-shirt as he pushed and pulled at her shorts and panties.

"Just for the record," he said, "I'm totally safe. I had a physical a couple of months ago."

"Good to know."

They slid into her new bed together, arms and legs intertwined.

"You feel so good," he whispered as he sent his hand down her back to squeeze her bottom.

She ran her fingers over soft chest hair and hard belly. His cock surged against her hip, making its presence known.

"I want to touch you and kiss you everywhere," he said gruffly, "but right now, I just . . . I need . . ."

Since she needed the same thing, she shifted onto her back and reached out to him. He came into her embrace and took her mouth in a series of deep, searching kisses as he pressed his cock against her, letting her know what he needed.

Grace cradled his hips between her legs, needing him just as fiercely. "Evan . . . Now. Hurry."

He grasped his cock, positioned himself and slid into her, his breath catching. "Oh my God," he whispered. "That's unbelievable. Grace, *God*."

She tried to breathe past the lump that settled in her throat at the sheer relief of being back in his arms. "Have you done it without a condom before?"

"No," he gasped. "Never. It's amazing." He moved slowly, as if trying to prolong the exquisite torture. Suddenly, he pulled out of her.

"What is it?"

"We never got to do it this way." He flopped onto his back, reached for her and arranged her on top of him.

Grace sucked in a sharp, deep breath as she took him in.

"Roll your hips," he said, nearly levitating off the bed when she did it. "*Grace* . . ." His jaw pulsed with tension, and his fingers tightened on her hips as she settled into a rhythm that he disrupted when his fingers delved into the place where they were joined, to coax her.

With the tension growing to nearly unendurable levels, she looked down to find him gazing up at her with so much love and affection that her heart filled to overflowing.

"I love you," she said, leaning down to kiss him.

"I love you, too." He took her hands and held on tight as he surged into her, crying out just as she reached her own peak.

As she came down from the unimaginable high, he wrapped his arms around her and pressed his lips to her forehead. Under her ear, his heart pounded out a steady beat.

"Everything is different now that I know you love me," he said.

"For me, too."

"I've never felt anything like this, Grace."

"I never imagined there *was* anything like this. Not for me anyway."

"It's all your fault, you know."

"I know, I know," she said, endlessly amused by him.

"So you won't go out with Seamus, right?"

Laughing, Grace smacked his arm. "How can I go out with anyone else when I'm madly in love with you?"

"Why didn't you just say that in the first place?" His indignant huff nearly set her off into a fit of laughter from which she might never recover.

She had a feeling that was going to be a regular problem where he was concerned. "Because it's so much fun to torture you."

Growling, he rolled them over so he was on top and looked down at her. "I never wanted any of this, and now I can't imagine a future that doesn't include you. How did you do that to me?"

"That's for me to know and you to find out," she said with a smug grin.

"It might take fifty or sixty years to figure it out."

She hugged him tightly. "I'm not going anywhere."

~

Thank you for reading *Hoping for Love*! I hope you enjoyed it. Keep reading for a sneak peek at *Season for Love*, Owen and Laura's story!

SEASON FOR LOVE

Chapter 1

*O*wen Lawry stood on the porch of the Sand & Surf Hotel to watch the last ferry of the day leave South Harbor for the mainland. He and his van were supposed to have been on that boat. With his obligations on Gansett Island over for the season, he'd planned to be heading for a two-month gig in Boston, the same autumn engagement he'd had the last five years. It paid well, and, after all this time, the club owners were friends.

His gaze was riveted to the ferry as it steamed past the breakwater into open ocean, where it dipped and rolled in the October surf. As the sun set on Columbus Day, officially ending another summer season on Gansett, Owen wondered what the hell he was still doing here when he was supposed to be on that boat, leaving for good-paying work on the mainland.

"You know why you're still here," he muttered, thinking of the blonde beauty who had him wound up in knots. He was at the point where he wondered if a man could actually die from pent-up desire.

It might've been better for them both if he'd left as scheduled, if he'd taken the gig in Boston and gone about his carefree existence with the same lack of responsibility that had marked his entire adult life.

What was he doing here pining after a woman who was still married to someone else and carrying her estranged husband's child? What was he doing spending every possible moment with a woman who'd made it clear she was unavailable for all the things he suddenly wanted for the first time in his thirty-three years? He was driving himself slowly mad. That was the only thing he knew for certain.

Before he met Laura McCarthy, he was perfectly satisfied with his life. He spent summers playing his guitar and singing on the island— the closest thing to a real home he'd ever had—worked autumns in Boston and winters in Stowe, Vermont, playing to the ski crowd. In the spring, he headed to the Bahamas for a few months off. It was a good life, a *satisfying* life. Watching the last ferry of the day fade into the twilight, Owen had the uneasy sensation that he was also watching that satisfying life slip through his fingers.

He usually felt sorry for guys who allowed themselves to be led around by a woman. His best friends, Evan, Mac and Grant McCarthy, Joe Cantrell and Luke Harris, had fallen like dominoes lately, one after the other finding the women they were meant to be with. Only Adam McCarthy remained untethered and seemed happy that way.

Owen, on the other hand, was stuck in purgatory, caught between the single life he'd embraced with passionate dedication and the committed life he never imagined for himself. He wasn't *with* Laura, per se. He just spent all his free time with her. Weeks ago, they'd shared a couple of chaste kisses that had been hotter than full-on sex with other women.

Since then, there'd been nothing but an occasional hand to his arm or a brief hug here or there. He'd continued to collect her off the bathroom floor each day until the relentless morning sickness suddenly let up as she entered her fifth month of pregnancy.

As he leaned against the railing he'd recently replaced on the hotel's front porch, Owen realized he missed that time with her in the mornings when she'd been so sick and he'd been there to prop her up. "You're such a fool," he said to the gathering darkness.

The autumn days were shorter, the nights longer and the chilly air a harbinger of things to come. Shivering in the breeze, Owen questioned his decision to stay with Laura this winter for the millionth time. Did she even want him here? Did she want company, or did she want *him*? If she wanted him, she was doing a hell of a job hiding it. For a while there, he'd thought they were at the start of something that had the potential to be significant. Now he wasn't so sure.

She treated him like a platonic buddy when all he did was fantasize about getting her naked and into his bed. Was he sick to be having such fantasies about a woman who was pregnant with another man's child? Probably. But as she rounded and swelled and glowed, he only wanted her more. At times, he even let himself pretend they were married and the baby was his.

"You're one sick son of a bitch," he said to the breeze. Sick or not, he wanted her with a fierceness that was becoming harder and harder to hide from her. One of these days, he was going to grab her and pin her against a wall and show her exactly—

"Owen?"

He sucked in a sharp, deep breath, ashamed to have been caught having such uncivilized thoughts about a woman he truly cared for. Attempting to calm himself, he turned to her. "Yeah?"

"Aren't you cold out there?"

No, he was on fire thinking about her, not that he could confess such a thing to her. "Not really. It's nice."

Laura tugged the zip-up sweatshirt of his that she'd "borrowed," around herself and joined him on the porch. Even though the oversized jacket swallowed her up, she was still his regal princess. She snuggled into his side, and it seemed the most natural thing in the world to slip his arm around her.

Resting her head on his chest, she let out a contented sigh. "It's so pretty this time of day."

His throat tightened with emotion, and his entire body ached from wanting her. "Sure is."

"It's pretty every time of day. I never get tired of our spectacular view," she said as a shiver traveled through her.

"You shouldn't get too cold."

"I'm fine."

"It's a good night for a fire." *Now where did that come from?* He'd no sooner said the words than he wanted to take them back.

"Oh, can we? I'd love that!"

Owen wanted to moan as he imagined how gorgeous she'd look in the firelight. With her around to look at all day, every day, he never ran out of ways to torture himself. "Sure, we can. Mac inspected the chimney last week and declared us good to go." Owen had collected a ton of driftwood off the beach that had been drying on the porch for weeks.

"I got marshmallows at the store. We can have a campout."

Perfect, Owen thought. More torture. Her childlike glee at the simple things in life was one of the qualities he liked best about her and part of what made him want her with a burning need unlike anything he'd ever experienced.

"Will you play for me, too? You know I love listening to you."

Here, wrapped around him, was everything he'd never known he wanted. And wasn't it ironic that he couldn't have her. He would've laughed at the lunacy of the situation if his growing ache for her hadn't been so damned painful. "Absolutely," he managed to say. "Let's go in before you catch a cold."

Was she reluctant to step out of his embrace, or was that just wishful thinking on his part? As he followed her inside, he took a last look at the horizon where the ferry was nearly out of sight and hoped he hadn't made a huge mistake by letting it leave without him.

LAURA'S ALARM DRAGGED HER OUT OF A DEEP SLEEP THE NEXT MORNING. Ever since she'd moved to the island right after Labor Day to renovate and manage the Sand & Surf Hotel, she'd been sleeping well again. That was a welcome relief following months of sleepless nights.

Discovering that her new husband hadn't quit dating after their May wedding had shocked the hell out of her—almost as much as discovering she'd been married just long enough to get pregnant. Months of restless nights, mounting anxiety and relentless morning sickness had taken a toll. By the time she arrived to start her new job, she'd been a wreck.

A month later, she was restored, energized, loving her new job and falling more into something with her sexy housemate with each passing day. She thought about the evening they'd spent together in front of the fireplace, roasting marshmallows and singing silly songs and laughing so hard she'd had tears rolling down her face at one point.

What would she have done without his steady presence to get her through these last few weeks? His care and concern had been a balm on the open wound her husband, Justin, had inflicted on her heart. And while she had no doubt Owen wanted more than the easy friendship they'd nurtured since they met over the summer, she didn't feel comfortable pursuing a relationship with him when they were on such vastly different paths. Not to mention, she was still technically married, which wasn't likely to change any time soon with Justin refusing to grant her a divorce.

With her baby due in February, her life would be all about responsibility for the next eighteen years. Owen's life was all about transience. He loved his vagabond existence. He was proud of the fact that everything he owned fit into the back of his ancient VW van. Other than the Sand & Surf, which his grandparents had owned and run for more than fifty years before their retirement, he had no permanent address and liked it that way.

His world simply didn't fit with hers, even if she liked him more than she'd ever liked any guy—including the one she married. Despite their significantly different philosophies on life, their chemistry was hard to ignore. She wasn't immune to the heated looks he sent her way or the overwhelming need to touch him that was becoming almost impossible to resist.

Standing with him on the porch last night, looking out over the ocean as the sun set, had been a moment of perfect harmony. They had a lot of those moments. Whether it was picking out paint colors for the hotel or discussing furniture options or reviewing advertising strategies, they agreed on most things. And when they disagreed, he usually said something to make her laugh, and she'd forget why she didn't agree with him.

She turned on her side to look out on the glorious view that was now a part of her everyday life. She'd loved the old Victorian hotel since she visited the island as a young girl after her mother died. Then it had reminded her of an oversized dollhouse. Those summers with her uncle Big Mac and aunt Linda had been the best of her life. They —and their island—had saved her from the overwhelming grief that had threatened to consume her. The island had saved her from the same fate earlier this year when she'd come for her cousin Janey's wedding and discovered a whole new life, thanks in large part to Owen.

With Justin fighting the divorce and still unaware he was soon to be a father, Laura should be spectacularly unhappy. As she got out of bed and dragged herself into the shower, she couldn't deny that the only reason she wasn't spectacularly unhappy was because she got to be with Owen every day.

She thought about that fact of her new life as she dried her hair and got dressed to meet her aunt Linda for breakfast at the South Harbor Diner. Maybe it was time she and Owen had a heart-to-heart about what was really going on between them. But how exactly did one broach such a subject? Did she say, "Listen, I know you want me, and you know I want you, but that's where our similarities begin and end. We can't build a relationship based on chemistry alone." *Could they?*

That question stayed with her as she went downstairs where Owen was sanding the hardwood floors in the lobby. At some point over the last few weeks, her project of renovating the old hotel had become *their* project, which was fine with her. Everything was more fun with him around to share in it, and besides, his grandparents owned the place, so it seemed fitting to have him involved in the decisions.

Owen turned off the sander, removed his respirator mask and hustled her outside to the porch. "You shouldn't breath the dust."

When he was always taking care of her in one way or another, how was she supposed to remember they wanted different things?

He took a closer look at her. "You look nice. What's the occasion?"

On regular workdays, she tossed her hair up in a ponytail and didn't bother with the light bit of makeup she'd applied to meet her always well-put-together aunt. "Breakfast with Linda, but I won't be long."

She felt guilty about leaving him to work when she was the one being paid to oversee the renovations. That reminded her she wanted to speak with his grandmother about getting him on the payroll. Since he'd given up his gig in Boston to babysit her this winter, it was the least she could do for him.

"Take your time," he said with a grin that made his eyes crinkle at the corners. "Believe it or not, I can manage on my own for an hour or two."

Looking up at him, she had to fight the ever-present urge to straighten the shaggy dirty-blond hair that hung low on his brow. "Owen . . ."

Amusement and affection danced in his gray eyes. "What's on your mind, Princess?"

As a modern, independent woman, Laura knew she probably shouldn't love that nickname quite as much as she did. "We need to talk." They couldn't go on like this all winter without one or both of them incinerating from the heat that arced between them.

"Probably." He bent to press a soft kiss to her forehead. "But not when you've got somewhere to be."

The loving gesture took her breath away. She wanted to reach up, grab a fistful of that unruly hair and drag his sexy mouth down for a kiss that would leave him as breathless as he made her feel when he looked at her that way. But then she remembered all the reasons why it was a terrible idea for her recently shattered heart to take a chance on a man who thrived on freedom.

She'd survived heartbreak once—barely. Why in the world would she set herself up for another trip down that hellish road? "Later, then," she said, her voice sounding as shaky as she felt. "We'll talk later."

"I'll be here."

Laura felt him watching her as she went down the stairs to the sidewalk. As much as she wanted to look back at him, she didn't. Rather, she took deep breaths to regulate her heart rate. The powerful effect he had on her was frightening. Nothing had even happened between them, and she already knew if he broke her heart, it would be way worse than the substantial damage Justin had done.

By the time she stepped into the South Harbor Diner, she'd almost gotten her heart to stop pounding, but the looming conversation with Owen had her vibrating with nervous energy.

Laura was surprised to find her friends Grace and Stephanie, along with her cousin Mac's wife, Maddie, sitting with Linda at a corner table. Grace had recently gotten together with Laura's cousin Evan, and Stephanie was hot and heavy with Laura's cousin Grant.

Everyone around her, it seemed, was newly in love and glowing with happiness.

"Hi, honey," Linda said, rising to greet Laura with a hug. Linda's love and affection had helped fill the awful void left in Laura's young life after her mother died. "You look so pretty. Come have a seat."

"I didn't realize we were having a party," Laura said, thrilled to see the others. Her new friends were also a big part of the reason she was so happy on the island. It was comforting to be around people who hadn't witnessed the thermonuclear meltdown of her marriage and didn't look at her with pity the way her friends in Providence did.

"Neither did we," Grace said, "and I'm kind of relieved to see you all. When Linda asked me to meet her, I thought I was in for a 'When are you going to marry my son?' inquisition." She punctuated the comment with a cheeky grin for Linda.

"Don't be silly," Linda said. "I'd never ask such a question."

The others laughed at the ludicrous statement.

"*Right*," Stephanie said, her tone dripping with sarcasm.

Propping her chin on her upturned hand, Linda zeroed in on Grace. "Since you brought it up, when *are* you going to marry my son?"

"Don't make eye contact," Stephanie advised Grace.

"You hush," Linda said to Stephanie, who she often said she would've handpicked for Grant. "I could ask you the same thing."

"You're not the one who has to do the asking," Stephanie said, arching a brow meaningfully at her boyfriend's mother.

"Touché," Maddie said, laughing at her mother-in-law's shameless quest for information about her unmarried sons and their love lives.

Sydney Donovan came rushing through the door and made a beeline for their table. "So sorry I'm late," she said, also seeming surprised to see the others.

They scooted chairs around to make room for the newcomer, who was Maddie's close friend from childhood.

"Luke dropped me off on his way to see Dr. David," Sydney said. "Fingers crossed this is his last appointment for the ankle injury from hell."

"Oh, let's hope so," Maddie said. "At least he's finally off the crutches."

"And he's walking much better since the surgery," Sydney said as she accepted a cup of coffee from the waitress.

Laura shook her head when offered coffee. "Could I have decaf tea, please?" Oh how she missed coffee!

"And when are you two tying the knot?" Linda asked Sydney.

Sydney's cheeks flushed with color to match her strawberry-blonde hair. "Soon."

"*Oh my God!*" Maddie said. "Have you been holding out on me?"

"Luke asked me a while ago, but I wasn't ready yet. I think I might be now."

"Oh, Syd," Maddie said, hugging her friend. "I'm so happy for you!"

After losing her husband and children in a drunk-driving accident more than a year and a half ago, Sydney had returned to Gansett

267

Island earlier in the summer and reconnected with Luke, her first love, a part owner of McCarthy's Gansett Island Marina.

"I haven't told him yet," Sydney said, "so keep a lid on it for a few days."

"Our lips are sealed," Maddie said, and the others nodded in agreement.

"I'm thrilled for you both," Linda said, reaching out to pat Syd's hand.

"Thank you," Sydney said. "I'm rather thrilled myself."

"No one deserves it more," Laura said.

They talked wedding plans and hotel renovations and kids for a while before Linda tapped her spoon on her coffee cup to get their attention.

"The reason I invited you all to come today," Linda said, "is I have a project I need your help with."

"Sure," Grace said. "What can we do?"

"You've all heard about the new lighthouse keeper—Jenny Wilks?"

"I've heard she's living out there," Stephanie said, "but I've never seen her."

"Neither have I," Laura said.

"Mac told me she has her groceries delivered so she doesn't have to leave the lighthouse," Maddie said.

"That's what I've heard, too," Linda said. "Big Mac was on the search committee, and when she sealed herself off out there, he said we should do something. And that's where you all come in." She leaned in and lowered her voice. "Part of the application process was an essay about an event in their lives that made them who they are today. Hers is so heartbreaking. Listen to this . . ."

Season for Love is available in print from *Amazon.com* and other online retailers, or you can purchase a signed copy from Marie's store at *shop.marieforce.com.*

ALSO BY MARIE FORCE

Contemporary Romances Available from Marie Force

The Gansett Island Series

Book 1: Maid for Love (*Mac & Maddie*)

Book 2: Fool for Love (*Joe & Janey*)

Book 3: Ready for Love (*Luke & Sydney*)

Book 4: Falling for Love (*Grant & Stephanie*)

Book 5: Hoping for Love (*Evan & Grace*)

Book 6: Season for Love (*Owen & Laura*)

Book 7: Longing for Love (*Blaine & Tiffany*)

Book 8: Waiting for Love (*Adam & Abby*)

Book 9: Time for Love (*David & Daisy*)

Book 10: Meant for Love (*Jenny & Alex*)

Book 10.5: Chance for Love, *A Gansett Island Novella* (*Jared & Lizzie*)

Book 11: Gansett After Dark (*Owen & Laura*)

Book 12: Kisses After Dark (*Shane & Katie*)

Book 13: Love After Dark (*Paul & Hope*)

Book 14: Celebration After Dark (*Big Mac & Linda*)

Book 15: Desire After Dark (*Slim & Erin*)

Book 16: Light After Dark (*Mallory & Quinn*)

Book 17: Victoria & Shannon (Episode 1)

Book 18: Kevin & Chelsea (Episode 2)

A Gansett Island Christmas Novella

Book 19: Mine After Dark (*Riley & Nikki*)

Book 20: Yours After Dark (*Finn & Chloe*)

Book 21: Trouble After Dark (*Deacon & Julia*)

Book 22: Rescue After Dark *(Mason & Jordan)*

Book 23: Blackout After Dark

The Green Mountain Series

Book 1: All You Need Is Love *(Will & Cameron)*

Book 2: I Want to Hold Your Hand *(Nolan & Hannah)*

Book 3: I Saw Her Standing There *(Colton & Lucy)*

Book 4: And I Love Her *(Hunter & Megan)*

Novella: You'll Be Mine *(Will & Cam's Wedding)*

Book 5: It's Only Love *(Gavin & Ella)*

Book 6: Ain't She Sweet *(Tyler & Charlotte)*

The Butler, Vermont Series

(Continuation of Green Mountain)

Book 1: Every Little Thing *(Grayson & Emma)*

Book 2: Can't Buy Me Love *(Mary & Patrick)*

Book 3: Here Comes the Sun *(Wade & Mia)*

Book 4: Till There Was You *(Lucas & Dani)*

Book 5: All My Loving *(Landon & Amanda)*

Book 6: Let It Be *(Lincoln & Molly)*

Book 7: Come Together *(Noah & Brianna)*

The Treading Water Series

Book 1: Treading Water

Book 2: Marking Time

Book 3: Starting Over

Book 4: Coming Home

Book 5: Finding Forever

The Miami Nights Series

Book 1: How Much I Feel *(Carmen & Jason)*

Book 2: How Much I Care *(Maria & Austin)*

Book 3: How Much I Love *(Dee's story)*

Single Titles

Five Years Gone

One Year Home

Sex Machine

Sex God

Georgia on My Mind

True North

The Fall

The Wreck

Love at First Flight

Everyone Loves a Hero

Line of Scrimmage

The Quantum Series

Book 1: Virtuous *(Flynn & Natalie)*

Book 2: Valorous *(Flynn & Natalie)*

Book 3: Victorious *(Flynn & Natalie)*

Book 4: Rapturous *(Addie & Hayden)*

Book 5: Ravenous *(Jasper & Ellie)*

Book 6: Delirious *(Kristian & Aileen)*

Book 7: Outrageous *(Emmett & Leah)*

Book 8: Famous *(Marlowe & Sebastian)*

Romantic Suspense Novels Available from Marie Force

The Fatal Series

One Night With You, *A Fatal Series Prequel Novella*

Book 1: Fatal Affair

Book 2: Fatal Justice

Book 3: Fatal Consequences

Book 3.5: Fatal Destiny, *the Wedding Novella*

Book 4: Fatal Flaw

Book 5: Fatal Deception

Book 6: Fatal Mistake

Book 7: Fatal Jeopardy

Book 8: Fatal Scandal

Book 9: Fatal Frenzy

Book 10: Fatal Identity

Book 11: Fatal Threat

Book 12: Fatal Chaos

Book 13: Fatal Invasion

Book 14: Fatal Reckoning

Book 15: Fatal Accusation

Book 16: Fatal Fraud

Historical Romance Available from Marie Force

The Gilded Series

Book 1: Duchess by Deception

Book 2: Deceived by Desire

ABOUT THE AUTHOR

Marie Force is the *New York Times* bestselling author of contemporary romance, romantic suspense and erotic romance. Her series include Gansett Island, Fatal, Treading Water, Butler Vermont and Quantum.

Her books have sold nearly 10 million copies worldwide, have been translated into more than a dozen languages and have appeared on the *New York Times* bestseller more than 30 times. She is also a *USA Today* and *Wall Street Journal* bestseller, as well as a Speigel bestseller in Germany.

Her goals in life are simple—to finish raising two happy, healthy, productive young adults, to keep writing books for as long as she possibly can and to never be on a flight that makes the news.

Join Marie's mailing list on her website at *marieforce.com* for news about new books and upcoming appearances in your area. Follow her on Facebook at *www.Facebook.com/MarieForceAuthor* and on Instagram at *www.instagram.com/marieforceauthor/*. Contact Marie at *marie@marieforce.com*.

CPSIA information can be obtained
at www.ICGtesting.com
Printed in the USA
LVHW010757180522
718911LV00014B/547